Praise for *The Round Dance*

"Carmine Abate's novelistic debut is a groundbreaking post-modern 'metaphor of the world.' This Italo-Albanian 'round dance,' brilliantly translated by Michelangelo La Luna, offers a blueprint for how to deal with cultural belonging in a globalized world while holding aesthetic as well as moral, religious, and social value."

—Dagmar Reichardt, coeditor of *Icone della transculturalità*

"The Arbëreshë community has made southern Italy its home for six centuries by renewing its identity as a distinct ethnic, linguistic, and religious minority. Masterfully written, *The Round Dance* opens their world for English-speaking audiences and is a welcome addition to the canon of migrant literature."

—Ines Murzaku, coeditor of *Greek Monasticism in Southern Italy: The Life of Neilos in Context*

"Through a lovely translation of Carmine Abate's poetic language, *The Round Dance* unveils to English readers the marvelous, centuries-long odyssey of the Albanian people in southern Italy and beyond, underscoring what some have called 'the powers of diaspora.'"

—Tullio Pagano, author of *The Making and Unmaking of Mediterranean Landscape in Italian Literature: The Case of Liguria*

T0285623

The Round Dance

Titles in the **Other Voices of Italy** series:

Other Voices of Italy: Italian and Transnational Texts in Translation

Editors: Alessandro Vettori, Sandra Waters, Eilis Kierans

This series presents texts in a variety of genres originally written in Italian. Much like the symbiotic relationship between the wolf and the raven, its principal aim is to introduce new or past authors—who have until now been marginalized—to an English-speaking readership. This series also highlights contemporary transnational authors, as well as writers who have never been translated or who are in need of a fresh/contemporary translation. The series further aims to increase the appreciation of translation as an art form that enhances the importance of cultural diversity.

A tangible testimony to the great diversity of Italian cultural heritage, *The Round Dance* features four intertwined stories creating a single macro-narrative. Its magical realism transports readers back to the adventures they relished in Gabriel Garcia Marquez's books, while its mythical twist whisks them into a distant yet very real and present world of a small Arbëreshë community in southern Italy. The Arbëreshë (or Italo-Albanians) are descendants of the people who were displaced from Albania to Italy starting in the fourteenth century to avoid the Ottoman conquest of the Balkan region. They have preserved their language and cultural heritage but have developed a distinct identity, which is neither completely Italian nor Albanian, and in recent times have been threatened by mass migration and globalization. Carmine Abate explores the deep-rooted traditions of these people and constructs a semi-autobiographical *Bildungsroman* around the coming of age of its protagonist, his own alter-ego who shares an Arbëreshë background with him. This is an original, gripping narrative that introduces English-speaking readers to the reality of a long-forgotten minority in the already neglected southern regions of the Italian peninsula.

The Round Dance

CARMINE ABATE

Translated by Michelangelo La Luna

Foreword by Francesco Altimari

Rutgers University Press

New Brunswick, Camden, and Newark, New Jersey

London and Oxford

Rutgers University Press is a department of Rutgers, The State University of
New Jersey, one of the leading public research universities in the nation. By
publishing worldwide, it furthers the University's mission of dedication to
excellence in teaching, scholarship, research, and clinical care.

Library of Congress Cataloging-in-Publication Data

Names: Abate, Carmine, 1954– author. | La Luna, Michelangelo, translator. |
Altimari, Francesco, writer of foreword.
Title: The round dance / Carmine Abate ; translated by
Michelangelo La Luna; foreword by Francesco Altimari.
Other titles: Ballo tondo. English
Description: New Brunswick : Rutgers University Press, [2023] |
Series: Other voices of Italy
Identifiers: LCCN 2023007324 | ISBN 9781978837430 (paperback) |
ISBN 9781978837447 (hardcover) | ISBN 9781978837454 (epub) |
ISBN 9781978837461 (pdf)
Subjects: LCGFT: Novels.
Classification: LCC PQ4861.B316 B3513 2023 |
DDC 853/.914—dc23/eng/20230224
LC record available at https://lccn.loc.gov/2023007324

A British Cataloging-in-Publication record for this book is available
from the British Library.

Copyright © 2024 by Michelangelo La Luna
Foreword © 2024 by Francesco Altimari
Copyright © 2005 Carmine Abate. This edition published
in arrangement with Grandi & Associati
Translation of *Il ballo tondo.* © 1991 Mondadori

All rights reserved

No part of this book may be reproduced or utilized in any form or by any
means, electronic or mechanical, or by any information storage and retrieval
system, without written permission from the publisher. Please contact Rutgers
University Press, 106 Somerset Street, New Brunswick, NJ 08901. The only
exception to this prohibition is "fair use" as defined by U.S. copyright law.

References to internet websites (URLs) were accurate at the time of writing.
Neither the author nor Rutgers University Press is responsible for URLs that
may have expired or changed since the manuscript was prepared.

To Michael, obviously
A Michele, naturalmente
natürlich für Michele
ne, Mikelit

Contents

~ Shkoi një ditë mjegullore ~

Foreword

Memory and Identity Performance
in the Imagined "Hora" of Albanians
of Italy or Arbëreshë

Since the last decade of the twentieth century, the writer Carmine Abate, thanks to the success of his novels, has earned a remarkable place, not only within contemporary Italian literature but also within the innovative transnational literary branch of "migrant literature."

It was his debut novel *Il ballo tondo*—correctly framed by literary critic Rosanna Morace for its thematic affinity within Abate's rich and multifaceted narrative, in the so-called "Arbëresh cycle"—to overbearingly bring the presence of a historical linguistic minority such as the Albanians of Italy or Arbëreshë to the attention of Italian readers. With the exception of those regions in the south, where the Arbëreshë population has been historically present for almost six centuries, this minority has practically disappeared from mass media attention and has been ignored by national public opinion.

This indifference towards the Arbëreshë did not exist at the end of the eighteenth century, nor during the nineteenth century, and not even during a significant part of the twentieth century; during these historical periods, the Arbëresh community was, although small, a great producer of ruling and intellectual classes. It often emerged as a vanguard in the main movements of thought and in the political, literary, and cultural history of Italy. In fact, these communities were never isolated; they were well integrated into the cultural and political progress of their era, which they owe to their intellectual elite. Some of the emblematic figures of Italian national history who have roots in these communities include: Domenico Mauro (in Calabria), Francesco Crispi (in Sicily), and Antonio Gramsci himself, whose family was of Calabrian-Arbëreshe origin, as well as Costantino Mortati, one of the authors of the Italian Constitutional Charter and, lastly, Stefano Rodotà, considered one of the most distinguished jurists of contemporary Italy. The intellectual skill collegially expressed by the Italo-Albanian minority can be defined as radical and forward-thinking, never submissive to the power of the historical moment. For example, during the institutional referendum of 1946, the Arbëresh expressed themselves in favor of the Italian Republic and clearly against largely monarchical southern Italy.

In *Il ballo tondo*, Abate speaks through his characters who are taken in part from his personal life but who, inspired by an autobiographical imprint that we might call communal, are paradigmatically representative of behavioral patterns that we find in the history of this minority. These characters share a common frame that constitutes the outline of the Arbëreshe collective memory, a cognitive and identifying heritage, rarely codified in written form, and predominantly oral. This heritage currently appears increasingly fragile, poor, precarious, and voiceless because of the depopulation that is wiping out a large part of Arbëria, not coincidentally located in the weakest areas of the already weak social fabric of the south. It is also affected by the disappearance of those intergenerational relationships that, over time, have ensured the continuity of a rich and resilient culture of Balkan matrix such as the Arbëreshe one. After more than half a millennium, this culture has had, precisely in its orality, the ability—while not necessarily exclusive, certainly privileged—to transmit its miraculous survival within Italy.

Carmine Abate, through several idealistic characters, manages to reconstruct in his debut novel an imaginary but also truthful Arbëria and, by using the plots of the collective memory of his people, narrates an extraordinarily magical world, related by some critics to the magic realism of Gabriel García Márquez. This is the same imagined world that the Italo-Albanian Girolamo De Rada represented in the nineteenth century; as the father of modern Albanian literature, his work served to promote the ideological basis of that political and cultural movement that brought back the ancient nation of his ancestors, the Albania that over the centuries had almost disappeared because of its long hibernation under Ottoman domain.

In *Il ballo tondo*, we discover the author's partial alter ego, Costantino Avati, at the center of the action. We find him in the same place—Marina—as a child of just nine years old at the beginning of the novel, and as a young man of eighteen in the round dance (or "vallja") that closes the novel. He is also at Marina on the occasion of two festivals: the "ethnic" one in which the Albanians, by kissing the sand where their ancestors landed, ideally turned their gaze across the Ionian Sea to the shores of the ancient homeland, abandoned physically but preserved in their memory; and his sister's wedding feast.

It is important to note the purposeful onomastic reference to the eponymous hero of clear Byzantine matrix, Costantino, who is the protagonist of the most beautiful and well-known legends attested in the different cultures that originated from the Balkan area. In the form of residual rhapsodies, they are still rooted in the social fabric and are well imprinted in the memory of the lower classes, the ultimate repositories of this rich "granary" of myths and legends. After having survived for centuries in the world of the Albanians of Italy, thanks also to ritual practices of a tradition protected and enhanced by the Eastern Byzantine church, these rhapsodies are rediscovered by Abate in the daily life of the novel's protagonists, also marking the novel's narrative rhythm, thanks to the author's extraordinary storytelling talents.

Nani Lissandro is the elderly repository of this collective memory and the holder of a language and culture considered "useless" because it is part of a tradition that is nonfunctional to a globalized society. His young grandson Costantino takes over the baton of this precious but often poorly understood cultural legacy, made up of songs, rituals, symbols, and this truncated language, provocatively revived by the writer who uses it in frequent passages of his novel. Other Arbëreshë characters, on the other hand, are almost unconscious victims of "Stockholm syndrome." They radically and masochistically want to erase their heritage, as if linguistic and cultural otherness were a stigma to be hidden or disguised.

Among these "renegades" of identity, there are those who do so from weak positions, out of ignorance, such as Costantino's father, Francesco Avati, also known as the Mericano. He is an eternal emigrant who thinks he can build a rosy future without a past and who aims to redeem a dark past of subalternity, harassment, and abuse that he attributes to his linguistic and cultural diversity of origin, and not at all to the weak social condition of his departure. Although at the novel's turning points, he seems to repudiate Arbëreshë traditions, in reality, he embraces and practices them. But there are also those who do so from strong positions, as a would-be bourgeois thirsty for power, like the Arbëresh teacher Stratigò who, in the conviction that he has achieved a dominant social position, places himself alongside his "masters" on the side of the hegemonic culture, paradoxically pursuing, as an acculturated person, the same goal as the poorly educated Mericano, striking the hands of those pupils who let a few Arbërisht words slip at school.

Fortunately, in the novel, we find a series of archetypal figures who defend these "few signs of tradition not yet obliterated by time." These are fragile yet resilient fragments of oral memory that from one generation to the next are, however, reduced more and more though characterizing a historically "migrant" community that continues to be, centuries later, still "migrating" between multiple lands, languages, and cultures.

In addition to nani Lissandro and Costantino, we recall, among the resilient models, other male figures such as the old "rhapsode" of Corone, Luca Rodotà, or even, albeit not without contradictions, figures from outside the community such as the young teacher Carmelo Bevilacqua: "He, a *Litir* from Belcastro, knew more about the Arbëreshë than all the people of Hora combined, including the parish priest and the other teachers." But except for Costantino's young fiancée, the "Romana" Isabella, who considers these practices old-fashioned and useless, it is mainly the women who, in the novel, represent the backbone of transmission of this memory, nourished at the community level by a deep sense of pride in one's ancestral roots.

Female protagonists are those of the Avati household, such as *zonja* Elena, the matron of the house, mother of

Costantino, and wife of Francesco "Il Mericano," with her two daughters: After troubled events that border on a crime novel Lucrezia married Maestro Bevilacqua, whom we find again in the final scene of the nuptial *vallja* (or round dance) that closes the novel; and Orlandina, who married an emigrant from Trentino, her father's workmate in Germany. It is she, in the distant Alpine land to which she moves after her marriage, who passes on the language with the historical trove of cultural traditions inherited from her Arbëreshë ancestors to her son Paolino. He is the one who becomes, in the diaspora of the diaspora, a symbol of what is, but also of what, after all, has always been Arbëria: an identitary, linguistic, and cultural hybridization in continual renegotiation that, without ever breaking apart, constantly develops, renews, and regenerates itself in the encounter with "the other"—never remaining enveloped in itself, nor identical to what it was before.

The paradigmatic figure of Paolino, living in the Alpine valleys of Trentino far from "Hora"—Abate's Macondo—stands as the symbolic heir of this Arbëreshe family at the center of *The Round Dance*. The writer gives us a plausible and convincing interpretation that allows us to understand the real reasons for this "Italian anthropological miracle," the expression with which a great intellectual of our time, Pier Paolo Pasolini identified a connotative trait of this minority. The Arbëreshe community remained in the shadows for a long time and was rediscovered by Carmine Abate with this novel, which is part of his trilogy with an Arbëresh subject entitled *The Seasons of Hora*.

I am sure that the present edition of this novel, masterfully translated into English by Michelangelo La Luna—a fine connoisseur of Italian fiction, and specifically of Abate, as well as of the Arbëreshe literary tradition and culture—will contribute to a better understanding and appreciation of the evocative Italo-Albanian world that the writer's fiction reflects for English speakers as well.

Francesco Altimari
Università della Calabria

Translator's Note

Il ballo tondo (*The Round Dance*) is the acclaimed debut novel by Carmine Abate, one of the most original Italian writers of our time. Released in Italy in 1991 by Marietti, relaunched by Fazi Editore in 2000, and then by Mondadori in 2005, the book has been translated and published in Germany, France, Albania, Portugal, Kosovo, Japan, and now in the United States. The novel won the ARGE ALP Readers' International Prize (2000) and was selected by Mondadori for the series "900 ITALIANO" (2016) as one of the one hundred best Italian novels of the twentieth century. In celebration of the thirty-year anniversary of its publication, *Il ballo tondo* was republished in 2021 in a new OSCAR Mondadori edition.

The book is divided into four sections by four Arbëreshë (Italian-Albanian) rhapsodies: two on the legendary hero *Kostantini i vogël*, and two on the national Albanian hero George Kastrioti Skanderbeg. It contains several stories that oscillate between chronicle and myth: stories of love and expectations, departures and returns, reality and legend, tradition and modernity. It is a unique *Bildungsroman* set in a small town of Southern Italy—a unique colony of the fifteenth-century Albanian escape from Turkish subjugation—transfigured into an area of the soul, magical and legendary, where time seems to stand still forever. It covers relevant themes such as education, migration, diversity, and inclusion, and gives a great picture of Arbëresh culture and of the socioeconomic condition of southern Italy from the 1960s to the 1980s. Moreover, it has a lot in common with the literary genre of magical realism, and in particular with novels by Gabriel García Márquez.

The story takes place in Hora, a village in Calabria where an ancient Arbëreshe community settles and where time, people, and events, seem to be wrapped in a magical atmosphere. It is here that Costantino Avati grows up and rediscovers the mythical past of his people and the roots of his restless present through a vision of the double-headed eagle. Around him are many unforgettable characters: his impetuous and melancholic father Francesco Avati, known as "il Mericano," who emigrated to Germany; his mother Elena, a great cook of spicy food and guardian of a secret torment; his two sisters, Orlandina and Lucrezia, with their convoluted love stories; Isabella, who makes Costantino's adolescent heart flutter; his teacher Carmelo Bevilacqua, a hunter of dreams and memories; his grandfather Lissandro, ironic and wise, the last custodian of an era and a world that are disappearing; and the mysterious Luca Rodotà, an interpreter of the old rhapsodies of the Arbëresh tradition.

The translation of *Il ballo tondo* was for me an act of love. Love for my Arbëresh roots and for a language and culture that are at risk of extinction. Love for a longtime friend and caring person like Carmine Abate, one of the most acclaimed contemporary Italian writers. In writing his stories, he uses the rhythm of the Arbëreshe oral tradition. He writes from the analogic rhythm of an oral language; it is an immense challenge to render that rich narration into a digital and exact language like English. In my translation, I tried to maintain the rhapsodic rhythm of the original text as much as possible, filled with repetitions, alliterations, allusions, anacolutha, verses, colorful idiomatic expressions, and words in Arbërisht, Calabrese, Latin, Greek, Neapolitan, Trentin, German, and so on. To respect the author's will and preserve the richness of the original text, I decided to maintain some of the foreign words as they are. To this end, all the characters' names and nicknames, as well as the names of locations, are left in Italian or in Arbërisht. This "translation adventure" started in 2016 and was recently completed after a lot of work and numerous revisions of the text. Its result would not have been possible without the help of several friends. A very warm "grazie" goes to Eva Benedikt, Domenic Caturello, Kyle Engel, Fabrizio Garau, Angela Pitassi, Daniel Shields, and Adam Vocatura. Finally, I would like to thank Carmine Abate himself, for all the patience and care with which he clarified some complicated passages of his book.

Michelangelo La Luna
University of Rhode Island

The Round Dance

Lojmë lojmë, vasha, vallen

Let's dance, let's dance, girls, the *vallja* of Costantino il Piccolo, married for only three days. Then he receives the order to join the army from the Gran Signore, Supreme Commander. He leaves. He leaves, of course, and fights for nine years without complaining, until after nine years and nine days, *ohi*, Costantino has a dream, a frightening dream: *e bukura*, the beautiful, was just about to crown another man as her husband. Costantino sighs; he sighs so loud that he is heard by the Gran Signore who, upon learning the reason for his sigh that morning, says to the trustworthy Costantino: "Take the ninth key, open the ninth stall, take the savage horse, the one as black as olives, the one faster than a kite; put the silver saddle on him, for the halter use the gold one, and go to Hora, where your bride is." And Costantino goes faster than a kite, hardly sleeping day and night, until he steps foot on his motherland, until he is in Hora. Here he meets *zotin pjak*, the old father, but he does not recognize him. "Where are you going, *zoti pjak*?" "I am going to throw myself off a cliff; this morning my daughter-in-law will crown another man." And the son to the father: "Go back, *zoti pjak*, for I am Costantino." And the father to the son: "Costantino, my son, spur your fast horse and you'll find her on the steps of the church." And Costantino moves forward, until he meets *zonjën pjakë*, the old mother. And the same scene occurs, the words are repeated, and Costantino wastes no more time; with his horse at a gallop, he flies faster than a kite, and finds her in church, just in time to shout at the priest to put away those crowns, because he is Costantino, Costantino of the first crown.

Prologue

This tale of *Kostantini i vogël* was the only Albanian story that my friend, Costantino Avati, knew before going to the fair in Marina with his grandfather. It was one of the few ballads that we, as children, had heard being sung at wedding processions after the marriage ceremony. Sometimes, if the crowd was in the mood, we would all take each other by the hand, children and adults alike, and dance in a circle to the monotonous yet cheerful rhythm of the vallja: *Lojmë lojmë, vasha, vallen*. And since all the valle started with the same invitation to the girls to dance, the only verse I remembered from Costantino il Piccolo was the first one. Costantino Avati, on the other hand, would have been able to recite entire passages from memory for two reasons: because the protagonist was named Costantino and because zonja Elena, his mother, after hearing the ballad, never got tired of repeating that she and her husband, Francesco Avati, had lived the same beautiful love story.

It went like this, zonja Elena recounted: upon returning from the military he, her future husband, saw her, a fourteen-year-old girl, the age at which she was blooming like a flower. Then and there, he didn't recognize her: she had been a young girl when he left, but now she was in the Avatis' household, delivered to him by destiny on a silver platter. There was no need for his relatives to recommend her to him. His eyes allowed him to see, and his refined brain allowed him to understand, and so he promised to marry her as soon as possible. Later though. After he had done what he had sworn to do as a young boy: lay a blessed olive branch on the spot where his father had died, in a coal mine in the *'Merica Bona*, the Good America. And so, while nearly all of his peers emigrated to France for work, he boarded a ship in Genoa in search of a tomb of black debris.

He was gone for nine months and nine days—nine months as long as nine years—and he came back just in time to break up the new engagement that her father, *zoti* Lissandro, was arranging with a young man from Puhëriu. Yes, with the same promptness of *Kostantini i vogël* to be loyal to the *besa*, the given word. In Hora, our town, they called him the Mericano right away because of that trip to America, which the proud young man never wanted to speak about with anyone, but maybe also because of his carefully groomed mustache, like Clark Gable, whose seductive charm had spilled off the silver screen onto all the women of Hora during the nine screenings of *Gone with the Wind*.

Over the course of twenty months, zonja Elena gave birth to two girls: Orlandina and Lucrezia. They then waited impatiently for the birth of a boy, even though everyone said they already had a little boy in the house: Lucrezia, a real *burraçë*. Since the first years of her life, she only played with the boys, and she peed like a boy, standing up, and whistled with four fingers in her mouth.

Eight years after Lucrezia, finally he was born.

Unlike his sisters, little Costantino was not a combination of his parents; he hadn't inherited his mother's physical exuberance and midnight black hair; nor did he have his father's chameleon eyes, the color of Cipollino marble, now with stripes of emerald-green or gray, depending on his mood and the weather. Costantino was delicate, with olive-toned skin and two dazed, big brown eyes. His personality may have more closely resembled that of his maternal grandfather, a man inclined to daydream and speak tirelessly for hours and then suddenly, and inexplicably, be silent for days on end.

It was his grandfather, nani Lissandro, who took him to the summer fair in Marina, replacing once again the Mericano who, after the birth of his son, had been forced to emigrate to Germany. And so, from that day on, Costantino's eyes began to grow even wider, like when you wake up in the morning after a long sleep, suddenly overtaken by a band of light. This band of light was the tale nani Lissandro told, uncovering historical and mythical roots that had been completely ignored before.

Something similar happened to many children of Hora, myself included. Until the day of the fair, we didn't even know that Hora had been founded five centuries earlier by Albanian refugees who refused to surrender themselves to the Turks who had invaded their lands. At home, we spoke *si neve*, like us, in Arbëresh, and then at school, from the age of six, we began to learn *Litisht*, that is, Italian. All this happened naturally; we didn't ask for rhyme or reason. Luckily for us, there was the fair in Marina; and then, who knows why, our chaperones felt obliged to tell us the approximate story of our distant past.

My friend Costantino was taken to the fair when he was nine years old. Today, when we go back to Hora on vacation from the foreign cities where we work, he talks to me about that day in the same epic manner of the old Albanian rhapsodes. But how else can he talk, since he spends all his free time collecting, organizing, and translating the old Arbëreshë rhapsodies into Italian, and then saving them on his computer in his office at one of the government ministries in Rome? I let him speak freely, and he goes beyond the day at the fair, ending with: "and then?"

When his story started, I was only eight years old, and I didn't see him as much as I would in later years. It was, therefore, just by chance that I also found myself in the *piazzetta* of his *gjitonia*, his neighborhood, when Costantino announced to the world with pride: "I saw the double-headed eagle flying in Marina yesterday!" And while he recounted the event in detail, I relived the scenes as though they were in a movie I had seen who knows when, immediately positioning myself as the protagonist.

Një

The second time Costantino Avati saw the double-headed eagle he was eighteen years old, and because he was afraid to be considered crazy, not only did he tell no one but he tried to convince himself he had been dreaming with his eyes open. However, he never doubted that the first appearance was real, and even though a quarter century has passed since then, he still has picture-perfect memories scattered here and there, on the background of a solid blue–colored sky, dotted with puffs of clouds.

That morning he had been brusquely awakened by the strident, nervous voice of his mother, just before the roosters of the alleyway began to crow. He had to hurry, she was saying, if he wanted to go to the fair in Marina with nani Lissandro. Without having to be begged, unlike the way he usually did when he had to go to school, he jumped out of bed and in a flash slipped into his patchless pants and the green nylon shirt he wore only on holidays.

In the alleyway dimly lit by the sunrise, old Baialardo barked at the cats curled up on the balconies, and nani Lissandro loaded two sacks of dried figs onto his mule, cursing the dirty devil that wore him down: old age is a bitch, *një pjak ësht si një fjetë e thatë*, an old man is like a dry leaf; once upon a time he could toss a sack of dried figs with one hand, nani kept repeating, whereas now at the age of eighty . . .

First, Costantino greeted him with a smiling "*mirëdita*," good morning, to let him know that he was the happiest child in the world; and then he helped him tie up the pack saddle to the four goats nani had managed to raise that year.

Then darkness.

Ten years earlier, at that same fair in Marina, nani had sold nearly fifty goats who survived a winter of heavy snow and arctic freeze sent by the dirty devil. One hundred and twenty heads had died: of hunger, of cold, or being torn apart by wolves that came down from Sila. He kept Chicchinella and Gigina for himself, the two most fertile and tame goats, and Baialardo, a big coffee-colored herding dog with large white spots around his black eyes. He would never have gotten rid of them for anything in the world; they were old friends—warm, physical memories. At the fair, he only sold the three or four kids that the generous Chicchinella and Gigina had given birth to and two sacks of white figs that he himself had harvested and set out to dry on his plot of land just outside the town.

Light again.

As they arrived in the piazza, nani Lissandro spat at the main door of the Palazzo of Don Morello, just as he had done each time he had passed by before dawn, showing his disgust for the rich people of Hora. Yes, once, during the time of the occupation of the lands, when it seemed like the world itself was about to turn upside down, he had tried to set fire to that heavy walnut main door, but it had cost him a pistol shot that grazed his right ear and a week at the Carabinieri station during which he had felt ashamed of himself for denying what happened.

Once out of town, they took the mule track that steeply and narrowly descended toward the coastal strip of Marina. One by one, the mule leading the way, the four goats clip-clopped along behind, then old Baialardo with his big, wide-open eyes, and finally nani who was tramping his heavy feet and thinking aloud, yelling something at the mule or turning to Costantino, or looking at the sky, at the sun red as fire that slowly rose from the sea spraying it with a long yellowish-red brushstroke. It was at that point, when Costantino was also staring at the horizon, that nani began to speak in a grave tone, as though he were revealing a sacred truth to him.

Beyond the horizon, on an August day just like today, the sea is calm, three galleys of refugees set sail: the first was full of young men, the second of girls, and the third of bread and wine. They went ashore in Marina, preceded by the large double-headed eagle that guided and protected them day and night ever since they had been forced to leave Arbëria, invaded by the Turks. We have the same *gjak*, the same blood, as those people.

He spoke with a different voice, grave and serious, with musical echoes at the end of each sentence, and such a thick accent that Costantino could hardly understand him.

It was Skanderbeg himself who advised his people to flee. He and a handful of brave men had been able to resist the Turkish army for years—the most powerful and largest in the world. Then, when he fell ill with malaria and after having met the shadow of wind that is death, he said to his son:

Abandoned flower, *lule e kësaj zëmër time*, flower of my heart, take your mother and three galleys, the best you have, and leave this place immediately, because if the Turk finds out, he will immediately kill you and your mother will become a slave. But before you leave, when you get to the dock, tie my horse to a cypress tree. Unfurl my flag and tie my sword to the middle. When the north wind blows and the horse neighs, the flag with the double-headed eagle waves, and the sword jingles. If the Turkish man hears them, he will be afraid, and fearing the death that lies dormant on my sword, he will not pursue you wherever you go.

Immediately, Costantino felt more at ease with this Skanderbeg than with Garibaldi, the Hero of the Two Worlds about whom he had studied in school, and mounted the mule as though he were riding the steed of the cypress tree. He took hold of the story, with a deep sigh and a solemn gaze into the emptiness. It was only many years later, as he was collecting Arbëreshë songs and rhapsodies, that he would notice that nani's story was a combination of ancient rhapsodies, the initial pieces of the mythical roots of his world. In the meantime, he understood why the language they spoke in Hora was so different from the one spoken by Zorro on TV, by the maestro at school, and by the *Litirj*, the non-Arbëreshë people of the area.

They reached the plateau and crossed the fiumara, after refreshing themselves at a rivulet that wandered off among the smooth, flat stones.

The air was getting muggy. The deafening hum of cicadas was growing louder as the day wore on, and the maddened giant flies and horseflies, followed by the clouds of gnats, rested on the mule's sweaty back, on the drool-covered muzzle of the goats, on Costantino's nose, on the damp edges of Baialardo's eyes, and on the old man's thin hands. They settled, buzzed around, settled again, and buzzed around again, tracing a zig-zagging path through the thick air.

Now that the sea was close, Costantino could no longer see it, hidden as it was by trunks of big plantains, and behind these by the crowns of orange, almond, fig, and olive trees. Basically, there was no way around it. There is no way around it. There's he who gets the grain, and there is he who sweats, thought nani Lissandro out loud, and it was as though he were speaking to Don Fidele Morello's gardens on his side or to the mule that walked in front of him, but certainly not to his grandson who was behind him and who heard those words drift through the haze.

The entrance to Marina left Costantino speechless. He turned his gaze to the sea he saw lapping at the end of the straight and dusty road. And he no longer heard nani's voice, nor the cowbells of the goats; he did not notice the droppings in the shape of olives and mandarins that dotted the road, and upon which he kept stepping, dirtying his new shoes; he barely perceived, as if from a car racing past, the stalls overflowing with sundries and peanuts set up along the sides of the road, and gypsies and other vendors from faraway towns selling decorated mules, Swiss cows, steel plows, velvet fabrics, piglets, Tuscan cigars, statuettes of Saint Anthony; and all he heard was the echo of the incessant, "*Huè, huè*, fresh fish, sardelles for salting," of the fishermen, or the soothing, "*Ohi, ohi*, what a lovely salt," of the women, or the rhyming calls of "The Palm Reader of Rossano, who reads the future in your *mano*." Costantino followed nani like an automaton, hypnotized by the blue of the sea-sky.

"Costantì, Costantì, wake up!" nani shook him two, three times, grabbing him by one arm. "Did you see that we sold the goats and the figs at a great price? Such luck this year!

Now let's go eat something on the beach; when evening comes, and the prices go down, we'll buy sardines and salt."

When they got to the beach, the old man struggled to take off his hiking boots and his heavy wool socks; Costantino imitated him, still a little dazed by the loud noises of the fair and the vast expanse of the blue water. They approached the shoreline barefoot, followed by Baialardo, who was wagging his tail like a puppy. When they were about a foot from the water, nani Lissandro knelt on the wet sand, placed his palms on it, and with eyes closed he kissed it with the same tenderness a little boy would use to kiss his mother. It was on this beach that his ancestors had landed five hundred years earlier, he explained to Costantino who, with a gaze full of wonder, had asked the reason for that kiss. For a moment, Costantino had been drawn to nani's thin lips, dotted with pearly grains of sand. But then his attention turned to the little waves that crashed at his feet. Each small wave brought him a new thought, a question: how did the Arbëreshë feel when they left Arbëria? Did they hope to see their motherland again someday? What did they look like? What work did they do? Where did they live in the early years? How did they live?

Nani calmly responded, as though he had been reading his grandson's thoughts: "The first thing they did was eat; they brought bread and wine, I told you about that, didn't I? We too have bread and wine. So, shall we eat? Do you feel like it?" And as they ate bread with goat cheese and fresh figs, they saw another old man, as white as nani Lissandro, repeating the kissing ritual. He was tall and skeletal, and he walked with a slight hop, as though with each step he hoped to take flight. Nani's eyes were shining: that crazy man, he said, was Luca Rodotà, the rhapsode of Corone, his dearest friend, he stressed with pride, whom he had met for over half a century every year on the day of the fair.

Costantino didn't pay attention to the old man's appearance, but he surely was thin and loony, with two eyes the color of the sky after the rain. He likely also had a long white beard and a sort of mandolin with a single string, the lahuta, that he wore constantly, slung across his shoulder so that it covered his red vest. That's how he would see him again some years later; that's how he remembers him today.

The two old men hugged each other like brothers. "*Skumetiri se ki ësht Kustandini*," I bet that this is Costantino, said the rhapsode and kissed Costantino as though he had always known him.

A small crowd quickly gathered around the three of them. There were Arbëreshë people from other towns around the area of Catanzaro and Cosenza. They had all known each other for years and immediately fell into a busy chatter in Arbëresh, and when they did not understand each other, they switched to a stilted Calabrian dialect. Even though Costantino was listening to them carefully, he was only able to understand a part of what the men were saying; each spoke in his own way, one saying *katundi*, while another *vend*, and yet a third *u paisi*, all meaning the same thing: the town. But the problems they had, which they brought up with an emphatic *po po*, were identical, like drops of seawater: the rent of the land increasing year by year, the mildew on the grapevines, the urge to go work in Germany, as so many were doing by now. One had simply to accept the facts: no one was going to talk about the double-headed eagle, nor would they talk about the mythical past that tied them all together. The everyday present crushed everyone mercilessly. But then: "Precisely in this cursed land the eagle had to rest!" a man shouted right in the middle of the conversation, who from his accent had to be from Puhërìu.

"Quiet, don't curse!" the rhapsode of Corone reprimanded him. "The land is never cursed; it's the men who are cursed, who are capable of sucking the blood from their own brothers. The eagle is not to blame!" As he spoke, he stared at the sun after having raised his face toward the sky with a slow and calculated movement. He might have lowered his gaze with the same slow intensity, as though offering a sort of bow to the crowd of admirers who shared his dissent, if Costantino hadn't called out in an eager voice: "The eagle! The eagle! The double-headed eagle! Look, there it is!"

Everyone looked in the direction that Costantino pointed to, and after a moment they burst into a peal of laughter.

"But that's not a double-headed eagle! Those are two gulls flying next to each other," said nani Lissandro, who was by his side trying to convince him. His grandson paid him no mind and continued to stare while squinting his eyes to see better: the eagle was soaring slowly over the sea, passing through the intense blue of the sky with his hooked beaks, and through the puffs of vanishing clouds as though they were soap bubbles.

"But how can you not see it? Are you all blind? It is a small white eagle with two heads!" Costantino yelled, angry, as though surrounded by a crowd of his taunting and jeering peers.

"Costantino is right," said the rhapsode of Corone. "The eagle is here among us. He is the one who can see it because he is young and free of malice."

Dy

The Avatis' house was at the end of two rows of houses that formed a semicircle; most were two-story houses, with stairs out front and small verandas that opened onto an area constantly crowded with children; they were old houses, placed next to each other at a steep incline so that the Avatis' home looked as if it were resisting the load of the other houses, preventing them from tumbling into the ravine below.

In the piazzetta of the gjitonia, the news of the double-headed eagle's appearance had the same effect as a stone thrown into a pond, expanding in concentric circles among the children of other neighborhoods, until it reached *rahjin*, the piazza. The younger children were amazed by Costantino's tale, but the older ones, those who had already turned ten, began to scoff and tease him, eventually infecting the younger ones.

The adults of the gjitonia who by chance had heard the news pushed the matter aside with the expression "*Ësht gji i jati.*" By pointing out that Costantino was just like his father, they recalled the reputation the Mericano had for being a prankster as a young man. Everyone remembered the time the Mericano had, with tears in his eyes, spread the news about the death of Pope Giovanni, while in fact, he was alive and well. Another time, the guy announced the start of World War III, tearing wildly at his hair, imitated by a group of crying and desperate women, standing out from which was his wife, zonja Elena. She was the only one who believed Costantino's tale without a shadow of doubt, even without listening to it completely. That's how she was; she followed the linear trajectory of her thoughts, even when engaged in a discussion, and she always gave easy answers, sweet and smiling, such as: *ne ne*, yes yes, *mir mir*, good good, *oh bukur bukur*, oh beautiful beautiful. And that's what she said to her son as she mentally organized the job she would soon be doing: salting the sardines her father had purchased in Marina.

Costantino's sisters, however, felt a shiver down their spines after hearing his tale, especially Orlandina, as she was the most impressionable. They soon got a hold of themselves, and Lucrezia, the youngest but the more cunning of the two—who claimed to understand people's malice—advised him not to repeat his story to anybody or he would become the town fool and everyone would consider him to be crazy in the head.

But Costantino was stubborn—and in this, he really did resemble his father—and instead of staying quiet, as his sisters advised him, he continued to add details to his story: the double-headed eagle had green and blue feathers, strong, curved beaks and red talons, and slowly flew through the air with majestic movements; a group of Arbëreshë people gathered on the beach had also seen it; it was, according to Costantino, the same eagle that led the Arbëreshë from

Arbërìa to Italy, an eternal eagle that every now and then mysteriously appeared over the sea and disappeared into the Sila mountains.

When schools reopened on October first, Costantino dove into the new geographical maps that hid the shabby walls of his classroom. For days, he examined all of Europe and the countries that overlook the Mediterranean. All summer he had imagined Arbërìa as a land of steep, snow-covered mountains, where double-headed eagles built their nests and where men, women, and children battled day and night against the Turks under the command of the descendants of Skanderbeg and of Costantino il Piccolo. Now, he was searching for a geographical reference point, something concrete and trustworthy, in which he could firmly anchor his story. No matter how hard he tried, even with the help of some of his classmates, he couldn't find a nation, or region, bearing the name Arbërìa. Yes, there were nations with similar and equally alluring names—Algeria, Albania—but there was not even a hint of Arbërìa.

Signor Maestro Stratigò, an elderly Arbëresh from Shën Kolli, turned the violet bags that clouded his eyes toward the center of the ceiling when the boys asked him where Arbërìa was, the one their grandparents spoke of from time to time. The message of the maestro was clear: Keep quiet or I'll get angry. However, Costantino not only repeated his question but he also mentioned the story of the double-headed eagle. At that point the violet bags became threatening, and the maestro, banging his fists angrily on the desk, yelled: "But what Arbërìa?! We live in Italy. Eagle my foot! You're all a bunch of jackasses! You don't even know how to speak Italian. It doesn't get through your thick skulls that by law you're not allowed to read or speak Albanian, at least at school, at the very least at school. You're a bunch of jackasses!"

From that day on, Signor Maestro Stratigò became even more scrupulous in his observation of the ministerial decrees, and for those whose ears were so dirty they couldn't hear, he said there was a sign hanging next to the blackboard, on which was written in capital letters: "It is strictly forbidden to speak Albanian."

Even the Litirj maestri laughed behind his back about the sign. They couldn't make sense of their old colleague's stubbornness—as he himself was Arbëresh or *Ghieghiu*, as they used to say—in punishing pupils who, in conversation with a classmate, let a *gjé*, listen, a *qetu*, be quiet, or a quiet *vre*, look, slip from their mouths, and whipping them with harsh strokes. When the children instinctively avoided his blows, the sound of whipping was also heard in other classrooms. But the maestro continued to strike them, deaf to their pleas and justifications of the young pupils who yelled: "My mouth just does it, I didn't do it on purpose, *më vete goja*, my mouth just does it!"

These whippings went on for a few months until the maestro, in a fit of rage, broke the oak ruler over Costantino's head, causing a bump of three fingers tall, and then he smacked Michele, Costantino's desk mate, who cried for the rest of the morning. Two days later, Signor Maestro did not show up to class anymore, officially because of illness. In reality, at around eight that morning, a little bit past Konicella, a small group of men led by nani Lissandro and Michele's father, waited for Signor Maestro's white Fiat Seicento. They were armed with piercing gazes (some say they had knives, but you know how people are), and full of conviction, they warned the maestro (with their blades pointed at his body) never to set foot in Hora again if he wanted to make it to the age of retirement safely. Signor Maestro didn't say a word; there was only an awkward noise that faintly snuck out, little by little, until it vanished, and then an intense smell of beans and rotten eggs filled the air.

Carmelo Bevilacqua from Belcastro, the new Signor Maestro, was a young, rosy-cheeked, chubby boy with thick glasses that left a red mark on his sweaty nose when he took them off. He settled in Hora in the home of a Germanese, an Italian immigrant in Germany, and like any good maestro, the first thing he did was get acquainted with the sociocultural environment in which he was now teaching. The thing he found most intriguing about Hora, as he told his colleagues, had to do with it being an Italian-Albanian community: an issue, an aspect, a problem, a phenomenon that cannot be ignored in conceiving a correct approach to teaching Italian, in a sense, as a second language. It was also a wonderment, a beautiful thing, a fascinating story, as he would say to the children and the people, bombarding them with questions about how, when, and why the Arbëreshë arrived in that arid area of Calabria. The information he gathered this way, poor in factuality, would be transcribed into the small withered notebooks that he always kept handy, inside and outside the classroom.

Signor Carmelo Bevilacqua was also affable, not only a maestro and scholar. Affable and kind, *i mirë si buka*, as good as bread. He was a poor boy, all alone, with no mother, said zonja Elena and other mothers with daughters whose trousseau had already been completed. The Signor Maestro didn't exactly look like a maestro, in fact, he was a bit unkempt; his shirt collars were poorly ironed, and as if that wasn't enough, they were covered in dandruff, he never wore a tie, and never had a clean shave, not even on holidays. Poor boy, all alone, with no mother. But everyone liked him, including the *burra* of Hora, old and young, who perhaps thought he was innocuous and well-mannered, and therefore incapable of touching or even thinking about touching their *gra*, whether it be daughters, or sisters, or wives, or fiancées. Furthermore, the maestro's interest in the traditions and daily life of the town, the fact that he played cards with them, the short time in which he acquired and learned to pronounce many Arbëreshë words clearly and correctly, and his small notebook in which he inscribed idiomatic expressions and episodes of local history flattered them and made them swell with pride; and it contributed to making him one of the few Litirj, sent from above, truly proper, "One of us, from Hora," as they would tell him, convinced they were giving him some sort of high compliment.

The pupils of the fourth grade loved their Signor Maestro. There was no comparison with the previous one. Carmelo Bevilacqua was as good and patient as an angel. One morning, in fact, when the pupils were tasked with drawing a still-life of an object or a person in the classroom, nearly everyone chose to sketch the maestro, with his rosy and rounded face like the "O" in Giotto. It was Costantino himself who thought to add white angel wings sprouting from the back of this model maestro. Come to think of it, those wings were a sign of gratitude, subconsciously of course, toward a maestro from another world who, on the first day on the job had already broken that despised oak ruler and thrown it into the brazier that heated the classroom; who allowed his pupils to speak Arbëresh without punishing them; who had taken Costantino's story of the fair seriously, of the things he had learned and seen, and of the eagle, the double-headed eagle; and so on and so forth.

One evening, Costantino was bursting with joy because his mother had invited Signor Maestro to dinner, as many other families in Hora had done. At first, when the maestro presented himself at the Avatis' house with a carnation for zonja Elena and two red roses for the sisters, Costantino felt embarrassed, and he stuttered and laughed for no reason. Later, however, he behaved as a perfect host, offering the guest some egg marsala and introducing him to all the members of the family: mother, grandfather, Orlandina, Lucrezia, Baialardo, and, of course, the Mericano: "This is my father," said Costantino, pointing toward a framed photograph hanging on the wall. That was his father. Costantino hadn't seen him for nine months, and as always happens after separation, the true image had begun to blur, giving way to the one in the portrait that dominated the bedroom: his father was pictured from the waist up beside his brother; both were young—about twenty-five years old—with white eyes and thin mustaches; both had black bands sewn onto their jackets as a sign of mourning for the death of their mother. When Costantino was three or four years old, his sisters showed him that daddy was the more handsome one, the one on the left with the chiseled, refined face. But Costantino would often get confused and kiss his uncle's face, as cold as the broken glass that protected the portrait. "This one on the left," Costantino specified, and the maestro, who perhaps that day was a bit more blind than usual, patted his clean-shaven nape and said, "You're the spitting image of your father. Two peas in a pod. Truly."

The girls, focused on setting the table in the kitchen, were marveling at the maestro's index finger as it traced Mericano's face in the air. They didn't say a word all throughout dinner, intimidated by such an educated man. Costantino, on the other hand, babbled on like a *mascìna*, a machine, and his mother said: "Let him eat in peace, the poor maestro!" Addressing her guest, she repeated to him for the umpteenth time to eat and not to worry about anything, because that was all organic food, from the garden, all homemade.

The maestro didn't know how to say no, and so he ate. He ate and talked, and he didn't fail to sneak a glance or two at the two girls in front of him. Nani Lissandro wasn't in the mood, he had heartburn, but nevertheless he smiled all the same and ate to keep the guest company.

From that evening on, Signor Carmelo Bevilacqua started to frequently visit the modest house of *za* Elena, as he now referred to Costantino's mother. Often, to justify his visits, he would say he was there because he had grown fond of little Costantino, a bright pupil with a good head on his shoulders who, with some tutoring, God willing and family finances permitting, could become a good maestro or, perhaps, a professor, or at least a bookkeeper, since he was an ace in mathematics. But sometimes he confessed he was there for *za* Elena's divine bread and beans, the best in Hora; and when, at Signor Giorgio's store, Signor Alessandro invited him to dinner, he didn't have to be asked twice. In reality, he was looking for Lucrezia's eyes there, those "sunny eyes" that "are the most beautiful in the world, I have never, ever, ever seen eyes like those," he would sing at the entrance to the alleyway to announce his impending arrival, full of furtive glances.

Lucrezia would lean her head on the quilt that she and her sister Orlandina were weaving on the loom and hide her eyes, which were the color of sea foam on a background of marble; they were beautiful, certainly, and shining, but it was the beauty and brightness of the marble, not of the sun. The two girls worked furiously, working the loom with four hands and exchanging whispered words followed by mischievous giggles.

Before leaving, the Signor Maestro would approach the loom, and, behaving as though he were an expert, he would examine the ancient warp of the multicolored quilt, running his fingertips over the little stylized bicephalous eagles, the color of red wine, and finally would proclaim: "I've never seen a quilt so beautiful, so precious, so rare: it is a quilt fit for a museum, of immeasurable value." Then he would cast a furtive glance at Lucrezia, who would immediately lower her gaze to the eagles, and he would say goodbye in a perfectly pronounced Arbëresh: "*Rrini mirë!*" Stay well!

Tre

One muggy day, toward the end of July, announced by Bai-alardo's whimpers and from a group of barefooted children shouting, "*Merikani, Merikani*," the Mericano appeared at the top of the cobbled alleyway of the Palacco neighborhood. As soon as he saw his wife and children excitedly waiting for him on the veranda, he was unable to hold back his emotions. He had watery eyes only on arrival, never on departure, because that scene catapulted him backward forty years of his life, calling back to memory the first time he saw his father return from America. He stood staring, baffled and happy at that man dressed in white with a wide-brimmed hat on his head, moving slowly through the heavy air, clean and with shiny shoes. He was as handsome as a king. "Go meet your *tata*, your dad, children," his mother had said, fixing with trembling hands her beautiful *çipulèt*, onion-shaped braids, and the *coha*, an embroidered skirt, she wore every day. But he and his two brothers stood with their backs against her skirt, intimidated by that giant white man with an upturned blond mustache.

Beside the Mericano waddled a lanky stranger who swung his pointy nose left and right toward the windows overflowing with carnations and begonias. Giacomino, the vagabond, trotted behind them, hired in the piazza in exchange for a bottle of wine. He trotted like a little mule, yoked to a wobbly cart on which stuck out, among others, a large, emerald-green suitcase, similar in color and brightness to the chest the Mericano's father had brought back from America.

When he was a couple of steps from his family members, the Mericano opened his arms and one second later clasped his wife and two daughters, while Costantino cowered like a featherless young eagle under his big wings.

Everyone, including the barefoot children, Baialardo, and a swarm of flies, entered the vestibule after the Mericano had hugged his old father-in-law, greeting him in Italian to make himself understood by the guest: "You're still nimble, pa. You really take care of yourself."

In the stifling heat of the room, the stranger was fanning himself and shooing away the flies with his hands as large as fans. With an embarrassed smile, he observed the children with their shaved heads like landing strips for the blue flies to land on; the newly painted walls already covered with a myriad of black dots; his traveling companion whispering into his wife's ear; and above all, the girls' beautiful braids that seemed almost blue in that blinding light. As for the words that fluttered about the small room, he had given up trying to grasp their meaning; the buzz of the flies sounded more familiar to him than that incomprehensible "African" dialect.

The children, after having watched the arrival scene of the Mericano with the foreigner in their dilated pupils, scampered off through the alleyways to spread the news, dragging poor Giacomino with them, who had just finished guzzling two glasses of wine.

"This man worked with me at Anelini, in the same colors unit," the Mericano explained to his family members as they listened attentively. "We even lived together for years in the same barracks. He's got a good head on his shoulders, he is a money saver and hard worker. He'll stay in town for some time as our guest."

Apart from zonja Elena who, informed by her husband, knew everything about the guest, the others thought that the foreigner was a true German: dirty blond hair, light little eyes, and tall enough to hang the sausages onto the rafters without having to climb up on a chair. But instead, "Nice to meet you, *me ciamo* Valentini Narciso. *Son d'en paesin en provincia de Trent*," I'm from a little town in the province of Trento, said the foreigner, deluding everyone at first. So, he was a Trentino. Aha! A Trentino, thought Costantino, who seized the opportunity right away to show everyone (especially his father), his geo-historical knowledge, bombarding the guest with questions: "Ah, so you are a paesano of Cesare Battisti? Did he live far from your town? Have you ever been to Campana dei Caduti? And to Castello del Buonconsiglio? And to the Dolomites? Is it true that there's a lake with red water over by you?"

The man from Trentino gave a monosyllabic answer: "Yes," repeated several times, immediately making it clear he was a man of few words. But eventually, he felt he had to commend Costantino on his excellent education. So, the Mericano first heard about the maestro, Signor Maestro Carmelo Bevilacqua, who gave lessons to Costantino for free and who was convinced that Costantino had a knack for learning. The maestro was away on vacation in his hometown, but he had the courtesy to send many warm greetings to Signor Avati, zonja Elena said. The Mericano had other plans for his son: to buy him some land with his savings from Germany so he could become an independent farmer with no masters, a landowner like Don Fidele, or at least a good artisan, like those who earn more than a Germanese and can build a house by working in Hora. The idea of having his son study seemed so far-fetched—and, as much of a realist as he was—that it hadn't even crossed his mind. The short recital given by Costantino in perfect Italian, along with the Signor Maestro's vote of confidence, made his eyes shine, totally green in that moment. "Alright," he started to say, solemnly in Italian, "I won't hold back. You will study, I promise you! But first I have a duty to settle these two daughters of mine down with two good young men." And he looked into the eyes of Orlandina and Lucrezia, who lowered their gazes, blushing. Then he pulled out a little ring of keys from the pocket of his pants and with the smallest one, opened the lock on the big emerald-green suitcase. Bursting from it came cotton T-shirts covered in incomprehensible print, velvet skirts, light-weight floral print dresses, wide-brimmed straw hats, knives, limes, axes of solid steel, polka-dot ties, lots of chocolates melted from the heat, candies, peanuts, packs of cigarettes, and nylon shirts for the family members and relatives. The Mericano's eyes continued to shine, green and prideful; his calloused hands seemed as light and delicate as those of a woman, and his tongue was the needle on a record player, stuck on the note: "Ehè," which was echoed by a chorus of "Oooh!"s. Ehè, oooh, ehè, oooh. The man from Trentino wanted to laugh, but he held himself back. The items were passed from hand to hand, they were patted or stroked delicately and admired with curiosity, and they became tepid, warm, alive until the last hand, zonja Elena's magical hand, made them disappear in the pantry, in the armoire, in the trunk, and in the little dresser drawers. "Everything in its place," zonja Elena intended to specify to the guest, because she loved a tidy house, and because hers was a small, humble house, but it was neat and clean, and because soon, friends, relatives, and neighbors would be stopping by to greet her Mericano with his well-trimmed mustache, her king with emerald eyes, just by the sight of whom her heart filled with joy, her eyes with tears, and her head with fluttering butterflies, butterflies that flitted back and forth in time, never still, these blessed butterflies, never still.

From every alleyway of Hora, the awaited army poured into the living room to embrace the Mericano, and they embraced him; to get news of the paesani in Ludwigshafen, and they got it; to meet the foreigner, and they met him; to know if by chance—but yes, of course you can tell us, we will stay silent as the grave—in short, if that gentleman was the boyfriend of the eldest daughter.

The Mericano answered neither *ne* nor *jo*. He smiled and gave great pats to friends, pinches to ladies and children, and cuddles to his little Costantino whose back was glued to the Mericano's legs and seemed that he wanted to defend him from the kisses and hugs of the invaders.

The Trentino now felt, more than ever, like a fish out of water, with his head that stood out over the army of dwarves. His little eyes watered, weary from the journey and from constantly diving into dozens of curious and smiling eyes. In that unfamiliar, noisy confusion, he was no longer able to make out the blue hair of the daughters of Francesco Avati, who was called, as far as he could tell, the Mericano. Which was Orlandina, the daughter about which Francesco had spoken to him at length, the girl who whistled now and again, or the other one, the more serious one, with the sad eyes and nervous hands? What did it matter? They were both beautiful, and he, at forty, certainly couldn't afford the luxury of nitpicking; he didn't have any time left, it was now or never. As a young man, he had planned on working and saving: that was why he left, wasn't it? He hadn't noticed as he slipped on the banana peel of time and tumbled forward, without having enjoyed anything during that slide other than the meager satisfaction of buying two plots of land in his region, two plots for a future that had already passed. His mind kept returning to those two plots of land, he dove his watery eyes into the living and lifeless points of the room, and he recalled his parents buried in the little cemetery in town, near his meadows—come to think of it, he had never thought about the proximity! On the plots of land, he would plant apple trees, Canadian and Golden, as his brothers had done; he would build a little villa and a stable, and he would raise some cows, rabbits, and children. Because children are the salt of life, his dear old mother had told him often, a concept that his friend Francesco Avati also reiterated: "A man without children is like a spent ember." So, was he waiting for children to fall from the sky? The *terrone*, the southerner from the Albanian town, with whom he shared a room for six years, had been clear, "I have an almost twenty-year-old daughter, as beautiful as the Madonna, and she is intelligent. In her dowry, she has the trousseau that she is weaving and embroidering by herself, along with the house we live in, or the equivalent in German marks. I am talking to you man to man; she's easy to digest, like a glass of water. Her only blemish is that she had an affair with someone, a piece of shit that wanted to marry her, in words he had already married her, but then, when it came down to it, he backed out because some hussies in his family, his mother included, said my Orlandina wasn't good enough for them. She wasn't, because they have two more hectares of land than we do, they have cows and houses, and therefore their son could go for one of the shallow daughters of the steward of Don Fidele. If you'd like, you can see her, my Orlandina. If you'd like, you can come with me to my hometown, no obligations. But if she says no, we'll still be friends, just as before. *Gut?*"

"Gut, gut," OK, OK, he had replied. And on that gut, with his eyes about to completely liquify and pour themselves out onto the floor, he heard Francesco Avati's voice, accompanied by a pat on the back: "Valentini, did you see how many lovely people came to greet us! This is nothing like Germany! Here, everyone knows and respects you, here you are not an *Itaker*, an Italian *Gastarbeiter*, you're never alone here! Well, now let's finally eat!"

Just the family was left now, sitting around the overflowing table. The plates of vermicelli steamed like volcanos, and they smelled of basil, garlic, fresh tomatoes, sausage, and pecorino cheese. The Trentino anticipated the taste of it, sniffing with discretion.

"*Peperoncino?*" asked nani Lissandro.

"Oh goodness, no!" answered the guest, recalling the Mericano's deadly sauces, and he covered his plate with his hands. Everyone else at the table began to chop those fiery red horns, one or two per plate, even the youngest, even the two girls with their delicate rosy little mouths; everyone sprinkling their volcanoes with little red circles and white seeds, which were so spicy that they would numb your tongue, light your mouth on fire, and rim your butthole with hemorrhoids.

Katër

To the Trentino, it seemed that all they thought about in that African town was drinking, eating, and shelter from the heat. By the fourth day after their arrival, the procession of visitors had yet to end. Calm and smiling, they would drink a few cognacs or glasses of wine, or almond milk or orange soda, and until lunch or dinner time hang onto every word of the Mericano in continuous movement. Francesco Avati was unrecognizable: he was no longer the taciturn, sulky, clumsy man that the Trentino knew in his German version, a man so insecure that he asked for his help even when he went grocery shopping. He was the Mericano now: cheerful, talkative, and arrogant, with eyes of another color, of a brilliant green. The Mericano, in an undershirt day and night, ate and talked, drank and talked. Everyone would have preferred to hear about Germany, but it seemed the Mericano's only audience was his Trentino friend, who already knew everything about Germany. So he talked about his past, and the Trentino ate with a miserable face, maybe without even listening to him—it could be that he was angry at his own shyness, because as of yet he had only been able to exchange six words with Orlandina: *buon giorno*, good morning, *buona sera*, good evening, *buon appetito*, bon appetit. The meals were the only times he had her in front of him; for the rest of the day, she stayed chatting separately with her sister or working at the loom.

The Mericano ate, the Trentino ate, and Costantino safeguarded in his memory all the details of those tepid, tepid late July evenings, with the cone-shaped shadow of Mount San Michele covering the Palacco neighborhood, his mention of the double-headed eagle, the hens pecking the crumbs off the red pavement bricks, the bellowing laugh of the Mericano and the more reserved one of the Trentino, Baialardo gnawing on the salty ham bone, and papa talking . . .

You must know, my dear Valentini, that on one December night, ten years ago, right here, above our heads, the charred beams of an abandoned old house came down, demolishing our kitchen and half the wall that separates this room from the next. We were truly lucky that time, right, Elenuzza? Fortunate in our misfortune. The sky dumped buckets of water, thundering and flashing like fireworks. We were sitting before the fireplace, enjoying the last embers and talking about the olive harvest of that year, which, without the help of Elenuzza who was nine months pregnant, seemed never-ending. Anyway, we were talking and perhaps guided by the hand of fate, we suddenly decided to go to bed. In fact, we had just crawled under the covers and we heard a loud ruckus, a tumbling of stones by the bed, and a shower of rubble on the bed. *Madonna mia*, an earthquake! Elenuzza began to wail and sob, and the girls, hearing their mother despairing, did the same. I told myself: the world is crumbling, but I tried to encourage them, yelling that nothing had happened. They clung to me like ivy around my legs and neck. I wasn't able to move, trapped in a box made from *tijlli*, wooden beams, fallen from the roof. I thought of the consequences that the shock might have on the baby my wife was carrying in her womb. I knew it was a boy. Everyone was saying so: with her round belly and her low saggy bottom, it had to be a boy. And I thought of my first son who might be stillborn, and inside me I despaired, without realizing the risk of another collapse, of the dangerous situation in which we all found ourselves. A shower of lightning bolts and the voice of my father-in-law yelling at me to get out of there brought me to my senses. I covered Elenuzza and the girls with a blanket, and by the light of the lightning bolts, after having removed the rubble with my father-in-law, we ran to Caterina Fioravanti's house, a neighbor as good as bread. My wife was feeling really bad, writhing around like a serpent. The old woman anticipated what was about to happen and didn't get discouraged. She sent the girls to the kitchen with their grandfather and had me heat some water, she gathered clean sheets, scissors, thread, and lots of scraps of linen, and she even found some comforting words: "Have courage, my daughter, everything will be fine." A shrill and prolonged wail, louder than the roll of the thunder, jolted me from my nightmare. Little Costantino was born. Costantino, my little one, was born, and I didn't give a damn about the collapsed house, I hugged the old woman, the grandpa, the girls, Elenuzza, and I saw that little black and blue guy, yelling and yelling, and searching for his mother's breast with his eyes closed.

The next day I found an old house for rent, a narrow, stuffy little shack. I lasted about three years there, but at the first chance, I packed my bags and left for Germany, intent on rebuilding my house with my savings.

According to Costantino, the past clouded his father's head, just like the strong wine he drank in abundance did, whereas the present only filled his belly and sometimes made him vomit.

Being born on the night of a downpour, and even on a Friday, would preserve the Mericano's son from the misfortune that had met his dear departed father, of whom Costantino carried the name: this was the Mericano's deep conviction. There had been no need to wrap the legs of the bed with rags, as his own mother had done when he, the Mericano, was born, to prevent those mule-footed women going to visit the newborn child from getting hurt and cursing him; nor had they laid a bountiful table in a corner to mollify them with food, since in doing so, as it was believed back then, they would bring good fortune to the newborn. In the modern age in which Costantino was born, these beliefs had disappeared almost completely because people had become more *'sperti*, aware. And if those fates had really existed, on that night of the downpour they would have remained in their home by the river or in the gorge. He would make his son's good fortune himself, with his own hands, with his own sacrifices. Costantino wouldn't go roaming around the world like his grandfather had, and as he himself was doing, for a piece of bread. He would stay peacefully at his home, working as a professional, as this Signor Maestro said, or maybe as a farmer, but at his home, among his people, and he would enjoy his children, he would have the time to cuddle them as they grew.

Everyone knew what the Mericano was getting at, everyone except for the Trentino. In fact, as often happened to him when he drank at least a liter of wine, he started on the story of his father who died in the 'Merica Bona, dead and buried all at once, under an avalanche of coal. He was four years old when he saw him for the first time, and he enjoyed his cuddles for about three months; then his father left Naples, forever. The Italian consul sent a telegram to the mayor of Hora, and he showed up at the house with that sheet of yellow paper to deliver the bad news. What struck the Mericano was not the desperate wailing of his mother, who was pulling her hair out in clumps, scratching her face with her nails, and beating her chest with her fists, making it resonate like a drum, but it was the *vajtim*, the funeral lament, which followed when his mother didn't have either her voice or her strength anymore: the vajtim, intoned by his grandmother who traced back the stages of life of her *figlio i ziu*, that is, her black, unfortunate son. It was impossible for him to remember what it was about since he was too young then, but the effect it had on him, that is something that he still carried inside of him. It was a lament that penetrated the skin, the blood, the brain, so much so that the Mericano heard it often when he was alone, he confessed. Around the old woman, with her stringy hair let down on her shoulders, was a room full of women in black and men with long beards. In place of the coffin, on the kitchen table with four lit candles at its sides, there was a portrait of his poor father: blond and with a thick, upturned mustache, in his thirties. But with blurred eyes, without light, as of one who is destined to die young.

From that day on, the Mericano's mother had rolled up the sleeves of her mourning coha and worked the fields for her entire life like a man, better than a man, and her children never lacked for anything, not shoes, nor clothes, nor bread and butter, and she never let them go work for the wealthy people of the town. They took off her mourning coha thirty years later, when all the sons had been working abroad for a while, and they dressed her, as it was customary, with the golden wedding coha, which was too puffy for the coffin, but it made her look twenty years younger.

Pesë

They had the Trentino stay in the kitchen for the night, sleeping on a mattress stuffed with corn husks, under linen sheets embroidered by hand.

"Valentini will be fine. In Germany, we didn't even have sheets, and we used our coats as blankets in the bitter cold," the Mericano said to his wife who had thousands of qualms.

As a matter of fact, the Trentino didn't complain, even though Baialardo often played with his bare feet that stuck out of the makeshift bed. With each tiny movement of his body, the dry corn husks crunched and sounded like shots in the heavy night air. No, the Trentino didn't complain, but he wasn't enthusiastic about spending sleepless nights and fruitless days in that hole far away from the world that was as dry and yellow as Baialardo's crap, waiting for an answer of utmost importance to him.

The Mericano didn't manage to speak to his daughter face-to-face to reveal his friend's intentions to her. He hoped his daughter would understand on her own, and that maybe she would like Valentini, at least a little. He probably couldn't find the right words, the Mericano, though he was a skilled orator when he wanted to be; he was just waiting for something to develop on its own, or maybe he was waiting for his guilty conscience to fade. But Orlandina didn't understand, or pretended not to understand, the half-spoken phrases, the quasi-allusions, the discrete praise largely made by her mother to the stranger, a man born to make a woman happy, a man without vices, who doesn't drink, doesn't smoke, doesn't waste money, who has two fields, a house in town and one in the mountains, and forty thousand marks in the bank, which is no chump change. In town, everyone talked about Orlandina's upcoming wedding, which she knew nothing about. Her head and heart were still packed with memories, emotions, and a love-hate that she, despite her best efforts, could not shake. That Judas (perhaps she called him this in her thoughts), that Judas whose name she was loath to pronounce, had tricked her, had minced her heart up and thrown it to the wolves. Why hadn't she heeded her mother's warnings? *Gjaku ësht giaku*, blood is blood, it never lies. Family is family. That is a family of pimps and whores. Don't trust them, *bijë*! Why didn't she stop after her mother, her grandfather, and even little Costantino had scolded her? Why hadn't they beaten her to death, why? Ah, if her father had been in town, he would have eaten her alive, and he would have beaten that man like an old drum, covered him in black and blue, banged him up like an old pan. Her mother had cried every day. And Orlandina, with the brazen boldness of her sixteen years and her face warm as a running oven, would meet him at night in the alleyway under the starlight, by day in her grandfather's barn, or in the cave near the pigsty. Any excuse was a good one: going to watch TV at a friend's, bringing grass to the rabbits or sludge to the pigs, and he was always on earth, in the sky, everywhere, just like Christ, leaning against the worn, snapdragon-covered walls, lying on the hay mixed with honeysuckle flowers, lurking in the cave hidden by the branches of a wild fig tree. They were a handful of seconds in which their hearts would rumble like thunder, and their lips would suck at each other with force, and their hands would explore the hot, firm ridges of their bodies in their clothes, and the groan was as one, suffocating and continuous, for a handful of seconds that seemed to enclose all of Orlandina's life, trapping her in an infernal circle from which she might try to escape, escape with the potion of agave, poppies, and copper fungicide, free herself forever from that Judas who was suddenly engaged to another woman, obeying his aunts' will like a dog. She had vomited pasta and greenish beans, poppy seeds, and copper fungicide foam for an entire night, and her mother had cried and pulled her hair, and cursed her husband for having abandoned her in that hell with a basket-case girl; she had cursed Germany and that *bir putërje*, that heartless family, that family of pigs; she had prayed to her family's dead to save her luckless daughter, while her daughter prayed to the same ancestors to make her die, to break that circle in which suffocating memories floated.

The dead had then listened to the mother, who had a mass said for them with altar servers, and the daughter appeared purged from that tapeworm that devoured her guts. She seemed to bloom anew like a cherry tree in springtime, and when she combed her blue locks and rinsed her smooth, shiny face with mint water in the morning, and brushed her white teeth with ash, she would have made the great-grandson of Skanderbeg himself fall in love if he had passed by. Her mother was pleased with her appearance, though the circle of sadness at the bottom of her daughter's gray eyes did not evade her, nor did the deep groove on her eyelids: the wrinkle of despair. *Më të ligtit ka skuar, bijë*, the worst is over, daughter, but it is known that a fire covered in ash still burns. In fact, that wound burned, yes indeed: it was deep and circular, for Orlandina's whole life.

The proposal made to her by her father a week before leaving with the Trentino was the stone cast in the lake of her memory, emanating ripples that multiplied all night long, now small now large, encompassing bunches of kisses, honeysuckles, and snapdragons, and finally they crashed beside the stranger like a window wide open to the world, far from that town she hated.

"I don't mean to impose my will upon you," her father told her, not looking her in the eyes. "I think you would want for nothing with Valentini, I would leave you in good hands. You must be the one who decides. You will give me an answer tomorrow. If it is yes, you will become engaged, he will arrange for the house and the business in his town, and you will be married a year from now."

Costantino was present that evening, he heard his father's muffled words, and to this day he remembers his sister's tearless sobs and her tossing and turning in the messy bed that night, unable to find rest.

The next day, zonja Elena and one of the Mericano's sisters made the rounds of the town dressed in their Sunday best, announcing the engagement of Orlandina and the stranger, "*me një burr të huaj*," as they said, "*nga provinçja i Trentit*," from the province of Trento.

Gjashtë

During the day, the door to the Signor Maestro's house was always open, as is custom in Hora after all. So, in the afternoon, the pupils would walk into the little front room without knocking and would place on a table, heavily laden with books and well-worn notepads, a *kulaç* of warm bread, or a bottle of wine, or two eggs of the day, or some fruit in season, or a bit of fresh milk, or some fresh ricotta, and then they would quickly run out again. They knew the maestro would not accept those gifts because he felt embarrassed, and if he caught them with a gift in hand, he would say, "Tell your mothers I thank them, they are very kind, though I cannot accept!" When they brought him a longhorn beetle, known in Hora by the misnomer of *çikalle me brirat*, they would call aloud, "Signor Maestro, a cicada with horns." He would come rushing from the bedroom and, happy and excited, would take off his glasses to get a better look. He had a collection of more than a hundred specimens, some living and some preserved dead. His pupils couldn't understand what he found so interesting about those mute little black creatures. Could they understand what a maestro feels? "Don't you see how elegant this little insect is? It looks like it's wearing a tailcoat. It walks gracefully, waving its splendid antennae and flapping its slender butterfly wings for long movements." No, they could not understand. The adults smiled at this oddity: it was the quirk of an educated man. Nothing too astounding about it. Yet, his pupils didn't just encourage him, but in many cases imitated him, collecting their own elegant, horned cicadas, while the more eccentric ones collected singing cicadas, two-tailed lizards, and ladybugs with no black spots.

For his part, Costantino contented himself with collecting new details about the appearance of that double-headed eagle, including it in his writing whenever the prompt of an essay offered him a chance to talk about it. In one composition for class, fortunately based on fiction, he wrote about a giant double-headed eagle carrying a bearded man wearing a helmet with a goat's head on top, wielding a large golden sword. A man, in other words, who bore a striking resemblance to that image of Skanderbeg the maestro had shown him one day. The latter, very seriously, read Costantino's essay aloud, while his peers mocked him, exclaiming with amusement, "*Po po po*, that stinks!" But Costantino seemed not to care about them. He cared about the Signor Maestro's opinion, only that. "Well, Skanderbeg on an eagle, it seems too unlikely to me, let's see . . . I mean, I would completely exclude an event of this sort, even though sometimes reality exceeds imagination. But . . ." the Signor Maestro said calmly, "I mean . . . let's see . . ." and he reflected for a long while, massaging the base of his nose, after having removed his glasses. "But there is nothing to laugh about the double-headed eagle. During my military service, in a museum in

Rovereto, I saw a taxidermied little double-headed calf. I mean, it is nature sometimes that works these wonders . . . I mean, it could very well exist, a double-headed eagle. I mean, it can exist, or it could have existed in other times. Well, I can't say whether it would be able to fly with two heads . . ." And Costantino stuck his tongue out, black from eating fresh nuts, at his classmates who had previously mocked him, taking partial revenge in his own way.

How many beautiful things Signor Maestro had seen, how many beautiful things he had read, and he knew how to explain them all! He, a Litir from Belcastro, knew more about the Arbëreshë than all the people of Hora combined, including the parish priest and the other teachers. Because he read, he always read. And he finally explained that Arbëria absolutely exists! It is right in front of Apulia and is now called Albania. Arbëria is the former name of what is now Albania, *Shqipëria* in Albanian, the Land of the Eagles to be exact, freed from Turkish oppression in 1912. In Italy, however, there are dozens of towns in which ancient Albanian, Arbëresh to be exact, is spoken, and these towns, located in Abruzzo, Molise, Apulia, Basilicata, Campania, Calabria, and Sicily, make up "Little Arbëria." Is it clear now?

Costantino nodded in class, full of admiration for the maestro, and at night in his home he would become Costantino, the Piccolo of the Signor Maestro, from whose lips he hung excitedly. The free lessons were fruitful, despite the constant interruptions of the maestro who, though not having been asked by anyone, had taken upon himself the task of appraising the art of weaving quilts. He would very often approach the loom and admire the stylized bicephalous eagles, always touching them delicately with his fingertips, while sending discreet, coded messages of love from the corner of his eyes.

Costantino learned how to use Pythagoras' theorem, a compass, an atlas, and how to solve equations to calculate the volume of a solid, and he could recite "Silvia, do you remember still/that moment in your mortal life," while the Signor Maestro would launch his fiery arrows of love at Lucrezia's heart, making it pound like crazy under her nylon blouse, and in *te zjarri i zëmërës*, in the fires of her heart, her emotions and desires burned, revealing themselves through colors on her face, now white, now pink, now red. Every once in a while, she would let out a little nightingale-like whistle, when the embarrassment spilled out of her smiling and darting eyes, but the sweet whistle that rose from her heart-shaped lips was a far cry from that savage sound of her past as a rude *burraçë*: it was the call of a nightingale in love.

Costantino didn't understand the subtle distinction the Signor Maestro made one evening, between "a heart with ventricles that pumps blood" and "a heart with wings that unlocks love." Zonja Elena, on the other hand, did not miss anything, even though it seemed like she was intently mending her father's thick woolen socks. She knew. She knew and she was glad in her heart. Let the women in the neighborhood talk. They had already done so with Orlandina, but after her engagement with Narciso, they were green with envy just like Trabekku. Let them talk. The grandpa was there, in the house. There was a *burr*. And nani Lissandro indeed was there: asleep next to the burning hearth, or busy whittling olive or walnut logs with an ax and a small knife, from which, as if by magic, would emerge large wings and heads with curved beaks of flying eagles that he would gift to the children of the gjitonia. But grandpa didn't notice the sparks of love that glittered in the large room under the sharp strokes of the loom. To grandpa, Signor Carmelo Bevilacqua was an educated Litir, lonely and far from home. Therefore, a man to host. Because hospitality is sacred.

On those mild spring Sundays, he would take him to the woods, along with his grandson and Baialardo. And then nani Lissandro was the Maestro, and Signor Bevilacqua was a diligent pupil who hung on each word he uttered and took endless notes. Despite his age and his constant curses against the bastard demon who had weakened him, nani Lissandro walked fast, and he had an extraordinary memory and skill to tell stories, as noted by the actual maestro who was in the mood for paying gracious compliments. But nani Lissandro didn't even understand some of those words. In the woods of Krisma, where for years he had pastured his goats, he felt at home, he knew the most remote paths, the hiding in the cavities of the most ancient oaks, the deepest caves, the springs with the freshest and cleanest water. It had been his world, his 'Merica, his Germany. In his free time, he had pottered around in his plot of land, and his family had never lacked anything, neither oil, nor wine, nor bread, because, not to brag about himself, but he knew how to work the land better than a man who was just a farmer. Don Nico Morello rented the Krisma olive grove only to him because he was the best at pruning the olive trees: the goats stripped the tender little branches that were pruned, and he was left with the wood to burn and chop, and if it was a good year, a few tons of oil to sell. Don Morello didn't want to hear shit: the quantity of oil was negotiated at the start of the blooming season; half of the calculation was made by his experts. He would come to collect it, even if a frost or hail had reduced the harvest to a quarter of the estimated olives.

The maestro would stop in one of the many clearings that dotted the woods to admire with his binoculars the mountains of Sila or the waterfall that flowed in the distance, only barely visible to the naked eye; and nani Lissandro sighed. He sighed and said that he had many memories whistling in his head. Memories of his youth in those woods, many adventures, so many. And since these were not adventures for children, one day he sent his grandson to go look for Baialardo, who hadn't been around for a while and who, he said, probably believed he had to find lost goats like he used to do when he was young, risking—with his heart in his throat—dying of exhaustion. Then he started telling his story in the present tense, as he always did when the memory was so strong and alive that it turned time upside down.

Now then, many women come out here to collect twigs for the bread-baking oven. Women from Hora and from Shën Kolli. He, the young nani Lissandro, herds his flock around here. In the early morning, he cuts the twigs and piles them in neat little stacks, ready to be loaded on the back. Someone thanks him and says he is a *burr i mirë*, and he replies, yes, he is a good man, but above all, he is a *burr.* Other women understand and play along, joking and laughing, because women like to joke about these things, and tell him he is very bold and that one of them has a husband or a fiancé or a father who, if he finds out, would cut him in half alive, but in the end . . . Just the thought of Filumena makes him horny. She is married but has no children, so she is slender. She is a *grua me kripë*, a salty woman. She is thirty or so, and he is twenty-one. She grabs him by the neck and wants to fight with him. They tumble in the grass, entwined. She laughs. Let's see who is stronger, she says. And she touches him just there, as they wrestle, as though she wasn't doing it on purpose. They roll all the way to the oak tree, and he lets her pin him down. And so, still laughing, as though she were joking, she sits atop him and unbuttons his moleskin trousers, she grabs his hands and places them on her firm *sise*, and he sees the foliage of the oak tree spinning round and round him as in a vallja, and the sun's rays and the paradise that he savors make him close his eyes tight.

Costantino started to snigger behind a bush; then nani started to chase after him, waving a stick in the air. "Ah, *bir putërje*, son of a bitch, if I catch you!" he said, laughing.

On the way home, nani Lissandro kept insisting on his idea about women with and without salt, *me kripë e pa*, while the maestro wrote, tirelessly, as he walked.

"Yes, Filumena is a *grua me kripë*, a real woman, unlike all those *pa* women. Yes, *grat me kripë* are dear and good and loyal, but they are dangerous, because they have fire in their hearts, under those firm sise. Filumena is like that," concluded nani Lissandro, and he sighed in the face of those giant evergreen oaks that adorn the entrance to Hora. The question had been on the tip of the maestro's tongue for some time: "And Lucrezia, Signor Alessandro, Lucrezia. What do you think she's like?"

"Lucrezia?" nani Lissandro replied. Lucrezia was a *grua me kripë*, you could tell by her cutting, experienced, and passionate gaze. He, nani Lissandro, imagined her like the Arbëresh girl that had bet against an evil Turk to see who of the two could drink more. The Turk would have bet the Arbëresh prisoner that he had tied up to him, while she would have bet her virginal bed. Feasting and smiling, the girl, before drinking, had someone put snow in her glass in secret, while the Turk, consumed by that dangerous excitement one feels when he is sure of winning even before he has won, drank with abandon; and so, drinking, he fell asleep.

Then she untied the prisoner, gave him weapons, and together they fled on a galley toward Italy.

The maestro diligently transcribed everything, but obviously he paid no attention to the words he wrote. If he had taken just a moment to reflect, he wouldn't have behaved as he did toward Lucrezia, with the same arrogant lightness as the Turk and regretting it sorely later.

Shtatë

Orlandina's wedding date was set for the second Sunday of October. But by early July, the Mericano was already in Hora. He had even worked during the *Freischichten*, the days off, he explained, just so that he could extend his holiday by a month or so. On his way there, he had stopped at the Trentino's house for a day: Narciso had turned his parents' old house into a villa, a palace even. "You'll be a princess," he told Orlandina, who listened to him without enthusiasm.

In October, the Maestro Carmelo Bevilacqua would be returning to Hora as well, and zonja Elena hoped to arrange her youngest daughter's engagement in the presence of her husband so that he would travel back across Italy, after Orlandina's wedding, with his soul at rest.

Lucrezia counted the days on the warp of that endless, wine-red quilt: a row of stylized bicephalous eagles, a day and a half less. October was closer, when her prince in bifocals would stand before the loom.

From time to time, her prince would send a letter addressed to Costantino. "Dear Aquilotto," he would write, but the rest of the letter was a series of references to her, "to your dear sister Lucrezia" who, he imagined, was surely weaving, and he thought often to . . . that quilt of inimitable and precious eagles, as beautiful as Venus de Milo, the quilt that he couldn't wait to touch with his fingertips. P.S. He felt nostalgia for those evenings by the fire, and of *za* Elena's bread and beans.

The Mericano was the least enthusiastic about those letters. "Well then, who is this Signor Maestro of whom you cannot stop stuffing your mouth? I mean, what kind of reputation does he have in his hometown? What are his intentions?" he would ask, while his wife and children opened the envelope, curious and excited; and even Baialardo wagged his tail happily and never grew tired of sniffing the letter that smelled of bergamot. The Mericano waited in vain for an answer until he lost his patience because his family didn't even understand the questions. To them, Signor Maestro Carmelo Bevilacqua was Signor Maestro, who else could he be? And what did it matter what his reputation back home was? And what did it mean "What are his intentions"?

"As long as he's not another son of a bitch, because otherwise I'll wring everyone's necks," the Mericano said abruptly as he was about to leave for the piazza. "As long as you don't go looking for spikes on the snow," he added on the doorstep. Then the girls, hit in the heart by those cruel bullets, burst into tears, and their mother consoled them with watery eyes.

Baialardo was the only one courageous enough to bark, while nani went off on his own to file down the beaks of his eagles, as if he did not want to get involved; Costantino didn't know if he should sit by nani or follow his father walking up the hill quickly toward the piazza; seen from down there, he seemed tall and haughty.

On one of those evenings when he had left the house with dark gray eyes, the Mericano returned home glowing. He got his family together, closed the door, and announced with a certain solemnity: "The estate of Castello del Piccolo is ours."

"Ours?" asked his wife, stunned and dismayed, while the others echoed her sentiments with faces full of wonder.

The Mericano smiled under his neat mustache and slowly stuck his thumbs in the pockets of his waistcoat, like a true gentleman, his green eyes shining bright.

Don Cesare had arrived from Naples, he said with a deep sigh. His car was parked in the piazza under the elm tree. He had seen him coming down with the notary from Marina. So, he had come, as had been said for a long time, to sell half of the family Palazzo to his brother Don Fidele, and likely also the estate of Castello del Piccolo, the last remnant of his inheritance. Don Cesare, after his father's death, liquidated everything quickly, estate after estate, half the fiefdom of Santa Vènnera, and retired in Naples with his daughters, who were of marriageable age and hated that desolate little town in Calabria, with dusty roads and the young men with pitch-black skin, who shrieked in that awful Ghieghiu dialect until late at night from the bar in front of the Palazzo. On the other hand, Don Fidele, who was a bachelor, had decided to live in Hora after spending most of his youth in three different university cities in Northern Italy, after he had satisfied all his whims, as he said. And he was able to live there as the Don that he was, having sold the constructible land in small plots around the town and maintaining possession of a modern agricultural business in the plains, where he employed a foreman and four or five laborers from Hora.

The Mericano had followed Don Cesare down to the front door of the Palazzo; he introduced himself and said in a decisive tone, "I heard you are selling the estate of Castello del Piccolo. I am here to buy it in cash, even in marks if you prefer."

Don Cesare had let him enter the interior courtyard; he looked at him warily before opening his mouth: "Four million, including the castle. Not one lira less. If yes, my good man, go home, get the money, and come back with a witness."

"*Gut*," replied the Mericano in German and left the courtyard with confident strides. "*Katër milliune! Ësht i regallarum!*" Four million! It's a gift! he was repeating now to his family.

"It is not so much of a gift," said nani Lissandro, contradicting him. "The land is rocky, and there are more or less ten olive trees and about twenty wild olive trees on a hectare of land. What they call a "castle" is a useless old ruin immersed in a thorn bush. But it is just on the outskirts of town, so it is worth four million. Not more."

"In Germany for four million you can't even buy the land to dig your own grave, you can't buy it. It is a gift, it is," the Mericano answered, annoyed. "And besides, it's important to buy, because money goes away and land endures," he added, and his father-in-law replied that on this point he completely agreed with him. Hats off on this topic.

Zonja Elena retrieved the money she kept pinned in the mattress, and after counting it three times, handed it over to her husband, while her father, who needed to be the witness, went to change his hat, jacket, and shoes.

The Mericano called Costantino aside and, clutching the bag of money close to his heart, addressed him in a solemn tone, his eyes shining green: "Come, bir, you come too. This is an important day, bir, and you shall not forget it as long as you live. One wonderful day, the Castello estate will be yours, bir. It's only right that you come with us."

So, Costantino too crossed the walnut doorway of the Palazzo, climbed the marble staircase, stepped on the carpet of a long hallway, and finally, entered a room with smiling, chubby, rosy-cheeked, little angels flying in the blue sky of the ceiling.

Behind the desk piled high with papers were Don Fidele and his foreman, standing, and Don Cesare and the notary, seated; towering above everyone was the sulking face of Don Nico Filippo Morello who, from the wall where his portrait was hung, was helplessly witnessing the crumbling of his fiefdom of Santa Vènnera.

"You've closed the deal of your life, Francesco Avati," said Don Fidele with a sardonic smile at the signing of the deed of sale. And the Mericano, without losing his composure, responded: "Don Fidele, one begins with a plot of rocky terrain. Your father, blessed be his soul, began with an ass and a hectare of woods, didn't he?"

Don Fidele forced himself to smile again like before, but a clumsy smile and a more strident and nasal voice came out. "Yes, but then there was still something to buy, unlike these days . . ."

"Well, you know, since I was a boy," nani Lissandro intervened slyly, "at the Santa Vènnera fiefdom, four landowning families have come, one after another, the last being yours, the Morellos. Families come and go, but the land remains, Hora remains. And maybe . . ." nani abruptly interrupted himself. And now we will have all the things we didn't get before when we occupied the land, with the Germanese's money: perhaps he would have said this if he had continued.

Instead, Don Fidele continued with a conciliatory tone, but with the same sardonic smile as before; he agreed with nani Lissandro and admitted that times had changed, everyone these days was equal to him, or even wealthier, like some of these Germanese who knew how to make two matches from one in order to save. And while his brother was counting the money, apparently uninterested in these pointless conversations, he prided himself in being a friend to everyone, a *compare*, a godfather and a best man to many in Hora, where he lived peacefully and didn't give a crap about living close to the San Carlo Theatre.

It was Don Fidele himself who accompanied the old man, the Mericano, to the door, and his son who trailed him like a shadow, and in taking his leave, he said: "Francesco Avati, if you decide to stay in Hora, my palace is always open to you. I will tell my foreman to rent you as many hectares of land as you like!"

Oddly, the Mericano reacted as though those words had offended him. In fact, pointing to the rolled-up scroll of the notarized deed at Don Fidele, he replied, "Do me a favor, go to . . ." but he didn't finish his sentence. "Ah, Don Fidele, Don Fidele!" he added, shaking his head. "Many thanks for the thought. My regards." And they headed toward home, where the women waited for them anxiously to celebrate, nani and Costantino ahead and the Mericano behind, with the notarized deed clutched against his heart and his thoughts on Don Nico: his arrival in town forty years ago, the people in the piazza celebrating him, welcoming him the way their great-grandparents had Garibaldi, as a liberator. The men drank and toasted to Don Nico's good health, the women in coha lightly danced a vallja, Don Nico, the new boss, a man to admire, *çë burr*, from lumberjack to landlord, the children applauded, hurray for Don Nico Filippo Morello of

Cosenza, Don Morello, the podesta and landlord, the percentage of harvest as a rent doubled, and the tax for the pasture turned into cultivated land tripled, the occupation of the land, Don Nico afraid, the agrarian reform, Don Nico with his head above water, once more, ten years ago, the collapsed house, Germany.

The next day, early in the morning, the entire Avati family went to Castello del Piccolo. Nani Lissandro and his animals were already there, having somehow penetrated the Castello Forest, a mass of intertwined trees, among which were holly oaks, sessile oaks, and Turkey oaks. The so-called castle that gave its name to the grounds stood farther up on the right side of a little domed knoll, but from the mule track, along which the Avatis were climbing, one could make out only a little island of brambles, surrounded by a sea of dry grass on which floated dense crowns of wild olive trees.

"Here is our castle," the Mericano exclaimed emphatically, ten steps from the bramble. "It is small, but for us it will do." And the meaning of these words, repeated not by chance in Litisht by the Mericano who felt like being on the world stage, was immediately grasped by everyone: make the castle livable and live in it! But if someone didn't get it yet, he explained his grandiose plan more clearly in Arbëresh, with grand gestures: slowly, little by little, with a few years in Germany under his belt and with some sacrifice, the castle would be brought back to life. The merlons and possibly also half of the tower would have to be restored: redo suspended slabs, doors, and gateways, but first of all burn all that goddamned bramble—actually no, his father-in-law was right, that would risk burning some useful objects, hidden in that tangle of thorns, wild figs, palms, and oleander—first of all, tear out that undergrowth and save the savable, call some good stonemasons, and little by little and with a lot of goodwill, yes, goodwill is everything . . . and, of course, plant some grapevines and sell the wine under the name "Vino Castello del Piccolo," then yes, one could go back to living like a decent Christian in Hora. And, while the Mericano was getting the family members to give consent, Lucrezia was whistling, echoing the call of the nightingales scared by all that human chirping. Finally, nani played the part of the wise old grandfather, using a proverb that says, when too many roosters are crowing, the day has grown late; and the Mericano repeated, just to conclude, first of all, that undergrowth had to be torn out, right away, now, *nanì nanì.*

Trimming against the grain of the castle's hirsute foliage lasted roughly ten days. By the end, even Costantino and the girls had become skilled at handling billhooks. They sang at the top of their lungs "Fatti mandare dalla mamma a prendere il latte," Have your mamma send you out for milk, while pushing away thorny branches of bramble; they swallowed blackberries and black figs while whacking their billhooks; they would prick themselves, suck their fingers, and sing at the top of their lungs "tell that guy I'm jealous."

The adults, on the other hand, were sweaty and sometimes swore because even before finishing the first task, they were thinking of the other million things that had to be done, and they sweated more just at the thought of it: the rocks spread across the ground, the hard terrain, unharvested for decades, *ohj Krisht i bekuar!* Oh, blessed Christ!

Finally, the big stones of the castle's outer walls glistened under the sun's rays; the entry gate had clearly been pulverized; of the merlons, only a few jagged traces remained, the tower seemed to have had its top mutilated. That construction with a sturdy structure, more than a castle, must have been one of those fortified towers used for defense during the time of the Saracen raids, but to the Avatis it was Castello del Piccolo, as it was called in town. They were devouring it with their eyes, their castle, it was there, in all its grandeur, or rather, smallness: twenty steps by twenty, give or take, the smallest castle in the world, already anointed by nani, with a malicious smile on his lips.

The Mericano seemed annoyed by that misplaced irony, because if one looked carefully at it, the castle was clearly more than twenty by twenty, he would bet his head on it.

"Oh, my dear Mericano, this was the castle of the dwarves, not of Costantino il Piccolo, who had a savage horse that was taller than this entryway," and by saying so, the old man gave a swipe with his ax at a pear tree that was suffocating under the thorny tentacles of a bramble that had grown up in place of the front door.

The hollow trunk split in two and freed a swarm of angry wasps that forced the instigator down the slope, his arms protecting his face, and then down, fast as a young man, slithering onto the lawn in search of shelter that was not there. Two or three suicidal wasps stabbed him mercilessly on the back of his hands, but luckily the bulk of the swarm buzzed past his head and was lost far away in the haze.

When the Mericano noted that his father-in-law was alive and well, on his feet, dusting off his clothes and touching the painful stings, he took his own revenge: a thunderous laugh that echoed from the gorge afar.

Tetë

To the Mericano, Signor Maestro Carmelo Bevilacqua didn't seem very likable. It was his way of speaking, always saying "that is," "let's see," "even though," his way of continuously laying out those stories of the Albanians of Calabria, or his thick glasses, slightly greasy like his hair. In any case, there was something that he didn't like about him. "That is," he would say, in a maestro tone and manner, "I'm telling you facts, not fairy tales;" only to then contradict himself with two "even thoughs" thrown in for effect, "even though, even though, fairy tales are often, deep down, truer than true facts." On his return from summer vacation, he brought a stack of papers and books from Naples containing the entire history of the Albanians in Calabria. According to Carmelo Bevilacqua, even they, the Avatis, were in those ancient pages; but there was nothing special about that. The real surprise was something else: the Avatis, once upon a time, had been a family of dukes, the Dukes of Avati. This was a big surprise. It was met with a long, collective "oooh" and ended with what sounded like a meow, which was interrupted by the Mericano's loud laugh, and then by his voice: "Don't make me laugh! We've always been a family of shepherds. Shepherds, not dukes! And besides, we're originally from the town of Campana!"

The maestro was visibly irritated by that presumptuous revelation, but he didn't back down from the task of showing everyone "proof," as he called it, of what he was asserting; it must be read to be believed.

They all carefully studied the shiny photocopies, staring wide-eyed and arching their eyebrows, but unable to decipher that tiny, tightly packed writing. Costantino turned them delicately in his hands, as though they were made of crystal, and for the first time in his life, he hoped his father was wrong and that, in the clash over these papers, the Mericano would be the one to succumb.

Annoyed, the Signor Maestro put all the papers and books on the kitchen table and ordered the Avati family to sit down and pay attention, just as he did in class with his pupils. He brought the papers under his nose and began to read and analyze out loud: *"Die dominico 15 Julii 1543 . . . Venimus a Terra Ypsigro et ivimus in casale Crisme seu Hora . . .* On Sunday, July 15, 1543 . . . We came from the Land of Ypsigro and went to the hamlet Crisme or Hora . . . Let's see . . . There were 21 households, for a total of 81 inhabitants. Of these, only five possessed *vineam et boves*, wine and cattle, Pietro Macrì, Yonna Masci, Basilio Caloyera, Domenico Scandrissa and—listen up—Kustandino of the Dukes of Avati, chamberlain of the hamlet, the only one to live in a stone house."

Those gathered stared at each other wide-eyed and astonished, while Lucrezia gushed admiration from every pore, in awe of that educated and charming Prince Maestro of her most secret thoughts who, among a "Let's see," a phrase in Latin, a year, and a name, never neglected to pierce her with his myopic arrows. "Let's see . . . the year 1596, 80 households, 170 inhabitants, *cum Graeco sacerdote*, with a Greek priest, this tells us that at the time, Hora had not yet bent to the Latin rite . . . let's see . . . last names of the family heads: Basta, Biase, Brasachia, et cetera, no Avati . . ." But the maestro wasn't giving up; he examined the copied documents and compared them to a book by a certain Zangari: in 1633, there were 36 families and 119 inhabitants who lived in hay barns and shabby earthen houses, but there was no trace of the Avatis; not even in the subsequent lists, but let's see. "Let's see . . . finally! Here it is: 1842, the last name Avati appears but without the noble title, Avati Francesco, fifty-six years of age, herdsman, born in Campana, married to Candreva Marneza, twenty-one years of age, born in Hora. In other words, I believe the Avatis left Hora because they had fallen on hard times and, driven by a strong calling from their bloodline, they returned to their hometown, having never completely forgotten it at least three centuries later."

How romantic the Signor Maestro was, an imaginative and persuasive man! He almost managed to convince the Mericano as well: "It could be, I'm not saying that it couldn't. But I do know that my great-grandparents were from Campana. This much I know. But anything is possible!" Then, turning to the women in the exquisite tone of a perfect host, he said: "My ladies, have you forgotten your duties toward our guest? We may be noble, but the law applies to every-one: a guest must be honored by offering him bread, salt, and heart," and fixing his gaze on Lucrezia like one who knows all, he added, "but not just the heart, one cannot live on heart alone; we need wine, prosciutto, bread, and salted sardines!" The ladies scampered away smiling, and the Mericano made the maestro move to the head of the table, "Here we say: the guest is always given the seat of honor."

The Mericano and the maestro spoke for a long time, about Costantino's future and that of Castello del Piccolo; even nani Lissandro jumped in now and then, but with misplaced observations; it was clear that he was distracted, as he often was in recent times. The women and Costantino listened in silence, chewing slowly. The maestro and Lucrezia spoke for a long time with their eyes. However, the Mericano spoke most of all; not only was he tipsy from the sweet, strong wine, which he was no longer used to, but also because of the bitter memories of his emigration, which he recounted, licking the crumbs from his groomed mustache. "Because if one lives there, alone, without affections, without these children that are your burning ember, without your partner to console you, alone and far away, an *Itaker* like many others, without a precise end in sight, without knowing why you are doing it, why you're sacrificing yourself like a mule for years, well then it's better to slit your throat with a razor blade, or to throw yourself off a bridge." But after this preamble, the Mericano immediately changed course: "These are stories that everyone knows, and nothing changes in telling them; they tell you: now this guy is going to complain again. It's better not to recount them. Everyone knows them. On the other hand, have you invited the Signor Maestro to Orlandina's wedding? She's getting married on the tenth of October. Tomorrow Valentini returns from Trentino."

Nëndë

So, lately, nani Lissandro was distracted. More than being distracted, he was absent, or absorbed in thoughts that seemed evanescent, like soap bubbles. Others would talk to him, and he would respond after ten minutes or more, having returned from his trips into the void of his mind. His only interest seemed to be whittling. He would shave away at the olive logs here and there with skillful movements, but he only managed to carve out misshapen and grotesque attempts at eagles, which piled up in a corner of the front hall of the house. So basically, with the exception of Costantino, who was too young to understand, the Avati family thought that by now nani Lissandro would never recover.

"He's old, and old people—you know . . ." his daughter would say with a compassionate sigh. "Maybe grandpa is sick and doesn't want to say it," Orlandina and then Lucrezia would say. "He's on a one-way road to losing his marbles," concluded the Mericano without mincing words. In reality, these were phrases uttered just because, and they would be lost in the dust of Castello del Piccolo, where the Mericano would work from dawn till dusk, or in the confusion of the small kitchen, or in the "Kënga e brumit," sung by all the neighborhood women at the top of their lungs, while Orlandina prepared the yeast: *Nga t'ënjtën ndaj mbrëma/na bëmi brumin/moj ti, zonja nuse,/tihj të kan martuar/se mir ësht të martuarit/me një dial të nderuar,* Around Thursday evening/ we prepare the sourdough/oh you, new bride,/they have married you/cause it's good to be married/to an honorable young man.

Orlandina was at the center of the world; her girlfriends would sing, over and over, that it was a great thing to marry an honorable young man; it is a good thing, *zonja nuse*, miss bride-to-be, Orlandina. But she knew that they criticized her behind her back, and deep down they envied her, gossiping about her past as a girl who *bëri hamur me një kupil e bukur si drita/e nanì ka martuar një arvull pa fjeta*, made love to a young man who was handsome as the sun/and now had married a tree with no leaves; her girlfriends laughed at the very tall Trentino, tall and therefore stupid, aged with no leaves, with just a few rounds left to fire, but with lots of money; lucky her, she would go far away and meet a kind mother-in-law who would dress her in a classy blouse, lucky her, but money isn't everything in life.

Orlandina perceived all this. In their shoes, she would have had the same thoughts as well. And yet, the one thing neither she nor her closest friends could have guessed was the feeling of tenderness she had toward Narciso. It wasn't love, not that. Nor was it physical attraction. But pure tenderness. Narciso was like a toy giraffe made of the softest, silkiest fabric. And soft was his right hand, which she had felt on those rare occasions when he had found an excuse to brush against her. Tender was the gaze that landed, above all, on the walls, or plates, or the prosciutto hanging from the ceiling, and when she lowered her eyes, on her hair. Her mother was right: "*Kështu do shortja, bijë*," this is what fate wants. And Orlandina had accepted the marriage proposal out of inertia, her head had nodded under the pressure of the heavy hand of *shortja*. May you have a white destiny, bijë. Your groom is like a star; he's a worker, a saver, and tested by your father; and the bride, like an April flower; the groom like a crystal, he's gentle, educated, he has land, bijë, bride, snow of the mountain. He's as good as bread, that Trentino. He is your prince. "*Fati i bardhë i nuses*," white fate of the bride, her female relatives wished for her, walking into the kitchen. "But a very shy prince, even though shyness is not necessarily a defect," Orlandina said, as she thought of that brazen pig who would paw at her as soon as they were alone and in public would stare at her with those milky eyes, and thinking back on it now, they disgusted her; at parties he only wanted to dance with her, holding her so tight it made her blush.

Narciso was so different! When he left for Taio, he offered his soft hand to her, leaving her face half-lifted, white and red with shame. He said to her "Bye Orlandina" and watched a blue fly zigzagging under the ceiling of that small room.

He had written her more than fifty postcards, one per week and each with the same mountainous landscape captured from different angles and in different seasons, with the same church bell tower standing tall in that blue. Narciso was concise: greetings to everyone and to my fiancée. And repetitive: greetings to my fiancée and to all of you.

When he came back, however, he kissed her *te gjaku e faqevet*, on the blood-red blush mark on her cheek, and she felt the tenderness of his lips and the mintiness of his breath. He wore a blazer with blue and white stripes, making him look even taller, and a light blue shirt buttoned to his neck. He brought her a little present, he said, stressing that it was a silly little thing and insisting that it was nothing. "A ring," he finally said, "I hope you like it." It was a gold ring, decorated with a tiny, brilliant emerald; it was stunning, a small, huge treasure, a lovely thing. Orlandina couldn't contain her joy and hugged her fiancé, clinging to his neck and kissing him everywhere she could, starting at his chin and then moving down to his chest, saying, "Oh thank you, thank you," and he, embarrassed, replied, "Oh, it's nothing, it's nothing."

And thus, thanks to the ring, they had broken the ice; so much so that later, when he gave her a basket of red apples, "*Stark*" he specified, from his own Val di Non: healthy, shiny apples. The hugs and kisses that followed worked a little better and lasted a little longer.

"*Ngë del illi o mos ngë del/ngë bën ditë o mos ngë bën/se na kemi kush na bën dritë*," The star doesn't come out, oh if it does not come out/the day doesn't come out, oh if it doesn't/ because we have who is making us light. Her girlfriends began to sing again, now that the yeast was ready; her gossipy girlfriends who knew nothing about the Trentino aside from his height. They held hands as they sang, dancing in a circle in front of the house door. The song spread down the alleyways, women came out of their homes, and children headed toward the singing. The Mericano, Costantino, and Narciso were just then coming back from the Castello del Piccolo, dressed in their dusty work clothes, just in time to admire Orlandina in the middle of the circle with her blue waves flowing down her shoulders, with a silk handkerchief tied to her arm, at the center of the world, dancing gracefully, and they thought: how entrancing, how blue her hair is, how beautiful, what a silver brooch she has! All the while, her dancing girlfriends sent her wishes of good health, a long life, long and rich, a full beehive, and a great destiny.

And nani Lissandro? Nani Lissandro was staring fixedly at the snake-like honey mostaccioli set out beautifully on the table.

Chicchinella and Gigina, the prized goats, had died, one after the other in the span of a week. And a few days later, Baialardo took off with two solidified snail trails of tears under his eyes.

"Maybe he was bitten by a poisonous snake," nani said to Costantino. "He'll go out into the woods to look for the healing herbs, and if he doesn't find them, he'll die."

"No, he won't die," Costantino argued vehemently, looking imploringly at Baialardo and stroking his wet nose. But Baialardo wasn't wagging his tail, he didn't bark, he didn't eat, and he didn't drink. Then, they saw him get up lazily, stretch out with a strange yawn, and walk off whining without turning back, his pace slow and unsteady.

That evening, they waited together, grandfather and grandson, huddled on the front stoop. They waited the following two evenings as well. The dog did not come back, and nani said with a sigh, "*Ka dekur*," he must have died.

"No, he isn't dead," Costantino yelled through his tears; the old man's only answer was to slap him on the back of his neck, to remind him that *një burr ngë qan*. How else was he supposed to make him understand that a man doesn't cry? With a guitar? And he gave him another slap that landed better than the first because now Costantino was trying to hold back his tears in vain with his head bowed. "You should know," nani said, "I've never cried in my entire life. Not even when Sidonia died. And I certainly had tears in me, enough to make Mare Nostro overflow."

The mention of his grandmother's death startled Costantino who abruptly turned his big teary eyes to his grandfather's thin, smooth lips. Zonja Elena had never told him about her mother, maybe because she herself knew very little about this woman with the uncommon name, dead when she was a two- or three-year-old *vajzarelë*; or because she was afraid of awakening a ghost that slept beside her, clutching her in its big, dead arms. Nani Lissandro didn't like talking about his wife either. On the rare occasions that he mentioned her, it seemed like he was talking about someone who died the previous day, not fifty years before; and not even really dead, just asleep in the next room, in her daughter's bed. In fact, he always talked about her in the present tense: "Sidonia does the laundry with ashes; Sidonia's laugh can be heard in the piazza; Sidonia puts a lot of ground *peperoncino* in her sausage;" or even in the future tense: "Tomorrow she'll be seventy-four, she's getting old too."

However, after that explicit statement, nani's lips didn't move in the direction that Costantino had hoped for: "Let's go eat, it's getting late," he said, and started climbing the steps of the house, out of breath as though he were scaling a mountain.

Despite the pain that irritated his stomach and the back of his neck, Costantino ate heartily; nani, on the other hand, slowly chewed the same mouthful of bread and sausage for the whole meal, never swallowing, trapped in the saliva bubbles of his own empty thoughts, which headed for the wall and could have drilled into it in the blink of an eye.

The energetic little crowd in the Avatis' house realized that Baialardo had disappeared from nani Lissandro and his grandson's grave faces, but they didn't seem very upset; and it wasn't because of the festive atmosphere so much as it was for a calming statement from the Mericano: "Hey pa, you're gonna get this upset over a dog? It's not like he's a Christian! I can understand this coming from Costantino since he's young, but from you, pa! And besides, I'm sure he'll be back, he's not dead, he's just on vacation. He's got seven lives just like you, pa."

Well, Costantino thought, it would be nice, but a week had already passed, and if that medicinal herb really existed, Baialardo would have found it by now. Baialardo was a pro, the best pro of all the dogs. So, Costantino stayed by his grandfather's side as much as he could, sharing that grief only the two of them felt. Sometimes he reported to him on the projects going on at Castello del Piccolo: with the rocks strewn across the ground, they had built a small dry-stone enclosure; the centuries-old well had been restored and now a plot of land could be farmed. But nani Lissandro seemed rather intent on listening to his own silence instead or on hitting the olive logs with the dull thud of his hatchet. Every once in a while, he would wince and furrow his white eyebrows or he would sigh while muttering something incomprehensible. He might have been saying, *"Jeta ësht si fjeta,"* life is like a leaf.

As dusk fell, nani Lissandro's vacant stare and lazy movements gave way to a nervous rolling of his pupils and an abrupt return to the land of the living: he noticed his grandson, he watched the sun disappear among the Sila peaks, he turned the chunks of wood over and over in his hands, threw them in a corner, and walked away without saying a word.

This subtle evening reawakening had escaped everyone, except for Costantino who, with his attentive gaze, decided to follow him one evening, driven by curiosity and boredom (the piazza and café were empty; his friends were at the movies watching "Per un pugno di dollari," *A Fistful of Dollars*, for the fourth time).

Nani crossed the alleyways of the Palacco neighborhood with small, quick strides, and took a dark, narrow dirt road that wound its way through the garden. The figure of a woman suddenly appeared before him, walking quickly with her head down, likely so she could see where to put her feet. Nani caught up with her; Costantino could hear their voices, but he couldn't make out the words, just muted sounds that got lost in the continuous buzz of the evening.

When the two arrived at a Sambuca hedge, Costantino noticed that the woman was taller than nani, and perhaps younger as well judging by the laughter that bounced off the hedge, resounding with all its freshness. They crouched and heeded the call of nature, as many people did in those years, either out of habit or because they didn't have a toilet in the house.

Costantino had, very quietly, positioned himself behind an agave plant, and from his new vantage point he could see the two hunched figures, but could not make out their faces. Then nani buckled his pants and the woman lowered her coha. They were gesturing, perhaps speaking excitedly. It was possible to gather little bursts of what they were saying. Nani's pleading voice: "Please, at least tonight." Nani's disappointed voice: "But why not? Why?" The woman's low, affectionate tone: "Come on, we can't, you're crazy you are . . . it's silly, we're old." Nani's determined voice: "An old bird still has flesh and bones." And finally, he grabbed her by the shoulders and pulled her into him.

The two figures melted together into one black body, with the woman trying weakly to wiggle away, and weakly mumbling her *jo, jojó, atì jo*. So nani led her away, under a fig tree in a garden. Costantino moved noiselessly behind an oleander bush. Now they were in front of him, two black figures contorting on the grass, silently, with slow movements, tangled in the coha, on the black grass of the garden, until nani took off his hat and mopped his brow with his arm.

Costantino intuitively understood exactly what the two had done there in the dark, but he never discovered the identity of the woman who had suddenly appeared, and just as suddenly disappeared in that dark alley, because the next night he didn't follow nani again. Or rather, he followed him until Baialardo cut him off, running and jumping on him with his paws on his chest and wrinkling his muzzle into a smile. His fur was dirty with clay and moss, and he looked like a Cirneco hound puppy since he was so skinny and small, and his ears perked up with emotion. The eyes were his though: black and sad.

Back at the house, they celebrated his return by washing him with soap and water, and feeding him *dijunelet*, spicy skewers of lamb intestine that the Trentino, despite all his best efforts, could not manage to swallow.

"What did I tell you?" the Mericano concluded triumphantly.

Dhjetë

On the eve of the wedding, the Trentino's three brothers arrived in Hora with their respective wives and children, daughters-in-law, sons-in-law, nieces, nephews, and grand-children: twenty-six in all, of all ages. The youngest, in his mother's arms, immediately became the center of general attention, the little victim designated to break the ice. The visitors felt suffocated in that room dominated by the large nuptial bed. The brothers and their oldest sons were taller and bigger than Narciso, so they towered over the room and shrunk it with the bulk of their bodies.

"You must be tired, what can I get you to drink, what can I get you to eat," zonja Elena repeated excitedly.

"Nothing, blessed lady, don't trouble yourself, just a bit of fresh water, don't trouble yourself," answered the guests in turn, and they glanced around in search of the bride-to-be, whom they had already seen in a black-and-white photograph.

Lucrezia and Costantino passed around orange soda, beer, and cans of Coca-Cola, while the Mericano distributed handshakes and welcoming smiles to everyone. Then from the upstairs room descended Orlandina, in her new dress, embroidered with small red flowers. The Trentinos widened their eyes when they saw that she was more beautiful and more youthful than they had imagined, barely containing oohs and ahhs of wonder; Orlandina smiled under the chandelier, surrounded by a green and blue halo.

Seeing the effect produced by the appearance of his bride-to-be, Narciso felt like the happiest man in the world, for he had been suddenly freed from that inferiority complex that he had in regard to his brothers, which had been his cross to bear for more than twenty years; and he thanked God for letting him reach seventh heaven all at once. He was so immersed in his own happiness that the Mericano had to resort to shaking him. "But here," he said, "we need to get busy, otherwise if we all stand around staring at the flies, night will come and the house won't be ready for the party!" Then he invited the women to go with Orlandina to the room upstairs to admire the trousseau displayed on the bed, while he and the men would prepare for the reception.

They moved the bed, the armoire, and the dresser from the biggest room. They lined all the house chairs and others lent by the neighbors in neat order along the walls. They placed a coffee table with a record player next to the door and a table with bottles of old wine, liquor bottles, a basket of *taralli*, a tray of sweets, and another of small chocolates in the kitchen.

That evening, after three rifle shots fired by Mericano, mainly relatives and numerous young people arrived with intentions of dancing. Orlandina and Narciso led the dancing clumsily with a tango at the pace of a waltz. The tango was stifled by extended applause and handfuls of confetti and small coins that jingled in the air like a small firework. The spouses-to-be looked like spinning tops, off-beat and wooden, but they were admired with sympathy, especially Orlandina in that fluttering dress with small red flowers and her waves of blue hair glistening softly on her shoulders. Many couples danced to the next waltz that followed.

Signor Maestro Carmelo Bevilacqua had arrived just as the party was at its height, dressed in his usual slovenly manner: a dark blue crew-neck sweater dusted with dandruff and a few stray hairs, blue velvet pants, slightly worn at the knee. Nani Lissandro and the Mericano, who were in the kitchen pouring drinks for the old folks, greeted him with wine and *taralli*, smiling and slightly tipsy; but zonja Elena was the one who coddled him most, who stopped going back and forth from the kitchen to the dancehall with a tray of small chocolates and put herself completely at his disposal: "Tell me, tell me Signor Maestro: would you like a beer, an orange soda, a little roll, *taralli*, a . . . ?" He just wanted to dance? "Go dance, Signor Maestro, go have fun, for you are very young, you are."

The maestro searched for Lucrezia's eyes through the crowd and found them immediately. Starting with the very next dance, without ever exchanging a word, they remained a fixed couple for the rest of the night. They held each other so tightly that Costantino, to avoid blushing in shame, left for the kitchen to help his father and nani until the end of the party.

The next morning, three shots were fired in the air announcing the wedding. This was immediately followed by the arrival of the entire town at the Avatis' house, on the doorstep, on the front stoop, and in the nearby alleys. The women crowded the room, in which the bride, dressed in white, stood at the center of attention, and they commented loudly: "Oh how beautiful, she looks like a princess, a doll, a Madonna!" Some elderly woman struck up the "Kënga dasmore": *Ulu nuse, e lumja nuse./T'erth hera ç'vete nuse*, Wedding banquet song: Sit bride, blessed bride./It's your time to become a bride. But the chorus of men did not replicate (and who could remember that nuptial chant anymore!), and so those three or four guttural voices, like suffering cats, were silenced by the Mericano: "*Rrini qetu*, please!" It was clear: he did not want to look ridiculous in front of the Trentinos with those confused remnants of the past.

Once the waves of people had finished filling the wicker basket with envelopes, legibly signed and full of well-wishes, stuffed with banknotes, the bride walked out on her father's arm.

Ignoring the stifling crowd and the admonition of the Mericano, Signor Maestro had caught up with the chorus of elderly women and now, in the midst of the bridal procession, he was transcribing the translation of the song in his small notebook, "what little we remember," the ladies said with modesty.

It was a modest ceremony, void of songs or long pauses in the new, humid church, cut through by gusts of wind and flies that entered through the doors flung wide open and exited through the windows with broken panes. The parish priest tolerated the children running and screaming, the men talking and laughing at the back of the church, the Trentinos' scandalized or amused expressions, and finally he repeated his favorite metaphor: "Marriage, dear newlyweds, is like a ship on the sea of life. The groom is the helmsman; the bride is the ship."

Later, the bridal procession headed toward Demetrio's house, one of the Mericano's cousins and a fellow Germanese.

It was a new house, empty and spacious, ideal for the banquet. The guests sat around the tables randomly in the four rooms, and while waiting for the courses, they began to toast the newlyweds, chalices raised.

On the faces of Narciso, zonja Elena, and the Mericano, one could read "it is done!" written by the satisfied smiles that appeared in the little wrinkles around their eyes.

Even Orlandina seemed calm now, with her face flushed with wine and emotion, a doll-like princess child whose expression, in church, had been sad and dull, even somber when, after the exchange of the wedding rings, she embraced her mother, her sobs resounding among the gesso saints, just like the bride in "Kënga dasmore": What have I done to you, mother of mine, to make you cast me from your breast, from thy breast and thy hearth.

The Mericano hadn't given a thought to expenses: he had hired the most well-known chef in the area for that day, a shepherd from Savelli who, with the help of five of the bride's relatives, had prepared tagliatelle with porcini mushrooms, roast and boiled veal, spicy skewers, *dijunele* of milk-fed lamb, chicken *alla diavola*, baby goat *alla cacciatora*, salad of lettuce and tomatoes, and a huge wedding cake topped with the bride and groom made of *mostacciolo*. Other female relatives began to serve these dishes: they did so with such talent and natural skill that the Trentinos thought they were waitresses by profession.

The guests from Hora never tired of complimenting the chef and the Mericano, and of toasting the newlyweds, while the Trentinos fawned over the welcome they had received. Such hospitality, incredible! Such lovely, kind people! Clean, and industrious people. And so they were bullshit, the stories that were told in Val di Non about the *terrone* immigrant who in his bathtub filled with soil, planted basil and parsley, since he didn't know what the tub's use was: huge and wonderful lies; there might have been one person, just one, because every family has a black sheep.

So, the Trentinos conveyed their appreciation, the surprises, and discoveries they made over the two days; and they danced with the others after pushing the tables—covered in plates full of little bones and half-empty bottles of wine—up against the walls. Finally, sweaty and exhausted, they even danced a Calabrian tarantella, imitating the wild groom who was jumping and kicking like a drunken horse, to the rhythm of a collective handclapping.

In the late evening, a little group of remaining guests walked the newlyweds back home, slicing the thick silence of the alleyways with a *Lojmë lojmë, vasha, vallen/Kostantini i vogëlith*, half sung and half whistled. It was that vallja, half yelled and finally danced in a circle also by the Trentinos who were entertained, one of the few marks of tradition not yet canceled by time and therefore worthy of being recorded by the maestro in his worn small notebook, two lines before the serenade of the night.

Eleven

The knight emerged suddenly and silently from the darkness of the alleyway. He was pulling a skinny mule by its bridle, its hooves wrapped in rags to muffle the sound. He approached the group of young men who were strumming the first song of the serenade under the windows of the Avatis' house, and he greeted them in their language: "*Mirëmbrëma*," good evening, he said, with a heavier drawl than the local accent. He was as old and scrawny as his mule, and he was wrapped in a gloomy wool cloak; but his eyes, the color of the sky after a rainfall, radiated bright, youthful sparkles under the yellowish streetlight.

When he carefully pulled a small, round mandolin from his saddlebag, many from the group no longer had doubts: the knight holding the lahuta in one hand, and the rounded bow in the other, was Luca Rodotà, the rhapsode of Corone. Clear to all was the motive for his unexpected appearance: he wanted to honor nani Lissandro, his lifelong friend.

The rhapsode began to sing a plain melody, expertly drawing his bow across the single string of the lahuta. Its handle resembled a double-headed eagle, with four eyes as clear as those of the rhapsode, and with the same sparkling gaze.

Mario shook Costantino vigorously because he had been talking to him for fifteen minutes and he seemed entranced, like he was sleeping with his eyes open, he told him.

The rhapsode lifted his gaze skyward to concentrate, and then chirped an *ohj* adorned with high and low trills: *Ohj vashë ti vjen te fera me mua/e si u vinjë ti çë më bien?* Oh girl, you come to the fair with me/and if I come what will you buy for me? It was a well-known song, so the young men sang along, too.

The melody flew through the sleepy alleyways, and it had the power to turn on lights, to open windows. The whole neighborhood woke up when the girl in the song accepted the ring from the young man, in spite of her mother and father. Nani Lissandro was surely tossing in his bed, with the forbidden urge to leap outside. Narciso was also restless, having been awake for some time, the basket of food at his feet, ready to be delivered to the best man just as soon as the serenade ended. But the serenade had only just begun. Now the rhapsode seemed to be declaiming, rather than singing, accompanying the verses with a sad melody. He recited strange tales of horses that told the Lady of her husband's honorable death, killed in battle after slaughtering many of his enemies; and the flight of two lovers who were followed and killed by the girl's relatives and are now reborn each spring upon their tomb: the young man as a cypress and the girl as a white grapevine wrapping around him; and of the nostalgia a young girl felt for her faraway homeland, where her father, mother, and brother were buried, a land she had not seen again since she left it: *Moj e bukura Morè/si të lé u më ngë të pé*, Oh, my beautiful Morea/since I left you I haven't seen you anymore.

The old man played musical interludes between each rhapsody and song, and the young men, standing round in a circle, tacitly praised his skill. They didn't understand all the words of the stories, but they grasped the meaning and became emotionally wrapped up in it, such that the rhapsode would, meanwhile, glance at them reassuringly, as though sensing their distress.

At the end of the serenade, the groom appeared on the doorstep with the basket overflowing with bottles of wine and cognac, prosciutto, sausage, *sardella*, cheese, and bread.

The young men invited the rhapsode to join them for a glass of wine, between *vëllezer*, brothers, they told him.

"I thank you, but it is already late for me," he excused himself. "I have a long night of travel before me."

Costantino was the only one left with the rhapsode, and he watched him wide-eyed, unable to find the courage to speak. He would have liked to introduce himself, to tell him: I am nani Lissandro's grandson, do you still remember me? Instead, he just watched in silence, as the rhapsode put on his cloak and stroked the muzzle of his mule, speaking softly into its ear as though to help him prepare for the long journey ahead. The mule stifled an affectionate whinny, nodding with his big, black head. They both seemed satisfied with the serenade and with themselves; and the night, at that hour, was extraordinarily quiet, the echoes of laughter, the crickets, and the sounds of breathing from the alleyways swallowed by the darkness.

"I bet you are nani Lissandro's grandson," said the rhapsode to Costantino, resting a hand on his shoulder. "How you've grown since we saw each other at the beach!"

Costantino managed a nod and a smile, but now his feet, having been pressed into the cobblestone, seemed glued to the ground, and he rocked back and forth awkwardly like a plastic puppet filled with water up to its knees. He could barely move, obeying like an automaton the invitation of the old man who had asked him to carry out the duties of host like a good Arbëresh and to accompany him for a stretch of the road. *"Poka je i nipi i Lisandrit,"* So, you are Lissandro's grandson, and from a dark alleyway that led to the piazza, a midnight blue rectangle opened, crisscrossed with luminous trails.

Ah, Lissandro . . . I would tell him, when we were young, that dreamers like us live a long time. Actually, they never die, because they are always looking backward and forward. The first time we observed each other astonished: we spoke with different accents, we came from faraway towns, but we both kissed the seashore, we were bound by the waves of the *giaku jonë i shprishur,* our scattered blood that flowed through our veins, just like brothers. I held the lahuta like a sword, and I felt like a prince under the curious stares of the Arbëreshë and the Litirj. An Albanian had gifted it to me, a true rhapsode who often passed through Corone. He fled Albania for trying to assassinate a vizier. He would move from one Arbëresh town to another, and people welcomed him with all their hearts, the way one welcomes a homeless brother. In exchange, he would play the lahuta and sing. He was always surrounded by a group of boys, like me, and he taught us to play his instrument with endless patience. He returned to Albania after hearing that the freedom flag waved over Vlora. He left me his lahuta, but I didn't want to accept it; and when he insisted, I asked him, "Why me?" He smiled, "Because you can look the sun in the eyes." Well, I never really understood what he meant, but since that day my life changed from this to that.

I started going around the way the Albanian had, sing-ing the old rhapsodies to the music of the lahuta. I went from one party to the next, I had fun and made others have fun, and at the same time, I reminded everyone who we Arbëreshë were, because even then people were beginning to forget. I felt important, helpful. But they called me a hobo in my town; my school teachers called me Don Quixote. They called me that! I, who broke my back on my plot of hard land to feed my family! They couldn't hide their jealousy when they heard me play, I don't know why. "Be careful," nani Lis-sandro told me, "The goat that leaves the herd gets eaten by the wolf," but I wasn't alone, and I'm not totally alone today, either.

With each passing year, as we'd count our numbers in Marina, we'd realize someone was missing. They would go off to 'Merica, they'd fly away. For a while, we tricked our-selves into thinking we could make 'Merica here in our towns: 'Merica means good work and good health, right? So, we thought, if we occupy the land, like the Reds say, and we share everything, your grandfather would repeat, then 'Mer-ica will be here; only it will be even better because our dead are buried here and this is our land; besides, what the Alba-nian said was true, one soul is worth just as much as another soul, and each of us is worth four hundred gold coins, there is no difference among men, right? So then, how is it fair that two or three families per town should own all the land, thou-sands of good hectares, while we rent and work the left-overs. We occupied the land, but they kicked us out at gunpoint and gave us back the most arid and rocky plots of land with the agrarian reform of the 1950s.

Your grandfather and I continued to meet at the fair in Marina, our beards and hair graying, each wearing the black tie of widowhood, our children or sons-in-law already abroad or in Northern Italy. And now? Well . . . I will keep singing as long as I have the strength. Singing and playing. And then?

When they reached the crossroads of Padreterno, they said goodbye. The rhapsode unwound the rags from the mule's hooves, and before mounting the saddle he walked a stretch of the mule path on foot. It was only then that Costantino realized that he was walking with a little hop, as though with each step he were trying to take flight.

Costantino was excited when he got back to the piazza, aware of having lived an unforgettable experience. Mario absorbed his tale, yawning, more asleep than awake. The young men who had been at the serenade were lying on the low concrete walls, snoring or singing to themselves, their faces serene, the ground strewn with empty bottles, until the first patch of sunlight struck their faces at an angle.

Shortly thereafter, Orlandina with her damp, gray eyes, the Mericano, and the sleepy Trentinos left on the five o'clock bus, leaving behind zonja Elena's waterfall of tears and dozens of fluttering white handkerchiefs.

Vú spërvjeret Skandërbeku

Skanderbeg unfolded the tents, under the shadows of spacious dur-masts. The warriors were seated near a clear shore, eating and drink-ing, when they saw a herald coming from Turkey.

"To you, prince of the Albanians, I was sent by the Signore Grande: where do you compete in battle?"

"Go and tell him to come to me."

As the herald returned, Muhammad jumped to his feet. He made the drums sound and gathered his officers.

"Now, my ministers, whose heart, amongst you, says that it will bring Skanderbeg to me, alive or dead?"

Everyone heard but no one answered. Then Balabani, the Alba-nian renegade, replied: "And what will my reward be?"

"Nine hundred thousand ducats and the Albanian provinces."

"Tonight you will have him dead or alive."

They dashed into the fight. Then in the middle of the street whence Skanderbeg was coming, the renegade dog emerged and stood in front of him.

"Now, renegade dog, either you will take my head, or I will have yours."

Skanderbeg slashed at him; but the rein fell from his hands; the renegade threw himself against him and wounded his arm, his arm and his horse. Skanderbeg leaped to his feet, and the Muslims shouted a loud cry of joy and rushed to surround him.

The hero raised his eyes to the sky: "Now help me, Christ God, thou who took me away, as a child, from the hand of thine enemies!" He then sheltered his back against an oak tree, and no one dared to get close to his sword.

But here they come, two thousand brave men, all young men chosen in the mountains of Albania: Ducagino brought them to him, Ducagino and Livetta. They broke in, routed, and stepped on the trampled people. When Skanderbeg saw them, he turned his mouth into a smile: "But you, Signor Ducagino, just watch my back, so that I will fight this dog; because he can see how I swing this sword, and how to wave a flag.

He made the sign of the cross and threw himself, grasping, and moving ahead like the fire in the stubbles, up to the point that he had filled up the roads and trenches with heads and cadavers. Only one he took and left alive: that renegade dog, so that he would bring the news. But his right ear was cut off, to keep it as a token.

However, when Muhammad saw him: "Balabani with a wounded head, where is that boast of yours that you would have brought Skanderbeg to me either alive or dead?"

"But you, Signore, Gran Signore, listen just a little bit, do not listen to too many things; it is not his arm that helps him, but the hand of our Lord."

"And now you bring your head closer, the head that contains false faiths; so I will take my pleasure with you."

They took him and forced him into fetters and cut off his head.

Viatrice delle fate

It was only as he was heading back to Hora, sitting on the mule's back, that Costantino doubted whether he had seen two conjoined gulls or a double-headed eagle flying around; thinking back to that blue scene, he would automatically lift his gaze skyward, each time surprised to see it dotted with millions of tiny lights, no sun, no gulls or eagles, just a yellow moon like a slice of melon.

The next day, in the piazzetta of the gjitonia, he talked about seeing a white double-headed eaglet twirl around in the sky. Any doubts? None, to the point that his friends were awestruck at first. But soon they got hold of themselves, and they all burst into raucous laughter when Vittorio said, "Yeah, and I once saw a flying donkey."

Costantino was too stubborn to give in to a joke. On the contrary, he never let a day go by without regaling his friends with his incredible story, in a setting full of increasingly realistic details. They started to think he might be a little crazy, and in a moment of exasperation, one of his friends gave him the nickname, "Aquila," Eagle, also referring to his piercing gaze that made everyone feel a little uneasy. And so, everyone in town knew Costantino as Aquila. He wasn't offended, he may not even have noticed it, feeling it stick to him like a tailor-made suit. It was his suit, there was no doubt about that, a suit he had chosen for himself and that others had put on him.

Three years after the fair, the only change was his appearance: he had a nice, oval face, he had grown taller and much more robust, and his dark brown hair had begun to curl like his thoughts. He attended Shën Kolli middle school for a year, and his Aquila reputation had spread among his new classmates as well. But they only had to put up with him at school, whereas the boys in Hora had to deal with him on the soccer field, at the bar, when they ran through alleyways rolling old bicycle rims, playing with wooden tops, with a double terminated wood point and a larger stick in *rassi e squigli*, or tip-cat, with bottle caps or lira coins in *sbattamuro*, with buttons and cards in *bottoni*, and hide and seek in *ika*.

Costantino had a reputation by then, just as he does today, for recording everything, even the most ordinary things, like the rhapsode's serenade that became memorable when he recounted them. It was as though he lived more intensely than other people, because he increased every experience tenfold, turning it into a myth once he lived it. His closest friends were simultaneously fascinated and exasperated by his man-child attitude: at times conceited, maybe truly a little crazy, seeking answers for them too, even when they just wanted to be left alone to spend their time playing and being lazy, as if they could tell that lazy days held the answers. If they were in a mood and he kept insisting, they would get mean, the way friends sometimes do, insultingly calling him "Aquila" to his face and loading their words with all the contempt they could muster. One day at the bar, the Mericano overheard them. It was bound to happen sooner or later.

"Now it's our turn," his father exclaimed in a threatening tone, and Costantino felt his blood turn to water. It was a warm evening in late October, warm and quiet, and his father let his words echo off the old wall of the Kurrituri that he was heavily showering with piss. They had left the bar together just three minutes before and were heading home for dinner. Costantino stood behind his father and looked up at the sky that, in that moment, was as red as his own face. "Knock off this crap about the double-headed eagle! I am telling you for the first and last time. I'm warning you for your own good," the Mericano said, buttoning his fustian pants. "Otherwise you'll become the town's laughing stock, and everyone will think you've lost your mind," unknowingly paraphrasing something Lucrezia had said long before. But he added to the advice his daughter had repeated time and again to Costantino, mentioning a name that echoed like another burst of urine: Sciales. "*Një paçë nga kroca si Viatriçe Shales*," a crazy man who lost his mind like Viatrice Sciales, he said. As soon as Costantino heard this name, he understood and turned the color of clay.

Viatrice Sciales lived in the same gjitonia as Costantino, in a one-room shack she shared with her aging mother. She wasn't yet forty, but everyone thought of her as being an old spinster, even though she had smooth skin, strong, white teeth, and a slender, adolescent body. When she was a girl, she saw three beautiful women emerge from the little hill of Ciccotto, their wavy blue hair loose across their shoulders. They wore the brightly colored holiday coha, and as soon as they spotted her, they began to laugh and started the round dance: they began as three, then doubled to six, and finally tripled to nine, dancing without singing. They put Viatrice in the middle of the dance and predicted a *fatin e mirë*, a good destiny for her. It was only then that she noticed their mule hooves crushing the honeysuckles on the Ciccotto.

"*Ke par fatat, bijarè*," her mother confirmed to her; so Viatrice went around town telling everyone that she had seen the fates; she never got tired of repeating what she had seen and heard, until after several months they began calling her *Viatriçe e fatavet*, to make fun of her. But she didn't care about the nickname, talking about the fates and to the fates, even until she was just old enough to marry. So, even though she was pretty, none of the serious young men of Hora ever dreamed of asking for her hand in marriage. She had received only two marriage proposals since the age of twenty, both from widowers in nearby towns; but she refused them with disdain, ignoring her mother's wishes. The night she rejected the second widower, screaming and crying was heard from her room, but the next morning, as if nothing had happened, she brushed her long dark brown hair on the doorstep of the house, not even trying to hide the scratches on her face and the livid bruises on her arms and under her eyes. It was the fates, "*kan qënë fatat*," she repeated, over and over.

They kept her in the Girifalco asylum for nearly four months. When she came back to Hora, she had a bewildered, childlike expression. She spoke only Italian, using the formal *lei* (you) with everyone, including relatives, neighbors, children, and even her own mother: "Gentle Lady, Dear Sir, Dear Child." She spoke obsequiously, and of course she spoke of the fates, and she did it in Italian. And so it happened that she was rebaptized with her nickname into Italian as well: Viatrice delle fate. Stupid fates, nani Lissandro would say ironically; he couldn't stand them. They had predicted a good destiny for her and look how she turned out!

To end up like Viatrice delle fate: Costantino covered his eyes to shield himself from that awful image. He had to stop talking about the double-headed eagle. His father was right, he had to stop. One should only believe in these things, the Mericano added, if they are handed down from father to son; you don't really believe in the existence of fates or the reincarnation of a dead man into a snake, like the witches said, but you kind of believe, just for the heck of it, for tradition, but not really, because fates with mule hooves don't exist, nor do talking snakes or double-headed eagles. However, according to his father, Costantino could still save himself, if he wanted, and this cheered the young man up.

From that night on, he lived the lonely life of the visionary without suffering. He knew no one would understand him—since his father did not—and he calmly awaited the day that he would be able to tell his children about what he had seen: the day when all this would become "a thing of the past." In the meantime, thanks to his father's intervention, he shed the reputation of the slightly mad boy and regained all his friends, resuming talking about soccer and Lassie's latest adventure. But in that moment, Costantino felt close to Viatrice delle fate, and so he was ashamed of having made fun of her as others did, "*Vre, Viatrì, vre fatat*," look, Viatrì, look, here are the fates, pointing to the wall of the shack whose stones had nothing but blooming snapdragons poking through.

The Green-Eyed Partridge

Ever since his hair started falling out, Signor Maestro Car-melo Bevilacqua sheltered his head with a dark blue beret, which he wore cocked over his left ear and never took off, not even in class or at the dinner table. The dark blue of the beret and the black glasses gave him a dark look, making him look like an eagle-owl with a big round head and large-rimmed eyes that looked like eyeglasses. In fact, the people in town had started calling him *gurgullea*—behind his back of course, because when they ran into him, they were always very respectful, using the formal "Voi," or "Signor Maestro," or "Signor Professore."

Lucrezia gave him a red wool beret she had knitted her-self that, in addition to being very stylish, would have given a little color to his face and taken care of his ugly nickname. But Signor Maestro was attracted to dark colors, so, even though he thanked her from the bottom of his heart, "I pre-fer my beret; it is less showy, my dear. I'll keep your beret as a souvenir," he said, not even giving her the satisfaction of trying it on. Lucrezia cried that night too, over her *gurgullea*-prince, stubborn as a mule.

The beret incident was the latest and least painful of the offenses Carmelo had inflicted on her. He said he loved her, he dedicated passionate poems to her, he promised his love to her for all his life, but the important and serious, that decisive step, the only one that really matters, he hadn't taken yet: he hadn't entered the house to ask for her hand. The Mericano, waiting for the maestro's step, had been in Hora since October 4th, making up the excuse for the townsfolk that he had some work to do at Castello del Piccolo. But the maestro, since Sunday, October 3rd, hadn't set foot in that house, not for his former student, nor for zonja Elena's bread and beans, not even for Lucrezia's green eyes. The Mericano was fed up and said, for the umpteenth time, "I won't say another word: just don't go looking for ears of wheat in the snow again."

He finally left for Ludwigshafen after All Souls' Day.

The following evening, Signor Maestro landed like an eagle-owl in the small Avatis' kitchen, handing out smiles and handshakes to all, even to Baialardo. Lucrezia and zonja Elena were very embarrassed by that unexpected visit, and they weren't sure if they should laugh or cry; nani Lissandro, on the other hand, stirring a spoon in the grain stew with wine that he was eating at that moment, looked him square in the eyes and said, in a very serious tone: "Young man, we say: *Kur zogu vete e vien, o bën o ka fulen.*" And, guessing that the maestro didn't understand, he repeated it to him in Litisht: "When the bird comes and goes, it either builds a nest or he already has one. Make your mind up, young man, make your mind up soon."

The maestro forced a smile and answered, "It builds, Signor Alessandro, it builds." Then he picked up the worn small notebook and jotted down the proverb that, he said, he had never heard before; bravo Signor Alessandro, a proverb to remember.

"I hope so, for your sake," nani Lissandro said, not at all endeared by the maestro's shameless flattery. Only Lucrezia seemed wooed, only she, with her bloodied cheeks and a fire in her heart, sitting in front of the fireplace. Zonja Elena kept her head bowed and sneakily pretended to be lost in thoughts of her own that had nothing to do with the guest. At that point, Signor Maestro couldn't think of anything better to do than to turn to his former student: he encouraged him to study "because your father makes a lot of sacrifices abroad for you;" and to study with a method "because if you know how to study, you learn more, or rather, better." In the meantime, he skillfully resumed weaving the velvet, soft glances with Lucrezia, which had been torn apart in recent times. "If you need books for research or help with your assignments, just let me know. You know you are very dear to me, and I would do anything for you," concluded Signor Maestro, dropping his voice on the last sentence, his *gurgullea*-prince eyes fixed on the girl. Lucrezia was melting like snow because of the burning fires that were hitting her cheeks and heart. Lucky for her, one of the two sources of heat, the maestro, left shortly, leaving an inexplicable smell of fresh almonds in his place.

After that night, Lucrezia started to hope again. Carmelo loved her; eyes don't lie. Sooner or later, he would walk into that house as her fiancé. Her mother warned her to be careful, bijë, because in the end you'll be on everyone's lips, just like your sister.

Each day, Carmelo came by to visit with the excuse of looking for Costantino or nani Lissandro. There were a few rare moments when they would find themselves alone and speak privately.

"But are your intentions serious?" Lucrezia would ask each time, wanting her hopes to be confirmed.

He would answer: "Trust me, love, trust me," and if zonja Elena or Costantino, or nani Lissandro, or Baialardo, or some other pesky neighborhood woman stayed away in those moments, then he would pull her to him and they would kiss, mushing their lips together, making their teeth chatter, letting their hands run free and quick under their clothes, getting entangled and unraveled, brushing, caressing, pinching, squeezing, until the footstep, the cough, the voice of someone approaching caused them abruptly to stop. Kisses and hands do not lie. Saturday night, Lucrezia was huddled in her little bed, eagerly awaiting the serenade; three songs, a symbol of love, would break the silence of that alleyway: "Partridge who flew from the hill to come land beside me, you looked at me with those eyes, and filled my mind. You walled yourself off inside my heart." It was him. He was singing beside her, in Italian, the ancient *vjershë*, accompanied by a friend with a guitar. "Only then will I leave you, golden crown, when my eyes will be covered in dirt." It was him. And Lucrezia was sighing and clutching her pillow tight. Then Baialardo began to bark, waking everyone, if they weren't already awake. "As much as all the sand and stones that these walls have, so much love I have for you, girl." Songs don't lie, Lucrezia thought, as she drifted off to sleep.

The next morning, she sat embroidering with her friends, her eyes puffy, her ears deaf, and inside she felt a strong desire to see him as soon as possible.

It went on like this for an entire winter.

"*Primavera dintorno/Brilla nell'aria, e per li campi esulta,/Sì ch'a mirarla intenerisce il core*," Spring around/Shimmers in the air and exults throughout the fields/So that the heart is touched at its sight, Signor Maestro recited to Costantino, his only listener. In spring, he thought, nowhere in the world was as beautiful as Hora. From his house's balcony, he could admire the town immersed in the green of the holly oaks, dotted with the yellow of the thorny Scotch brooms; and the countryside beyond, with cherries, almonds, and flowering hawthorns. "This is poetry, Costantì," he said, puffing out his chest with pure air. "Look, look what a paradise!"

Little patches of town opened before the boy's eyes, old rooftops covered in moss, and here and there the flat new houses of the Germanese cut through the top floor with bare pillars, arms stretched out to tickle the sky with six iron fingers; farther down, bushes and ravines that tumbled toward a tree-lined basin, and on the left olive groves, vineyards, and desolate and barren peaks that seemed on the verge of jumping into the sea.

Costantino didn't fully understand where Signor Maestro's joy came from, but he willingly allowed himself to let it rub off on him. He visited him every day on his way back from Shën Kolli, bringing him a warm loaf of bread or a bottle of wine, or some fresh ricotta, or the first ripe cherries from the Castello, gifts from his mother and sister. Rather than helping him with his homework, Signor Maestro mentored him, explaining methods and making his encyclopedia available to him. And while Costantino was studying, he would close himself in a tiny, makeshift laboratory, testing and retesting—the instruction book open on the coffee table—the way to stuff the bodies of dead little birds, swallows and robins especially, that his students captured with traps, at times catching them alive but injured in one leg. And since the results were very disappointing, Signor Maestro, who tended to be a perfectionist, would throw those semi-stuffed bodies away, with the ruffled feathers and two black holes in place of the eyes, in the trash can; then he would wash his hands and join his guest, drowning him with that strange scent of fresh almonds.

Once he decided he had become an expert taxidermist, he wanted Costantino to watch him work. That day, a white partridge with brown splotches on its back was on the coffee table. Costantino watched him use a surgical scalpel to make an incision from the sternum down to the tail, pulling away the meat and slicing open the skull; but then he closed his eyes, disgusted. He reopened them when the taxidermist-teacher, sweaty but satisfied, began the tanning process, rubbing a dense oil he called arsenic pomade that smelled like almonds.

The white partridge, perched on a dead branch hanging from the ceiling, looked sorrowfully at the empty house entrance with its eyes of green glass.

How could Costantino justify the maestro's taxidermy work to others, or to himself, if not with the maestro's own words? "Taxidermy is an art: the art of making eternal something that is destined to die; in other words, allowing a beautiful white partridge to live forever, while everything else becomes dust, dust to dust, blown away by the wind." Like a living parrot repeating ideas that were bigger than he was, he repeated these grandiose concepts to his friends who couldn't understand him. If he insisted on playing the part of the little maestro, they became annoyed, and in response, they warned him, "be careful, or sooner or later you'll find yourself stuffed, too, because you are an Aquila." Or, even more viciously, "then he'll do it with that *copë lesh*, piece of hair or beauty, you call a sister, right before your glassy eyes." In response to which Aquila, foaming at the mouth, would tell them all to screw off, along with their innocent parents: *"Ecni e mirrni te bitha ju e kush ju ka bënë!"*

What really bothered him was that in town people were gossiping about his sister, and his friends knew that he knew but said nothing; actually, he didn't do anything to stop it. Did he have something to stop? Signor Maestro would go visit them in the evening, and they would sit around the hearth in the winter, or on the doorstep in the spring, and would talk about this and that. What harm was there in all this? Or in the Saturday night serenades that made Baialardo bark?

The Smallest White Castle in the World

The Mericano arrived at night in a beat-up old taxi he caught at the Crotone train station. They were expecting him the next morning, his family said almost in unison, sleepy and not totally sure they weren't dreaming. Baialardo wagged his tail slowly, yelping and yapping, without the strength to jump on him to welcome him home as in the old days. The Mericano was *Kaputt*, *stunat* even, and didn't notice that his son had grown nearly as tall as he, not even when he took him in his arms to carry him back to bed.

Before falling back asleep, Costantino heard nani Lissandro, who had begun to snore again, and the hushed voices of his parents and sister that overlapped with the clutter of the donkeys in the stalls.

In the morning, he felt a sting on his cheek from the shaggy beard of an unknown figure, which startled him. He opened his eyes and realized it was his father. He whetted the thick saliva in his mouth, and, torn between happiness and embarrassment, he kissed his father's hand and sobbed for a while, tearless.

"*Ç'ke, birarè?*" the Mericano asked him, moved. But he knew. He also knew that sense of half-defeated anguish that takes you when you dream of grabbing a beautiful white horse by the tail, and you hold it still for a moment, being certain that it will then gallop far away. A dream, or the same memory of kissing his father's hand upon his return from 'Merica, galloping five months later towards death? The Mericano sighed deeply and pulled away from his son as though from a bittersweet memory, returning to the old tradition of opening the magical suitcases before the relatives, neighbors, and friends flooded the house.

That time, Viatrice delle fate came to greet him, dressed all in black from head to toe on account of her mother's passing. The Mericano began by offering her his condolences, but she cut him short: "Dear Signor Francesco Avati," she said, "now that I am alone and I don't even have my mother's meager pension, I thought I could come to work in Germany. You have a big heart, everyone knows that: you must find a position for me and then I will come on my own. I know you will do this and I thank you in advance."

Flattered, the Mericano answered with the same kindness: "Signorina Viatrice Sciales, the truth is I am not planning on going abroad anymore. I would like to try to live here. But if for some reason I should return, rest assured that I will find a position and call you. I swear on my dead relatives."

Late at night, when he was alone with his family, the Mericano began to unveil his plans: the first was to stay in town forever, just as he had told Viatrice delle fate, enough of this solitary life, that was the most ambitious plan; rebuild Castello del Piccolo, which would eat up a lot of money; buy a car, maybe a used one, and go on a real vacation like a gentleman, to the beach in Marina; marry off his daughter: this was his cross to bear, the thorn in his side, his poison to drink, the real concern, the Mericano said, of my nights alone in the barracks while thinking of you all.

Lucrezia wished she could just sink through the floor rather than listen to that same old story she knew by heart. But that evening her father continued: "I heard that your dear Maestro Carmelo Bevilacqua is the son of a bitch; I heard it from some of his townsmen who work in Ludwigshafen. The mother had him when she was very young, by an Irish tourist; then she was supported by an elderly lawyer in Reggio, who put the bastard through school. In the end, she ran off with a man from Vibo. And the son, having finished his college studies, sought a position as far as possible from his hometown—where everyone admires him as much as a false lira."

In that moment, Lucrezia hated her father with a frightening intensity: sharp drops of pure rancor flowed from her steel-gray eyes.

The Mericano didn't seem at all put off by his daughter's tears. He had done his duty as a father, he had informed himself about that man—whom he had deemed unreliable even before leaving town—and now he had presented his daughter with the results of his investigation, as though to say: Apple of your father's eye, you've been warned; don't come telling me later that you didn't know.

Zonja Elena took pity on Lucrezia, and, for the first time in her life, she openly contradicted her husband who, in her view, put too much faith in people's gossip; and besides, even if the information was correct, what fault was it of Signor Maestro? That poor child with no family, that young man as wholesome as wheat bread?

Everyone expected a furious reaction from the Mericano, who was well known in the family and throughout the town for the sudden bursts of rage that came when he felt he had been stepped on. Instead, the Mericano responded with a conciliatory tone: "Fine, maybe you're right. Let's not fight. As far as I'm concerned, she can marry whoever she likes." And, adding somewhat bitterly, "Even the son of Sorrarello," the poorest man in Hora.

"If that is what destiny wants . . ." zonja Elena said, closing the question with her fatalistic wisdom. The Mericano gave an ironic smile and happily changed the subject, affectionately ruffling his daughter's blue waves of hair. He spoke of the reconstruction work to be done at the Castello; work he would entrust to Master Cenzo, the only one of the town's masons he acknowledged as honest. "But first," he said, "let's put something in our bellies. An empty sack won't stand upright!"

Everyone welcomed the invitation to eat with a smile; even nani Lissandro smiled. But not Lucrezia. That evening, she didn't smile, didn't speak, didn't eat. The only thing that passed her lips was a whistle-like gasp, a sound she hadn't made in quite a while.

It was a hectic summer for the Avatis. The Mericano's Germanese energy was infectious, even spreading to that old dormouse, nani Lissandro, who now sat awake not only under a setting moon but also under a burning sun.

For a few days, father, son, and nani Lissandro helped Master Cenzo and his workers clean the castle's exterior and interior that, after two years of neglect, had again become overrun with weeds, brambles, vines, ivy, bindweeds, wild roses, and snapdragons. Then the bricklayers began preparing the scaffolding and transporting the material for the renovation: one floor, for now, with three rooms and the washroom, the Mericano said, fashioning himself a surveyor, showing his little project sketched on the page of a notebook: interior partitions, rustic plaster, and new floors; on the exterior, a nice white cement coat to seal the cracks that let the rainwater seep through; the finishing touches could wait for another year.

Nani Lissandro and his grandson tended to the olive trees, clearing the weeds from the surrounding plants, while the Mericano, in addition to overseeing Master Cenzo's work, was preparing a vegetable plot using so much manure, he said, that even a desert would become fertile with it.

The women came to bring a bite to eat. "*Po po po, ç'ësht i bukur nani,*" my word, how beautiful it's now, they called from afar; and they saw young tomato plants growing and blooming, as well as bell peppers, eggplants, cucumbers, and *cucuzza* squash before their eyes, while the house and garden took shape around them. *Po po po*, look how Costantino eats, working is good for him; bread earned with sweat tastes sweeter. This way he will learn how to earn his bread, the Mericano interjected, tireless and lean, whose total control depended on his mood swings.

Costantino ate with appetite, working harder than his grandfather and admiring the Mericano, his father, who was so dynamic and quick at work and cards, and who didn't let anyone step on his toes: Costantino himself had seen him, one night at the bar, throw his cards in the face of that cheater Patrù; he had heard him yell at Master Cenzo that he was doing it wrong, that he had to follow the plan and not make things up himself: that dividing wall in the middle, he had to tear it down and rebuild it at his own expense, because that one seemed like it was built by a shoemaker. So, the good

Master Cenzo admitted he made a mistake, and to ease the tension he said, "Fine, I'll rebuild it, but only if you offer us a cold beer first."

The Mericano nodded and his son flew into town to buy some beers, as he did every day: he liked his friends to see him in his workman's clothes, and he showed his joy through his crazy races across the three kilometers of dust to town, deafened by the chorus of cicadas and the humid heat of the early afternoon.

When his father arrived in the piazza in a used car, purchased in Crotone, Costantino could not contain his joy: strangers were gathered 'round the khaki-colored Fiat 124, and he stood stiff as a board, as though exerting an enormous feat, his leg muscles practically ready to burst. Luckily, his father let him get in the car, and focused and satisfied he drove all the way to Palacco. All it took was two honks of the horn. Neighbors and relatives ran after them, chanting in unison: "*Vrè, ç'ësht e bukur*," Look: how beautiful it is, and they threw confetti, candy, rice, and small coins into the cabin of the car as a sign of good wishes.

They went to the beach every Sunday that summer, following a long, winding road full of potholes and hairpin turns that would make zonja Elena throw up. When they arrived, the poor woman was more dead than alive. But as soon as she stuck her feet in the sea, she would come back to life.

Costantino was the only one who knew how to swim: he had learned at Bosco del Canale, in a stone tub that had, for years, served as a pool for the children of Hora. But as soon as he got a little farther from the shore, he was forced to endure a chorus of, "be careful, careful, don't go far or you'll drown, and then I'll finish you off." He laughed when he heard this unintentional joke and darted around his parents' feet, splashing water with his fists, specifically aiming at Lucrezia, who was afraid of the sea.

His sister was beautiful in her bikini, toned and slender, her skin dotted with pearls of salt water, like an actress from a commercial. His mother, on the other hand, hid her excessive flesh in an oversized, sleeveless nylon shirt, prematurely appearing like an elderly village woman.

They even managed to drag nani Lissandro to the beach, and it warmed the heart to see him there in his bathing suit under the beach umbrella, with his crooked legs thin as wires and whiter than milk.

In the evening, they would return home with sunburned shoulders and noses, except Costantino, whose tanned skin grew ever darker. That was the last summer he would wear a *marsin* around his wrist, a bracelet of colorful cotton threads he had woven together as he did each year, on March first, so the sun wouldn't turn him black. However, it had never served its purpose.

After dinner, Costantino would play cards on one of the doorsteps, or on the step of a staircase with his peers; later, with Mario and Vittorio—his closest friends—he would hide behind the Kurrituri, where the women from the poorest families would go to relieve themselves, standing in a row, with their skirts pulled halfway up their thighs. And, as the women conversed, the boys narrowed their gaze, spying their gleaming knees under the moonlight, and in between the sudden bursts of liquid, they could make out tufts that were dark like moss opened like sea urchins. Sometimes all it would take was the hiss of a bat in the distance or the trampling of a dry branch by one of the boys to make them dart away with their hearts trembling and their pants unbuttoned, tumbling down the mossy hill. They would stumble about blindly until someone was able to find the path that led through the vegetable patches and back to the safety of the piazza.

The next day, at Castello del Piccolo.

Work was going slowly because of Master Cenzo's constant interruptions, on account of his being busy with many other Germanese clients. By the time they were laying the first layer of plaster, it was already autumn: having prepared the mortar with white concrete, coarse sand, and a lot of water, the masons forcefully spread it over all the castle walls.

"This plaster should last forever," the Mericano said, just to say something.

The masons began to laugh, sprayed in mortar from head to toe, and Master Cenzo, struggling to open his cement-sealed mouth, tried to contradict him: "What do you mean, eternal?! We ourselves don't last for eternity, let alone plaster!" And he added, joking, "And if it's as you say, where will we find work in a hundred years?"

But the foreman hadn't understood the hidden meaning of those words that came forth from the Mericano's soul; to understand, he should have closely observed the Mericano's face, the way Costantino did, when the work was finished, when from the Kriqi, he enjoyed the white speck of the smallest castle in the world gleaming with reflected light. Just like his emerald-green eyes.

The Little Ladies and the
Bored Little Soldier

Signor Maestro Carmelo Bevilacqua appeared at the Avatis'
house at the end of the Christmas holidays, leaving everyone speechless, even the talkative Mericano who, on more
than one occasion, had wagered the castle against a lira with
a hole in it on the odds that this son-of-a-good-woman would
never again set foot on their doorstep so long as he—the
Mericano—was in town and since he was done emigrating.
No one, not even Lucrezia, felt confident taking that bet of
a lira, as it would surely have meant enduring a million self-
righteous jabs from the spiteful Mericano. But instead, the
maestro was at the front door with two bouquets of red roses,
one for Lucrezia and one for zonja Elena, and an illustrated
history book for Costantino.

The awkward tension in the kitchen could have been cut
with a knife: no one moved or said a thing. Lucrezia felt
faint but forced herself to endure, leaning on her brother's

shoulder and letting him support, unbothered, her dead weight. Her grandfather broke the silence, shooting an arrow at the Mericano, just like in olden times: "This turned out well for you, it did. If we had been braver and had trusted more, you'd be poor and crazy by now, without a castle because of a lost bet."

They all forced a smirk. Even Signor Maestro, although he didn't understand the old man's joke. He took advantage of the momentary distraction to free his hands, distributing his gifts. Then he approached the Mericano, and with a tremble in his voice that was inconceivable for a man like him, said: "I am here to ask for your daughter's hand," and as he said this, he took off his new cap—the red one Lucrezia made by hand—revealing his nearly bald head in public for the first time.

It was Signor Maestro's unexpected appearance, as opposed to his words, that struck everyone. Everyone, that is, except Lucrezia who clutched the roses to her chest, nearly smothering them in anxious anticipation of her father's reply.

"Put your cap back on," the Mericano said, meaning to put the man at ease. Then he came to the matter at hand: "If Lucrezia wants it, why not?"

All eyes turned to Lucrezia, and they noticed the shower of rose petals that burst from the fire in her heart and that old Baialardo—now nearly blind—sniffed at, having mistaken them for bits of meat.

"I see she does want this; in that case, so do I," the Mericano added, in the solemn and faintly artificial tone of one who has prepared his answer long before, rehearsing the facial expression and tone of voice.

From that evening on, zonja Elena had another son to look after, and the Mericano another mouth to feed. Signor Maestro went back to his own house only to sleep and stuff local birds, or the exotic ones that arrived in little cardboard cages.

In the span of a few days, Lucrezia rid herself of all the anxiety and insecurity she had carried around since falling in love with Carmelo. They would celebrate their engagement in the fall because Carmelo wanted time to prepare a traditional celebration, complete with a round dance—as he called the vallja—and celebratory cohe to please the ancestors in their tombs. No one tried to contradict him, not even the Mericano, because by now the bond was official and that was enough, according to Lucrezia, to silence everyone, even the cicadas that had chirped behind her back. The girl was at peace with all the saints and the fairies in the world, riding atop an extraordinary feeling of physical and interior well-being, evident in the overflowing exuberance of her body and some sparkles of light at the bottom of her eyes, which are enduringly green. She spent every minute of every afternoon and evening with Carmelo, except when her taxidermist prince was busy immortalizing a jaybird or a red kite that some friend of his had killed in the groves of loricate pines in the Pollino Mountains.

The Mericano wanted to be a modern man: he knew about life, he said, and he knew a woman follows her natural disposition, even if you chain her down; and, since he trusted his daughter blindly, he didn't see why he should present himself to the teacher, a learned man, as a backward, jealous Arbëresh. As a result, he didn't watch over his daughter directly, nor did he ask his wife to do so. As a bare minimum of precaution (but really, he said, it was just to avoid hearing criticism from his relatives), he begged Costantino to accompany the engaged couple when they ventured out of the house together: "You're her brother, Costantino, your sister's honor is yours as well."

And so it came to pass that Costantino lived through one of the dullest periods of his life. On Sundays, he had to get up early, dress in his new clothes and chaperone the betrothed couple to church. His father had told him to stay by their sides like a little soldier. In this new military life, the only chances he had to have a little fun came in the morning, at school. It wasn't just the wonderful geography lessons, but even the boring hours of Latin seemed like a stroll in the park compared to the long, exhausting walks to Trelisset, with the two lovers gazing into each other's eyes, fencing with their noses, and whispering little words that Costantino considered stupid and childish: *Të dua mir*, I love you, *lule e vogël*, little flower, *zëmëra jime*, my heart.

Sometimes the betrothed couple, pretending to head toward Trelisset, would instead cut down one of the narrow alleyways around Palacco and would end up at the teacher's house. They would close themselves in the maestro's bedroom, leaving the little soldier in the vast front room, offering an excuse that wouldn't even fool a child: "Your sister has a bad headache; she wants to rest for ten minutes. In the meantime, I'll read the paper. You can look at the birds."

The front room was like a piece of dead sky, with birds of every kind, caught by poachers on the Pollino and at the mouth of the Neto, and frozen here while migrating. If Costantino had had a magic wand, he would have freed them from that spell, letting them fly through the sky over Hora: kites, woodpeckers, cranes, herons, gulls, storks, partridges, black-winged stilts, a swarm of multicolored birds that would be joined by the double-headed eagle that would lead them far away. Far, far away.

Just as he arrived at this conclusion, the doors of the bedroom would open and the lovers would emerge, their hair tangled, their cheeks flushed, their eyes aglow. Signor Maestro only needed a minute to put himself in order: a quick comb over the back of his head, and his cap on top. Lucrezia, on the other hand, would spend a long time gazing in the mirror that stood by the front door: she would brush her rebellious curls, powder her flushed cheeks, and dab her already red lips with the lipstick she started using since she got engaged.

Zonja Elena didn't care for lipstick or the other ladylike eccentricities: her daughter would wake up late in the morning and dress like an actress, with tight skirts that stopped above the knee, and when she wasn't immersed in her sewing or out with her fiancé, she read *Grand Hotel* or other scandalous photo-romance magazines featuring couples that kissed on the mouth. The one good development was that she no longer whistled like a *burraçë*. If her mother tried to scold her or threatened to tell her father everything (which she would never do for fear the Mericano would react violently), Lucrezia would respond unabashedly, saying they needed to leave her alone, she didn't have to answer to anyone; now she was accountable only to Carmelo, only to her fi-an-cé!

They all went to await his arrival at the Marina train station. They were crammed, nearly to the point of suffocation, in the khaki-colored Fiat 124: the Mericano, his wife, his kids, nani, Baialardo, everyone was in good spirits because the dog had peed on Costantino's knees, possibly excited about their road trip. Orlandina got off the train with a suitcase and three packages. She was wearing a baggy tracksuit that seemed to highlight, rather than hide, the roundness of her belly. In her sixth month of pregnancy, Orlandina looked like she had been drawn with a compass: round face, round breasts, round belly, round bottom. She said she wasn't tired, even though she had traveled for eighteen hours; only her feet felt swollen, like two balls. She couldn't wait to take off her sneakers and walk barefoot on the cool tiles of the house, just like she did as a girl. Zonja Elena gave her the front seat, the most comfortable spot, and courageously piled in with the others in the back seat of the car.

"*Te Hora, jam te Hora*," in Hora, I am in Hora, Orlandina kept repeating, drunk on the warm air and curvy roads. She could hardly believe she was back in Hora after three years. Three years? It was as if she had been away a century. The Mericano was the only one who could have understood her, but he was focused on driving carefully: he didn't listen to his daughter, didn't hear a word of the compliments from the people piled in the back of the car. The Trentino air did her good, she exuded well-being from every pore, the belly suited her, it made her look like a real lady. Orlandina thanked them with a distracted smile and repeated, "*Jam te Hora*."

Old Lissandro was the first to comment on the astounding resemblance between Orlandina and zonja Elena. "You look like twins now, you could go hand in hand," he said. He was right: with her round belly and round breasts, Orlandina had her mother's body, she even had the same full face, with a few, very thin wrinkles, the same ladylike back-combed hair. But nani Lissandro wasn't just talking about their physical appearance; he thought mother and daughter were twins in the slow, regal way they walked—just like zonjas—and above all, in the way they kept a beautiful smile firmly on their lips as they argued, paving the way for the sweet, easy answers that were often off-topic.

Orlandina made the rounds of the relatives, accompanied by her little soldier of a brother. She told everyone she would be in town until the end of her sister's engagement party: that was why she was in Hora. But she was also in Hora for the taste of pomegranates, her mother's pickled vegetables, oil-cured olives and peppers, and salted sardines; otherwise, her child would be born with a thousand cravings. She laughed. She laughed with gusto, and with that same gusto, she ate all the delicacies she had listed for her relatives. And her husband? "*Mir, mir*" Orlandina would say curtly, turning their attention to the red apples she brought from Trentino, four for each family of relatives, fabulous apples, beautiful, delicious, shiny. Yes, but your husband? the relatives would insist. Right, the husband. She couldn't complain. Because in the end, Narciso was as wholesome as wheat bread. He trusted her (my lady, as he called her), to run the house. Because in the end, men from there are like *burrat* in Hora: they work the fields, and in the evenings, they play cards and have a drink with friends. They work a lot there, too. But there, the work pays well. Narciso planted some apple trees in his fields, and he cared for them as if they were his own children. He's there now, poisoning the worms or doing who knows what. That's why he couldn't come to Hora. Because of the apple trees. Sure, one doesn't live like a king, but money isn't wanting. She helps her husband with the harvest and then goes back to being a lady. It would be a paradise, with fields of green, and in springtime blossoming apple trees, if only it weren't so far from Hora. If only it weren't so different from Hora. Different in that it . . . Well, she missed the view of the sea, the horizon between the sea and the sky. Because in the end, mountains suffocate you.

The Round Dance

When Lucrezia descended the stairs the evening of her engagement party, dressed in the splendid gown her fiancé had ordered from Garrafa, the guests were speechless, their mouths agape, noses all turned toward her. "*Ç'je e bukura, bijë!*" how beautiful you are, daughter, zonja Elena whispered. Full of pride, her breath caught in her throat. Lucrezia glowed like a princess, wrapped in an indigo satin corset under which one could see her breasts throbbing like unripe quinces. She walked slowly, letting her coha trail, a gaudy skirt of coral red damask satin trimmed with a braided ruffle. Her head was held high and stiff, more like a statue than a princess; it was as though she were afraid of opening the floodgates on that undulating river of hair that was just barely held in place with the *keza*, a gold-embroidered head-covering secured with a long silver pin. The guests tossed confetti and coins and wished her well—*urime urime*—and kissed her delicately so as not to muss her up.

At exactly eight o'clock Signor Maestro appeared at the front door. Everyone looked at him, stunned. And then they all broke out into laughter, barely concealed with hands placed over mouths. Even Costantino and Orlandina allowed themselves to laugh, while the rest of the family didn't know where to direct their gaze. Signor Maestro, not at all embarrassed, gave Lucrezia a bouquet of orchids, took a few steps back—blocking the doorway—and blinded the crowd with the powerful flash of his camera. That dazzling light silenced the guests, and they admired the fiancé in his unusual attire: heavy black woolen pants that stopped below the knee, a white linen shirt with a rounded collar, and a black jacket that reached a large, handmade leather belt. But what had got everyone laughing were the rigid, black, cone-shaped hat, and the goofy goatskin shoes awkwardly tipped. This was the traditional garb for Arbëreshë men, and who knows where and how that devil of a Maestro had procured them. Then, ignoring the fact that he himself was already the evening's surprise, he said, as though announcing a show: "Ladies and gentlemen, I give you the evening's surprise, the man that will bring us joy with his sweet melodies, his pure Arbëresh music: and I stress 'pure.' My future grandfather should consider this a gift in his honor."

Everyone applauded, enticed; and there, at the door, stood Luca Rodotà, the rhapsode of Corone, with the lahuta in his hands. Costantino barely recognized him: he had grown thin as a bird, his nose hooked, his shoulder blades protruding, with a big beard like that of an orthodox priest, and long unkempt hair, like feathers. But his gaze was the same: clear and blue, like the sky after the rain.

"May the days and years extend before you, fiancé, together with your queen," the rhapsode said, in Litisht, out of respect for the maestro, his voice resounding in its usual baritone. *"Mirë së erdhe,"* everyone said in unison, welcoming him, while nani Lissandro walked toward him, filled with emotion.

The two old men hugged each other while everyone else fell silent; overcome by emotion, they averted their gaze until the flash of the maestro's camera brought them all back to reality.

Like a true professional, the rhapsode positioned himself in a corner of the room and began to sing: *Më dërgon ti ajrin!/ Qetu, trim, se t'e dërgoj,* You send me the wind!/Silent, young man, because I will send it to you. Just then, as if on cue, nine girls walked in dressed in their grandmothers' *cohe,* ready to recite the prayer Signor Maestro wanted for his traditional, old-school engagement party.

"This is what remains of the noble and beautiful cohe; all the others are rotting in the cemetery" observed the maestro. "But away with sadness; now is the time for the round dance."

The girls formed a circle and, guided by the engaged couple, gave life to an endless, rhythmic dance. After the first demonstration, all the other guests joined the vallja, and when the circle grew too big to fit in the room, two smaller concentric circles were formed. The young people danced the round dance with ironic smiles on their lips, and not having anything else to grab hold of, they clutched the sweaty and cold hands of their girlfriends. The only one not sweating was the old rhapsode who was singing and playing for three hours without taking a break; after all, what could his shriveled skin possibly exude? The old man's pluck and youthful strength were incredible. He had to cross the Sila on his mule just to get to Hora, descending to Umbriatico and finally climbing up along the Kapedirti i Dramësit. It was a gift, the rhapsode said, for Lissandro, his *vëlla giaku,* blood brother, his lifelong friend. Then he turned to the couple and said he had one last song for them, the song of beautiful death, beautiful because if one dies in one's sleep, like the song says, death is beautiful, it is not even death, it is a dream. Don't take it personally, I always close with this song. It is sad, but it is a good omen, like when one dreams of dying.

The song was accompanied by an enigmatic—rather than sad—chord on the lahuta. The song told the story of a girl who had a flax plant in her window. Oh, how I tended it, and watered it, the girl sang through the rhapsode's mouth. Until it grew big as a tree. And then I gave it to Rosa, my friend. Rosa said she didn't want it. And then she came with me, slowly down the street. The young man found out and disguised himself as an old man; and the old man walked with us, slowly, until we reached the convent, and there we met Hurandina. Hurandina is my sister, said the old man. I want to marry someone, I want to marry the little red one. I was very frightened: I might burn my heart, I might melt crack like a pomegranate. I want to marry someone, I want to marry the little white one. I was very frightened: I might go pale in the face, I might melt like the snow. The old man came to you in your sleep, and in your sleep, he hit you with the clasp of your braids, wrapped in flax thread.

None of the guests understood the meaning of that confusing song. Who was the little red one? Who was the little white one? Who had the old man hit in their sleep? But many of the guests seemed disturbed, and a deathly silence dominated the room even after the last note had sounded. Luckily, Signor Maestro was ready to dispel that cloud of sadness that seemed to cover everyone, he yelled to the young ones that they could now dance their *geghegè*. The response was a wild twist, which sent the sadness away to other times, and it drove Baialardo crazy—locked away in his doghouse—and excited the other dogs roaming free in the streets. After that, it was just slow songs until late in the night, when the close relatives dragged their daughters from the room.

Zonja Elena offered the rhapsode a bite to eat and a bed to sleep in, but he accepted the former—a bit of bread and cheese—and refused the latter. "I will set off with my mule," he said, "and by dawn I'll be in Corone."

The rhapsode chewed slowly, and as he chewed, he spoke about the past, using words others didn't always understand. Before leaving, he made nani Lissandro blush by talking about when they were still fresh-faced boys and they would have fun wrestling on the beaches in Marina. Lissandro would always win, but I had the strongest imagination, right Lissandro? I would dream about the trip across the sea, all the Arbëreshë together, because by then there were no more Turks, there was freedom and land to be worked, or at least he and I, on a sailboat, out to start our lives anew after more than four centuries. Was I crazy? Yes, I am still a little crazy.

Costantino's eyes were closing on their own, but before falling asleep he heard nani talking about the old rhapsode: "We won't see him again. He talks about the past with the same nostalgia as the living dead."

But there was no sadness in his voice.

Skanderbeg's Bust

In January the Mericano left again for Ludwigshafen, pub-
licly making two solemn promises: to find a job for Viatrice
delle fate and to return permanently, he repeated: definitively,
for his daughter's wedding. This final year of sacrifices would
allow him to finish the living quarters of the castle, where,
if they liked, the two spouses-to-be could live as king and
queen. He had some savings to support Costantino with his
studies; and then, to live well, the vineyard and the olive trees
would be enough.

Costantino held back his tears because his grandfather,
having noticed his eyes were about to explode, had repeated
një burr ngë qan, a man doesn't cry; but he felt thousands of
bubbles of anguish rise in his throat. And he envied his
mother and sister who sobbed in peace on the way home,
consoling each other.

The maestro was not with them. For some time now he had
been organizing the unveiling of the bust of Skanderbeg,
which he had wanted more than anything. He had convinced

the mayor, the public officials, and all the city councilmen, including those of the opposition, with a simple but effective speech: an Arbëresh town without the bust of Skanderbeg is not an Arbëresh town. Then he wrote to the Albanian embassy in Rome, and six months later a heavy wooden crate arrived from Albania. The bust was a bronze reproduction of a work by the famous Albanian sculptor Odhise Paskali, preserved in the National Museum in Tirana. It was placed on a granite pedestal and covered with a green tarp, awaiting its unveiling.

The maestro was frenetically busy: had he wanted it, the bust? Now he had to help his friend the mayor for a successful outcome of the inaugural celebration. It was up to him to prepare the posters and give a speech on the life of this Skanderbeg, and therefore read all the books on the subject. Oh, how many things he had to do, the maestro; he didn't even have a spare moment to stuff his birds, to be alone with his Lucrezia, to correct his students' homework. Sometimes, he ate while he read. With his fiancé, he exchanged more or less two sentences and two pecks of greetings. Then he would run away to his home to read and take notes.

If any family member dared to criticize or mock Signor Maestro's unusual behavior, Lucrezia became aggressive and vicious: she defended her fiancé with a drawn sword because he knew what he was doing, because he was a maestro, not an ignorant like you, nani, she cursed one evening, earning herself a slap from her brother. A violent brawl followed, with pulling of each other's hair and low blows, kicks to the shins, and spittle from her; from him loud backhands and "don't you dare again." All to the accompaniment of her mother's "*nanì basta*," that's enough, and the amused laughter of nani Lissandro.

The inaugural celebration was welcomed by everyone as a liberation.

The mayor lifted the tarp from the bust: frowning and proud, Skanderbeg cooled the audience with a steady look of reproach. From a small stage adorned with wildflowers and an array of fluttering posters (on which stood out the writing: Presentation by Prof. Carmelo Bevilacqua), the sharp voice of the maestro started by thanking the people of Hora, the gathered authorities, and above all the first secretary of the Albanian Embassy in Italy. Then he read his "Summary of Skanderbeg's life." Costantino saved a copy. It is a panegyric worthy of Signor Maestro: factual, sentimental, rhetorical.

He began on the night in 1404, when Skanderbeg's mother gave birth to him after an enormous snake appeared to her in a dream that from Albania went to the country of the Turks. The Maestro described the figure of a hero more heroic than the one sung in the rhapsodies. In this manner at Hora, it was learned that Skanderbeg was a nickname for Gjergj Kastrioti, which in Turkish means Lord Alexander. He had grown up in the Turkish court of the emperor Murad II, held hostage along with his three brothers, ever since their father John, prince of Krujë, had been defeated in battle.

The audience, as advised by the maestro, imagined the suffering of this family forced to split up from the most despicable blackmailing. However, immediately after, the audience rejoiced, because in the meantime Skanderbeg had become the strongest of all his comrades in the military art, and at the age of twenty, he was appointed commander of an army of five thousand soldiers with whom he had defeated the rebels in many areas of Asia. In short, Skanderbeg, according to the maestro, was born to win and furthermore was also very handsome, large in stature, broad-shouldered, muscular, and light-skinned, with two delightful and sincere eyes. Therefore, a great conqueror, not only of lands but also of women's hearts.

One day, an angry elephant hurled itself against the very beautiful princess Frosina, an odalisque of the harem of Mehmed, the sultan's son. But Skanderbeg stopped it and saved the woman. Frosina embraced him with tenderness, and with words that flew from her heart, she revealed her love for him.

Upon his father's death, in accordance with the agreements signed at the time, one of his sons was to ascend the throne of Albania. But what did Murad do? He didn't give a damn about the word he gave and poisoned his three older brothers. He spared only Skanderbeg, because he was interested in his physical strength and cunningness as a commander, ignoring that by leaving him alive he had secured his own ruin.

Skanderbeg, when he learned of the death of his brothers, did not react instinctively. Intelligent and astute as he was, he armed himself, above all, with patience, which has always sustained and governed the world. In fact: he continued to serve the sultan better than before, without letting anything that he harbored in his mind and in his heart slip.

Finally, one day he realized that the moment of that long-awaited vendetta had arrived. Sent with his army to suppress the prince of Serbia rebellion, naturally he succeeded, but the hatred toward the sultan was so strong that, in a surprising move, he allied himself with Christian opponents. Like lightning, he got to Krujë and with just five hundred Albanian soldiers he took control of his never-forgotten homeland, defending it for years, first from Murad and then from his son Mehmed.

The maestro mentioned each of the twenty-two battles fought and won by Skanderbeg, killing, he happily highlighted, the lovely number of four hundred thousand infidels. Only once he asked for a truce, and having obtained it, he crossed the Adriatic with nine thousand Albanians and went to the Kingdom of Naples to help King Ferdinand of Aragon fight the rebel barons. He immediately defeated them and the king and, out of gratitude, donated three Apulian towns to him: Trani, Siponto, and San Giovanni Rotondo. In this way, guided by the hand of fate, Skanderbeg found a way, albeit a painful one, for his own people who, defeated by the Turks after his death, would prefer to live in a foreign land but free, rather than as slaves in their own home.

"But of his death," the Maestro concluded, "I choose not to speak because it seems to me that Skanderbeg never died. He lives. He is here among us. And he observes us with his proud gaze. Look at him." And the people obeyed, admiring with due respect that bearded man, his cap topped with a goat's head, and his bronze gaze. "Here, friends, is what I wish in conclusion: that his presence, here, among us, can serve as a spur to the rebirth of yours, actually of our moribund country."

The applause was long and sincere. The Signor Maestro could not have been clearer or more concise: even the elementary school children had understood him and were already saying that this Skanderbeg of theirs was a hundred times stronger than Garibaldi.

The first to contradict the maestro was nani Lissandro, but he did it very tactfully, in a low voice, while people applauded: "But one time Skanderbeg was defeated in a battle in Belgrade against Mehmed's Hebalia Bassà. Too numerous were his adversaries, he was forced to flee, after seeing five thousand of his strongest men die, including his friend Musacchio, his first captain."

Costantino heard him and, still clapping, asked: "And how do you know this?"

"I just do," nani Lissandro replied and added nothing else.

The echo of the applause had just died down when from the crowd of adults a firm voice of protest was heard: "Instead of spending so many millions on an iron statue, you could have spent it on us unemployed people!"

Most of the people, including the mayor, reacted to the solitary voice with a laugh and a shake of the head in a sign of disapproval. Patrù was the one who had spoken, a good-for-nothing who had come back from Germany for good after just one year, saying the air was bad for him, but in truth, people said, he does not like to work, because Patrù was one of those people who doesn't want a job, even as a dead man, and he lives off unemployment; how did he muster the courage to speak up! But some people, here and there, agreed with him.

Signor Maestro felt that the core values of his soul were under attack. The smile on his lips faded, and when the authorities congratulated him on his beautiful, wonderful *shumë e mirë*, outstanding speech, he could not even say thank you. That comment, he would say many years later, was like a kick that sent him far from Hora. He walked away from the crowd almost running, without saying goodbye to anyone, not even Lucrezia who, unsure of what to do because of her embarrassment, leaned on Skanderbeg with all the weight of her heart.

The Christmas Hearth

Orlandina gave birth to a handsome boy of almost four kilos whom they named Paolo. Hora got the news ten minutes after the telegram arrived, thanks to the three gunshots fired by nani into that crisp March sky. That same day, the Mericano poured a round of drinks for the hundred and twenty comrades in the barracks: wine from Castello del Piccolo he brought to celebrate the happy occasion, and beer and schnapps galore.

Ten days later, a portrait of Paolo with his bald head and Costantino's big eyes dominated the living room in the Avatis' house, positioned next to the portrait of the Mericano as a young man. Zonja Elena was pleased: she had predicted the birth of a boy based on the roundness of her daughter's belly; and most importantly, she had wished it with all her might: better a boy, bijë, because girls only make their families suffer; and they suffer, their hearts suffer too, like a mountain covered in snow, as the old saying goes.

Indeed, Lucrezia was suffering. Even the walls of the house had noticed. Her fiancé was unrecognizable. All because of that cursed unveiling, Lucrezia said. But the maestro was no longer thinking of that day; he had closed the door on it, or at least so he said. At the table, he would engage in long monologues about the events happening in Italy and around the world: recounting the facts (stories of repentant addicts in New York and Milan, of doors slammed in the faces of ex-convicts looking for work in Turin, of Australian aboriginal women who thought they would get pregnant by touching the rocks in the fertility cave), he offered his opinions and moral lessons to his silent dinner companions, and he ate. He ate with increasing speed, without even chewing.

Lucrezia felt misunderstood and neglected by her teacher-fiancé, even though in front of her friends and family she bravely wore the happy face of her engagement party. Sometimes, when they were alone, she forced herself to complain, with words veiled in sadness, with feeble protests dispelled as soon as they were formed or softened with nervous smiles. But the maestro, at the end of that exhausting school year, about to turn thirty, told her, his dearest, that he felt the call of all the world's suffering; they were pleading voices that echoed in his head like an endless litany. "And my voice? Can't you hear it?" Lucrezia yelled in his face for the first time, crying at him as her fiancé finished saying that Hora was just a grain of sand in the endless desert of the world. He calmed her with a kiss and a hug, and inexplicably cried with her.

After the summer break, Lucrezia began to lose her patience. Once a week, her fiancé had her come to his house, with zonja Elena's permission, to have his house cleaned. Costantino refused to accompany her: by now he was a high school student at the Istituto Magistrale, and he said he had too much schoolwork to do; the truth is, he was tired of being the little soldier.

Lucrezia dusted the old stuffed birds, put the books back on the shelves that had been scattered across the unmade bed, stacked old newspapers and magazines in the closet-laboratory, cleared the taxidermy table of the mouse droppings, and waited. She made the bed or changed the sheets dirtied with sweat, swept the ants from the wobbly terracotta flooring and the cobwebs from the ceiling corners and behind the armoire, and waited impatiently. She waited, sometimes, sitting beside him as he read, letting out an imperceptible sigh.

The fiancé ignored Lucrezia's sighs and impatient waiting, and he lived his own eclipse as a lunatic in love around the planet of world hunger. For some time now he had even stopped going to Lucrezia's for meals. He preferred a quick lunch at home, a slice of bread and cheese, or bread and ham and a piece of seasonal fruit, rather than zonja Elena's abundant, fatty cooking, with her desserts made bitter by the guilt of considering the millions who have died of hunger.

The fights began quickly. Or rather: Lucrezia would fight and yell, listing the obligations of a fi-an-cé, the love and devotion she had for him that was no longer reciprocated, the plans for an Arbëresh wedding that went up in flames, the gilded coha and a folk group that he promised would have arrived from Albania. He tried to calm her with the usual pill of a kiss, but she wouldn't fall for it anymore; she wanted to know his true intentions, that's what she wanted to know. So he tried to explain in simple terms his ideas on the world's issues, but she turned vulgar, she didn't give a fuck about the world if the world was choking their love; in the end, he went back to the heartfelt resolutions that he had made during their happy times together, to the wedding with the coha and the Albanian group, and she seemed to grow calmer, looking into his kind eyes behind his muted glasses, his sweet face. She allowed herself to be touched by his smooth hands, as though nothing had happened.

When the Mericano returned in mid-December, the quarrels between the two fiancés suddenly ceased. The Mericano had this wizard-like power: he made problems disappear, suffocating them with his physical presence. In just half an hour he had repainted a smile on Lucrezia's lips, the time it took to settle on a wedding date with the maestro: next Christmas. Meanwhile, Carmelo had to spend Christmas with them. By now he was part of the family, and this way he could finally see the spectacle of the *zjarri i Natallevet*, the big fire that was lit in front of the church; what was he going to his hometown for? He didn't have anyone there; it would be a perfect Christmas, the Mericano promised in conclusion.

The happiest about the return of family harmony was zonja Elena. She had carefully followed the secret sufferings, the loud arguments, the nightmares, and her daughter's hysterical crying. But those moments of apparent tranquility, brought about by the Mericano's magic wand, could trick zonja Elena or Costantino, but not nani Lissandro. In fact, since the death of his mule, the old man had opened his mouth only to repeat that *jeta ësht si fjeta*, and one night he made his daughter cry: "Deceiving yourself is pointless. This engagement will end badly," he said. And, despite zonja Elena's accusations, he wasn't jinxing it, because even if nani Lissandro couldn't tell the future, he could read the present.

It really was a white Christmas. It snowed delicately from the first night, and the coldest of the roof tiles were already white. In the churchyard, a heap of wood was dusted in snow. For a month already, groups of children filled the dark alleyways with their echoing of their "*Cuka-dru dru-dru*," and if some family didn't immediately respond to that noisy call with even just one log, the kids wouldn't get upset; they would continue on their way, asking *cuka-dru*, while the older ones, with steps as light as ghosts, crept into the yards or doorsteps or sheds, and would take the biggest logs from the woodpiles—one or two each. "It isn't a sin; it's for Baby Jesus," they would tell the younger ones.

When they lit the Christmas fire, thick flakes fell from the sky like large feathers that bounced off the invisible curtains of the evening breeze, as though they were afraid of dissolving on the ground or being swallowed by the halo that rose from the flame. Costantino stared at the scene, transfixed, as though he had lived it all before: the fire, the feathers of snow, the people on the steps of the churchyard, nani, his parents, Lucrezia and Signor Maestro by the fire, even the old zonja with the holiday coha who was singing by herself: *Lojmë lojmë, vasha, valle/Krishti u le te ato Natalle*, Let's dance, let's dance, girls, the vallja,/Jesus was born on Christmas day, while Don Emilio sang "Tu scendi dalle stelle," You Come Down from the Stars, into the church microphone. Mass was over, and the holiday bells were ringing, drowning out the singing and the happy voices of people wishing one another a merry Christmas.

The churchyard was empty later on; a small group of old men and another group of young men remained by the fire, huddled on the steps. That night Costantino smoked his first cigarette, imitating his friends; he smoked until morning, coughing from all the smoke he inhaled and drinking Coca-Cola to keep himself awake. He felt waves of heat on his back and now and again would turn to look at the fire, seeing it die out.

At dawn, when the Christmas fire had become a circle of embers and ash, he headed toward home with Mario and Vittorio. He felt dazed and satisfied, his mouth bittersweet with smoke and Coca-Cola. It had stopped snowing some time before; in fact, over there, in Marina, a little sliver of light was starting to show, slicing that winter sky in two. It was at that moment that he felt a sense of nostalgia for his double-headed eagle, and he would have liked to see it fly above the sea, if only with his imagination: a brief flight toward the Sila mountains sprayed with snow, a quick fluttering of wings in the light that was spreading as far as the eye could see, like an upside-down cone. But suddenly, the Mericano's burst of urine echoed in his mind: Sciales.

After the Epiphany, they killed the hog. Zonja Elena was to thank for those one hundred and thirty kilos of meat: she had fed him, her *derk* with abundant soups, three treks each day, along the stinky road of the *zimbe*, pigsties, rain or shine.

When the last *soppressate*, soupies, were hanging from the poles in the kitchen, a wedding-like feast was prepared, with wine and meat aplenty. The guests drank to the health of the Avati family and challenged one another with toasts of coarse rhyming couplets. The Mericano answered every toast made in his honor, and on request told stories of Viatrice delle fate. He had found her a job in a food processing factory, but within three months she was washing dishes in an Italian restaurant, and four months later she was waiting tables in another restaurant. Recently he hadn't seen her, but his paesani said she was going steady with a Turkish man.

At the next table over, where the women were sitting, zonja Elena gestured to her husband to stop drinking, that was enough, enough. By the end, the Mericano was blind drunk. The wine he drank like water had a special effect on him: he would slap anyone who came near him, he would mourn his prematurely deceased parents without shedding a tear, and he pitied himself because, as he had been saying for decades, he would be dead within two years' time. In times like these, Costantino would run off to the piazza, not because he was afraid of his father's blows but because it made him sick to see him in such a condition.

That night, Carmelo Bevilacqua was the one who had to pay a price. Despite Lucrezia's warnings, he approached his future father-in-law, and using his maestro's voice with his arms spread wide, he said: "Now then, be good, papa! Now I'll bring you to bed." With the first slap, his glasses flew off; the second one sent his navy-blue beret flying. It left him petrified, shocked, his near-sighted eagle-owl's gaze staring into nothing, listening to the laughter from the other guests; he stood like that until two children returned his beret and glasses with a broken stem.

The next day, the Mericano didn't remember a thing, but he believed his wife's story; and because she was very worried about the consequences of those slaps, he apologized to the maestro, much to Lucrezia's satisfaction.

The maestro answered like a gentleman: he hadn't been the least bit offended, he said. That unfortunate incident was nothing compared to the lovely evening. In fact, he took the opportunity to thank him because, thanks to that banquet, as well as other ones, he had found peace again in the warmth of the people, and a newfound smile.

Zonja Elena would have liked to give her Mericano twenty-four thousand kisses for creating that well-balanced harmony: all on his trimmed mustache and on his emerald-green eyes, like she did when she was young; she wanted to suffocate him with kisses so he wouldn't have time to leave again. But the only thing that was suffocating was her desire for tenderness, while her kisses dampened the latest picture sent from Trentino: Paolo with his father's blond hair and Costantino's big brown eyes, sitting in front of his first birthday cake.

The Fake Mericano

Why the solemn oath to take a blessed olive branch to his father's grave in America? Well, who could know? Who? But an oath is an oath, and he, the future Mericano, for years and years thought of nothing but that journey.

Following his military service, he goes to Genoa to embark, with the olive branch in his suitcase. As soon as he got off the train, he realizes that he no longer has his wallet containing his money and passport. He retraces his steps, he gets back on the train, he searches every corner of the compartment in which he traveled; he begins to tremble; where did I lose it, where? "They stole it from you, Sir," they tell him in the offices of the railway police. "If they are honest thieves, they will let you have your documents back." Some consolation! How is he supposed to board without a ticket? And how could he live without money? Should he go back to Hora? Not a chance. Who knows how his friends would have teased him.

He remains in Genoa for nine months, nine months as long as nine years. With the intention of saving money for the trip, he washes dishes in restaurants, sleeps at the station, works at the port, sleeps on the beach, sells contraband cigarettes, sleeps in filthy little boarding houses. But the money is only enough to feed himself. So then one night a beautiful young man appears to him in a dream and tells the Mericano to follow him, because he'll bring him home, *biri jim*. It must be his father if he calls him that. Of course, it is his father: he is dressed in white, with a wide-brimmed hat, also white. He walks in slow-motion, and his shoes are shiny, of course it's his father. He has a blond mustache pointed upwards, and his eyes are glazed over without light: "I'm not in America anymore, *biri jim*, there's no use in looking for me. I go around, around, and around, and then one day I will stop forever. You return home now, or it will be too late, bir." And he can't help but follow him, but the whole way he asks his beautiful father only one thing: "What will they say in town?" But his father doesn't answer, and he walks oddly ahead of him, in slow-motion.

When he wakes, he goes onto the beach and tosses the olive branch into the sea. If there is a Christ, he thinks, he'll bring it where it needs to go. The next day he goes back to town, and to those who ask him, "So, Mericano, how is this 'Merica?" he, the Mericano, answers with a big smile.

Throughout the story, Costantino felt chills all down his back. They were alone at Castello del Piccolo, he and his father, and his father had talked while continuing to hoe the garden. Why did he tell him this story? They asked themselves at the same time, the Mericano aloud. "Well, I don't know, it just came out, involuntarily. But it is better this way, I feel lighter now, as if I'm free of a secret that weighed tons. And besides, if a son can't understand his father, who can?"

Costantino understood him; oh, did he understand him! And he would push himself to understand him all his life, because that is the destiny of children, he now repeats ad nauseam: understanding fathers who cannot return the favor, or who don't have the time, or the will.

The day he left again for Germany, the fake Mericano gave his son some final recommendations: to study, of course, and to give it all he has because, if he was out there making unspeakable sacrifices, the whole point was to give his son a better tomorrow, not a stick or a hoe, nor a suitcase or a pistol, but a nice paper to frame on the wall that would pave the road for his life; not to follow the maestro, who is obsessed with these ancient stories and makes the whole town laugh at him. Since I work abroad, what do I care that the Avati family was once noble, or about the richness, as he calls it, of speaking Arbëresh? I'll give you riches with this (and he slaps his forehead) and these (and he smacks his arms). Learn Italian well, because that's the language that will earn you bread; maybe even English, which might serve you one day, but what good is Arbëresh? The funny thing was that all these recommendations, even the last and most important one, he gave in Arbëresh: act like a father, bir, because now you are grown and grandpa is too old.

Costantino saw him board the three o'clock bus on a dreary winter afternoon and for the first time in his life, he was conscious of the invisible, twisted chain that tied him to his father. He felt the weight of those last recommendations in his stomach, and the chain of their separation around his throat more intensely than in years past, when nani Lissandro would have to forcibly hold him back because he wanted to leave with his father. He would kick and scratch and yell like a lunatic, his face lined with long tears and sticky snot dripping from his nose.

The bus disappeared behind the bend. Zonja Elena was quiet and absent, her eyes watery but not desperate like they had been at her husband's other departures. Signor Maestro had his arm around Lucrezia's waist, and the two returned home with their rediscovered lover's gait, gazing into one another's eyes, exchanging smiles and winks from times past.

Despite the distance, the Mericano waved his magic wand through his letters so that his words, the timbre of his voice, and his green gaze camped in the Avatis' house all through the spring. Lucrezia regained her confidence as a little engaged lady, future wife of Signor Maestro, and with this came the pleasure of feeling the flame of her twenty-three years reignite, especially the brilliant green of her eyes, and the blue waves of her hair shone like a rushing torrent.

After Easter, she resumed the work to finish her trousseau, assisted by her mother and aunts. In the evenings, she embroidered her initials and those of the maestro in lace, among the red and blue flowers of the pillows. During the day, she would weave the latest quilt on the loom. She was set on producing the most beautiful quilt in town, with stylized double-headed eagles forming a crown over two mountains covered in flowers that came together in the blue sky. In other words, a quilt made in the old way, she said to her fiancé, explaining the plot, in which a modern love triumphed. The idyllic atmosphere wasn't even ruined by the fact that the maestro had resumed his monologues on the problems of the world, because now he spoke of them with a certain detachment, only getting heated when nani Lissandro poked him with his disarming proverbs: Stretch your legs the length of the bed. What is said is more than what is done. How is it possible that the maestro didn't understand? A stone falls and the wall crumbles.

When school let out, Carmelo went to his hometown, leaving Lucrezia with her head bent over her loom, working frantically and thinking back on their last encounter, his velvet fingertips in the foreground, in the warmth of the locked bedroom.

That summer, with the women concentrated on the trousseau and nani busied with watering the garden at Castello del Piccolo morning and night, it was only relaxing for Costantino. He had passed to the third year of Magistrale high school with, as he said, excellent grades. His father had telegraphed him a money order of fifty thousand lire through the post office to reward him, and he, like all his peers, passed the time by watching it pass, playing cards until late in the evening, going to serenades under girls' balconies, sleeping until lunchtime until he was dazed. It may have been then that he, too, let that sort of restless laziness take over, letting time do as it will without the strength to achieve what had been planned, at least not until much later.

In the afternoon, he would go lay down on a large old sack of corn husks in one of the unplastered rooms of the castle and, covering one eye with the palm of his hand, he would spend hours tracing the bizarre lines on the ceiling with the other eye. The dead face of a giant man, the profile of a naked woman whose bosom hung to her feet, and a myriad of winding and twisting roads came together before his open eye, while the closed eye traced the body of Marcella and her thighs spread beneath the moon.

When the maestro unexpectedly returned in September, he pointed out a thick fuzz on Costantino's upper lip and teased him about his nose swelling with pimples, making him blush with shame.

Zëmërgùri

It was time for the grape harvest, and everyone in the Avatis' house took Signor Maestro's early return as his laudable desire to help them pick the grapes at Castello del Piccolo. At first, Lucrezia also had this impression, and she was happy about it.

They worked for two days in the vineyard, singing and laughing because they told the maestro that Costantino had found a girlfriend and he serenaded her from under the balcony. Costantino denied it, embarrassed, or he claimed that the girlfriend they were talking about, this Marcella, was four years older than him, and he blushed at the maestro's amused conclusion: "Love has no age!" But in the following days, the uncertainty in Lucrezia's fiancé's gaze did not evade her, poorly hidden by his glasses, nor did the trembling of his cold fingers when they grazed her. She tried to understand that polite silence better, during meals, but it seemed to her as though she were looking into an iron mask. Thus, the first time they found themselves alone, she at the loom, he on his feet bent over the warp, she decided to ask what was bothering him. "*Ç'ke?*" What's the matter? she said in Arbëresh, because by then the maestro understood the language of Hora perfectly.

He answered after calmly admiring the pattern of the nearly finished quilt. "Whatever you want it to be. Nothing. It's just that . . ." And he interrupted himself to continue looking at the quilt.

"It's just that . . . ?" Lucrezia repeated with apprehension, trying and failing to meet his gaze.

"I don't know . . . for some time now, this little town . . . it feels oppressive . . . I mean, I notice that I don't grow here . . . that is, I don't take part in what's happening in the world . . . That I'm not useful here . . . I'm not needed," the maestro said to her in a cracking voice.

Lucrezia was relieved, having foreseen, after the "just that" left hanging in the air, irreparable catastrophes; and so now she thought she would set everything right, reminding her fiancé that she was in that little town and that he was useful and important—in fact, extremely important—to her and to his students who loved him and admired him like a father.

"You don't understand . . . you can't understand," her fiancé answered with a tone of affectionate arrogance, like a misunderstood maestro. He turned his back on her and left without saying goodbye. Lucrezia found herself with the delicate circle of her thoughts undone in her head, and preparing for the worst, she let out gasps of anguish to keep from crying right away.

That night she slept little and poorly. She thought over all the moments and words of the discussion, from the initial "*ç'ke*" to his cruel "you can't understand," which burned within her like a flaming ember. But she was unable to find a plausible explanation for Carmelo's words and his behavior; and among the hundred guesses that rolled around in her mind, she ended up discarding the most probable one to avoid jinxing herself: that the maestro didn't care one bit about her anymore.

On the following morning, a still-summery sun shone, and through the open windows overflowed waves of carnations, geraniums, and basil. As if nothing had happened, her fiancé spoke to her with his usual sunny Sunday face after mass: luminous and rested, eyes smiling behind his glasses.

Once back at the house, they studied each other as they ate lunch with inquiring gazes, in between banal comments about zonja Elena's homemade tagliatelle and banal jokes about Costantino's eyes, still puffy from sleep. Nani Lissandro had eaten lunch already, and from the doorstep came the sound of an axe against a log of wood. The fiancés chatted briefly with him, and then they left to go for a walk— they said—to take advantage of the sun. Instead, once they arrived under the wall covered in snapdragons, they squeezed down a very narrow alleyway, and in three minutes they were at his house. Carmelo closed the door with his back and pulled her firmly to him. With their eyes closed, zigzagging down the wide hallway with their lips glued together, beneath the glazed gaze of the birds, they arrived on the bed and stripped, continuing to kiss each other on the mouth, the neck, the chest.

When the beam of dusty light that wandered around the room hit him in the face, the maestro put on his glasses and got dressed again in a hurry. It was the end of the deceptive spell. He stood before her with his legs apart, he held onto the headboard for courage, and with his head bowed, he confessed: "This summer I sat for an exam at the Minister of Foreign Affairs . . . an idea I have been sitting on for some time . . . it went well, I'm going to teach in Somalia . . . there are people there that need me."

He raised his head and waited for Lucrezia's response. But she just looked at him with eyes wide, a dead smile on her lips, incapable of any reaction. "Do you understand . . . I want to escape from this hellhole. I leave . . . Sunday . . . I've already decided . . . I already have a one-way ticket," the maestro added. It was at that point that Lucrezia felt chills shattering her insides: she covered herself up to her neck, rested her face on the pillow, and burst into a rhythmic and uninterrupted cry. She cried for so long that the maestro lost his patience. "Say something, by God! Don't cry like a girl who's been caned! It's not like I said I am breaking up with you . . . I said I'm leaving!" And since Lucrezia didn't answer, he yelled into her hair: "I should want to slap you! Do you want to get dressed and get out of my house or do I have to throw you out by force?"

Lucrezia got dressed like an automaton and quietly broke her silence: "*Zëmërgùr.*" Then she repeated it to him in Italian: "*Cuore di pietra,*" heart of stone. Finally, she yelled, "You have a heart of stone, but I'll break it in two!" and she jumped on him to scratch his eyes and face. The maestro defended himself: "How dare you, bitch! You're a viper, that's what you are!" He hoisted her up and flung her onto the bed, making her bounce on it twice. Lucrezia seemed to have calmed down, and in that fetal position she said, to the damp sheet, that none of this was right, that she didn't deserve it. Christ, how she felt stabbed in the heart, she said, how she felt her family was humiliated. And the wedding? The given word? The oath? The wedding for which her father was in Germany and the dowry in the chest? And the party with the coha and the group from Albania? And all those years of blind love?

Trampled in a moment, forgotten so he could feel useful somewhere else. Heart of stone, egotistical pig, tapeworm, coward, traitor, assassin . . .

"That's enough, now! Now, that's enough!" the maestro tried to interrupt her. "You don't understand anything, you have a thirteen-year-old head; I love you and I've shown you that in a million ways, even today. But this is stronger than I am . . . I mean, it is a calling I feel from the bottom of my soul . . ."

". . . Cheater, scoundrel, rascal, heart of stone . . ." Lucrezia continued tirelessly. "You don't love me; if you did, you would marry me and bring me with you, traitor, assassin, heart of stone . . ."

"What, do you think it's easy for me to take this step? But if I stayed here, I would be the unhappiest man in the world," the maestro interrupted her again.

They talked at length still, but it was as though they were talking to themselves since their words ran on two planes light years apart. Lucrezia kept up the unstoppable list of apostrophe and unearthed certain beautiful moments in their relationship in a final, desperate attempt to defeat the fiancé's monstrous foreignness who, for his part, clumsily pretended to be misunderstood, and repeated that he was, by now, decided.

When Costantino went to get his sister, because it was late, he said, and mamma was worried about her, he found himself scared to see her aged by ten years, with a streak of white hair on her forehead and the dull gray eyes of a dead woman. He led her home through the least used alleyways, persistently asking her what was wrong, if she felt unwell. Lucrezia staggered, leaning on her brother without answering him.

Back home, she threw herself on her little bed and closed herself in a stubborn silence. For more than an hour, she kept her hands over her ears to block out her mother and nani begging her to talk. Finally, her mother asked her, crying, "Do it, bijë, for the souls of our dead, for your father, bijë, for all the love we have for you, do it."

So Lucrezia was forced to free herself of that mouthful of poison: she threw up everything with anger, in a second, and then began to sob but shed no tears.

"We have no luck, bijë," commented zonja Elena dumbstruck, while nani Lissandro burst out furiously, "I'll kill him, I'll kill him," brandishing his fist before his face like a saber. Costantino stared in awe at his sister's lock of white hair, and so he said nothing: Signor Maestro was already dead to him, killed by the secreted bile of that same Mister Traitor; yes, dead, and amen.

Early the next morning, everyone was awake and in a daze. Lucrezia hoped the malaise she had was owing to a nightmare, but she surrendered at once in front of her reddened eyes and lock of white hair that reflected in the mirror. Her family members probably also wondered if they had dreamt that awful scene with Lucrezia half-dead on the bed. Costantino certainly doubted it. But the answer was bouncing around in the kitchen under the guise of old *za* Maria, who, with the air of a suffering Madonna, wanted to know all the details of the noisy separation, which the whole town was already talking about. The old woman's curiosity was liquidated with a "Who says these ridiculous things;" the door was closed, and the key was removed from the keyhole to prevent a procession of people from coming in.

Costantino didn't have the courage to go out that day, even though his team was supposed to have an important soccer game; the other three seemed nailed to their seats, immobile and silent.

Five days later, in the late afternoon, they heard the maestro's voice saying, "Open up, it's me!" while knocking loudly on the door. They opened and saw the maestro with his navy-blue beret over his glasses. "I have come to say goodbye," he said, "I leave tomorrow," and he extended his hand to old Lissandro. "No, you're not leaving," Lucrezia yelled, barely held back by her mother's grip on her skirt; and she slammed the door in his face. Then she went back to her unmade bed, dejected and inconsolable, with the other three at the headboard, as if she were about to die, hearing her mother repeat: "We never have any luck; who will tell that poor guy up there, how will he take it?"

No one knew how to answer, nor did they answer her, until the room grew dark and they understood it was time to try to get some sleep.

That night seemed to be made just for lovers: complacent stars were sparkling in the sky, and the moon, round as a melon, smiled down, splashing brushstrokes of waving lights in the distance, onto the sea; and then the crickets! Oh, the singing crickets encouraged a total stunning of the senses. The dark alleyways were steeped in the tranquil sighs of those who were, in that moment, dreaming of nights made just for lovers; those passing under the half-opened windows could sense the smell of breathing. A shadow stopped for just an instant to listen to its breath together with that of someone else, beneath the moon, and then went back to walking, rapid and agile. It walked up the steps to the maestro's house, and a couple of minutes later, was inside. It was never known if the maestro was the one to open the door, after the shadow knocked and said its name, or if it went in through the open balcony instead, risking its neck with such a jump. Later a scream was heard, barely louder than the chirps of the crickets, and the shadow retraced its steps, without haste, enjoying the night made just for lovers.

The maestro stumbled in the darkness of the bedroom, clutching his chest with his hands; then he fell to the floor, spent; he dragged himself down the hallway, he arrived in the foyer, and he opened the half-opened front door, pushing it with his head. Finally, he gathered all the breath remaining in his lungs and yelled into the night: "Help, I'm dead!"

Two Fingers of Honor
on the Forehead

Early the next morning, the piazza was already brimming with groups of men of all ages, standing at the bar, heatedly discussing the bloody events of the previous night. Nothing like this had happened in over forty years, the elders recalled, not since a *burr* from Hora killed the tax collector, *i huaj*, an outsider. The small groups competed for the attention of the maestro's two neighbors, who had been the first to run to his aid, and the driver that had taken him to the hospital in Crotone after calling the town doctor. Signor Maestro was found on his doorstep, white in the face and not breathing, lying on his back, spattered in blood. From his chest protruded a sort of hairpin, a dagger thin as an awl: it wasn't clear what exactly that thing was, each of the three witnesses claimed in turn, given that more than half of it was lodged in the flesh, and the part that protruded was almost entirely covered in dark, thick blood. The doctor had arrived out of breath and, having taken his pulse and cast a pitying glance, had sighed, "Let's load him in the car very slowly; in any case, it's a waste of gas."

No one could say with certainty whether he was already dead. The only one who could know was the doctor, but he was still in Crotone. It was Sunday, and the women who were going to church, crossing the piazza, slowed down their pace to hear the latest news. But news there was not: it was just a rehashing of the original story, with the bloody and dying Signor Maestro, but they left out the motive and presumed perpetrator of the crime.

As soon as they were approached by one of the outsiders who was married to a local, the old men would stress that Hora is a peaceful town, there isn't even a Carabinieri station in town, that's how peaceful it is. Forty years ago, however, the outsider tax collector was killed for far less, because one fine day he showed up at the door of a newly wedded young woman, and when she didn't have the money to pay him right away, he ripped off her wedding necklace; but that evening, the husband noticed it and made her recount the details of the encounter, after a lot of insisting, because the wife knew the customs of the time. Indeed, the next day, the husband loaded his pellet shotgun, positioned himself behind a bush on the slope of the road, and when the poor outsider walked by there, he was shocked by a single shot to the chest. Then, for forty years, nothing. Until last night.

The Carabinieri from Shën Kolli arrived in the late morning: they visited the maestro's house and even snapped some pictures of the stuffed birds; they spoke to women in the alleyways and to the men in the piazza. Then they went back to the station, bringing with them the three men who had first rushed to the maestro's aid. The three repeated the story told in the piazza, and as they were signing their statements, they added that it may have been thieves. Thieves from out of town, as nearly everyone who was interviewed in Hora had said. The Carabinieri never even came to learn that the maestro had been engaged to a girl in town.

After lunch, the piazza repopulated even more than before: now the people had amassed around the doctor and the news bounced from mouth to mouth that Signor Maestro was, for the moment, alive: alive by a miracle.

"Luckily, that kind of awl or pin didn't damage any vital organs," the doctor said. "It is a miracle it missed them: but the maestro has lost blood, too much blood. Now, they are giving him transfusions. If one of you wants to donate blood, you may come with me to the hospital. I'm leaving right away."

More than twenty men stepped forward, and the doctor found his smile again: "I have a car," he said, "not a bus. I need four of you."

Once the doctor and his four volunteers left, the groups of men formed again, standing in the middle of the piazza, or sitting on the little semicircular wall, their faces turned toward the warm sun. Everyone seemed calmer, thank goodness, thank goodness, they said, let's hope he makes it. The tax collector, on the other end, died instantly, and as he fell, he hit his face on a rock, breaking his teeth.

Of course, honor is honor, many people remarked. Imprinted on our foreheads were two fingers of honor; if we lose that too, we're done for! In other words, the tax collector was asking for it: tearing off the wedding necklace was a grave offense, too grave. But to kill him for it, that poor devil: that not everyone supported. They said that it is primitive to impose justice by oneself. It's primitive, some responded, when you're judging others. But if something like that happens to you, what will you do?

No one had the time to reply. The shouting in the piazza slowly faded and then fell completely silent: from the ascent of Palacco emerged the Mericano himself with his smiling son at his side. His *compari*, friends, and relatives went to greet him. They were more embarrassed than he was. "To what do we owe this surprise, *compà*, when did you arrive, how are you?" they asked as one, and at the same time they studied him carefully: his eyes were gray and tired from the trip, but he looked nice, freshly shaven and rejuvenated, with a new set of dentures that stood out with its shine.

The Mericano replied that he had arrived that night; oh, what a comfortable trip this time; the trains were empty, totally different from traveling during the holidays. He had come back to work on the castle. He still had two weeks of vacation logged, and he didn't like to stay in the barracks twiddling his thumbs. Others studied his hands and discovered them to be covered in calluses, like their own, rough and cracked from the chemical garbage he handled, the Mericano said, and he invited them to the bar to drink to his health.

No one had the courage to tell him about the events of the previous night, not even his closest relatives. They were waiting for him to bring it up. But he spoke of other things: of work in Germany, tough and dirty but well compensated; of the gray, drizzly weather; but what I miss, when I'm there, he repeated four or five times, is the warmth of people like this. And with similar phrases, driven by the beer and the circumstances, he went on until late evening, when he was forced to hear a young man who had just walked into the bar saying to the bartender: "The doctor called from the hospital; Signor Maestro is out of harm's way."

Once again, all eyes were on the Mericano: waiting for a reaction, a comment. And the Mericano said: "But the beer is better in Germany," and he let slip a dry belch, to make the point.

Ish një jëmë shumë e mirë

She was a very good mother; she had nine *hadhjarë*, joyful sons, and the tenth, a girl, whom they called Jurendina. To seek Jurendina's hand in marriage, sons of gentlemen and knights came and went, until finally there came a young man from a faraway Hora. The brother Costantino was the only one to agree: "Come mother, make this marriage."

"Costantino, my son, why do you want to send her so far away? For if I want her in my joy, in my joy I shall not have her; if I want her in my suffering, in my suffering neither shall I have her."

"My Mother, I will go and bring her here."

And they married off Jurendina.

A *keq i rëndë*, very cruel, year arrived that reaped that zonja's nine sons in a war. The house was left dark and empty.

She dressed in mourning for ten years; then on the Saturday of the dead, the mother went to church. On each grave a candle and a *vajtim*. But on Costantino's grave, two candles and two *vajtimë*. "Costantino, my son, where is the *besa*, the Word you gave me? That you would bring Jurendina back to me? Your *besa*, underground!"

When the church closed, Costantino arose from his grave. The stone covering it became a horse; he mounted it, bones on top of bones, and went to his sister's house.

In the piazza in front of the palace, he met Jurendina's sons. "Where has zonja, your mother, gone?"

"She's in the vallja, the round dance, for Hora."

And he went to the first vallja. "You are beautiful girls, but you are not meant for me. Is Jurendina with you? Jurendina, my sister."

"Go further and you'll see her; with the jacket and the velvet coha."

Having arrived at the other vallja: "Costantino, my brother!"

"Jurendina, get out of there, we're leaving, you have to come home with me."

"But tell me, my brother, because if I need to come in mourning, I'll go get dressed in black; if we are going in joy, I will get my party clothes."

"Come, sister, just as you are." And he sat her on the horse.

All along the way, the birds were chirping: "The living goes with the dead!"

Costantino answered, "That bird is *çiòt*, stupid, he doesn't know what he's saying."

His sister addressed him: "Costantino, my brother, a bad omen I see. Your broad shoulders are moldy!"

"Jurendina, my sister, the smoke from the rifles turned my shoulders moldy."

"Costantino, my brother, another bad sign I see, your curly hair is covered in dust!"

"Jurendina, my sister, your eyes are making you see this way, because of the dust on the street."

"Costantino, my brother, why don't my brother and the sons of *zoti lal*, Mister uncle, grace us with the light of their presence?"

"Jurendina, my sister, they are there, maybe *te rrolet*, at the circle, because we arrived tonight and they weren't expecting us."

"But another bad sign I see: the windows of our house are closed and blackened!"

"The wind is blowing from the mountains."

They arrived and passed before the church.

"Let me enter the church to pray."

She, alone, walked up the stairs, to her mother.

"Open the door, my mother!"

"Who are you, here, at the door? Stay away, *bushtra*, ferocious death, which took nine children from me, and now, with my daughter's voice, has come for me."

"Oh, open, zonja mother, because it is I, Jurendina!"

"Who brought you back, my daughter?"

"Costantino brought me back, Costantino, my brother!"

"Costantino? And where is he now?"

"He went to the church to pray."

"My Costantino is dead!"

And the mother held her daughter close, and the daughter held her mother close.

The mother and daughter died.

Twelve

"And this would be the Aquila guy?" the Romana said to her cousin, pointing her index finger toward Costantino who was just a few steps away. She should have yelled, that Roman, to make herself heard over the rhythm of "Avevo un cuore (che ti amava tanto)," I had a heart (that loved you so), that ten or so couples were dancing to, holding each other very close at Mario's house. Costantino pretended not to hear: with his mouth open toward the record player he sang softly, "*e si è perduto nel volerti bene*," and it got lost in loving you.

He hadn't gone gladly to that soiree put on by his clique of friends on Christmas day. He figured everyone would stare at him because of the still-fresh story about the wounding of the maestro. "Who do you think cares about that anymore, though?" Mario had said to him, lying, and forced him to accept. He had threatened him: "If you don't come, *mbrì*, we'll be enemies till death."

So, there he was, in the heavy, hot air of a little room pretending to have fun while everyone else pretended to treat him as though nothing had happened.

Signor Maestro Carmelo Bevilacqua had left for Somalia after two months of recovery in his hometown. He never set foot in Hora since. His house, which had been left open for months, had also been respected by even the most hardened thieves, who knew that they could find valuable objects there, apart from the small, worn notebooks and dead birds; even respected by the ants and the chickens. Only the spiders continued to weave between the beaks of the stuffed birds and to nest in the dusty feathers or in the eyes of eroded glass. That's what Costantino's friends had told him, who avoided walking past that house as though he were afraid of catching a glimpse of the bloody Signor Maestro in there.

"So, you're supposed to be the Aquila guy?" Now the Romana was standing before him, looking at him the way one looks at a disappointing painting, slowly pacing around him. Then she turned to her cousin beside her: "The only handsome thing about him is his eyes, big and with long lashes. The rest of him looks to me like a plucked, frightened eagle." They both laughed, amused, while Costantino didn't know what to do, what to say. He really was scared in front of that aggressive, ironic girl. Bitch. Bitchy and cocky, Costantino thought. He answered her with a smile that he intended to be ironic, but under those flared nostrils as rigid as a mule's, just seemed pathetic.

Providential as a summer shower, the record player let out booms of sound like lightning and thunder, and a watery American voice, so the Romana was pushed by a boy onto the dance floor, and she went wild in a breathtaking dance. Costantino did not lose sight of her even for a moment. Cocky bitch, he muttered to himself, awkwardly tapping one foot to the beat. He had seen her dance before. Actually, rather than dancing, it was more letting herself get strangled in the iron clutches of his horny friends, getting fondled left and right. And she was all for it as though it were nothing: she hummed along to the record, her eyes pointed upward like a saint. *Putërë.* Arrogant like her father. Always the center of attention since she was a child. She came to town at the start of summer, and a few days later she would go to the shore with her mother, hosted by an uncle who was an engineer. Her father would stay in town with his elderly parents and would go visit them now and again. Employed by some ministry of the government, he preferred to spend his time in the piazza pontificating about the "dolce vita" he led in Rome: the concerts of the great singers, the Serie A soccer games, the film premieres, the Chinese restaurants, the female tourists from Sweden, America, and Germany, and the pope's homily at San Pietro. Just like his daughter. Arrogant.

She was more or less the same age as Costantino, and when they were little they had played *me skravaijet*, a children's game, together on some doorstep, with five pebbles as small and smooth as confetti. Then they ignored each other for years. Costantino noticed her again when she started unbuttoning her shirt to show her two pointy nipples, held up by breasts that grew bigger and perkier each year. Yes, he remembered her as the Romana with the upturned nipples and nose. They never spoke and she didn't even dignify him with a glance. She returned to Hora in the middle of summer, for the feast of Saint Veneranda, and she would walk with her cousin up and down the Kona, wearing white shorts that showed off her tanned thighs, always followed by a host of admiring and jealous glances. She would sprinkle her luminous trails around like an August meteor, and then she would go back to Rome, leaving judgments, impressions, and assumptions swirling behind her nude shoulders, as if she were a little diva from Cinecittà. She had never been to Hora for Christmas, Costantino remembered it well. Never had he seen her with the pallid face—pallid as ricotta—of the winter. Who knows why she had stayed there this time, off-season and out of place, shaking her butt to the beat of the twist, undulating her breasts higher than ever, and busting the balls of precisely him who was carrying a sea of anguish within him: in other times, my dear Romana, I would bust your ass, he thought, and he would repeat it to her ad nauseam years later, unable to forgive her for that arrogant approach.

"Why do they call you Aquila?" It was her again, standing before him. A tick.

"And you, why do they call you the Romana?" Costantino replied nervously, touching his curls.

"What a dummy!" she answered, amused. "It's because I'm from Rome!"

"Well for me, it is because I once saw an eagle, actually, a double-headed eagle. Are you happy now?" Costantino said, in the same tone as her: aggressive.

She still had that brazen smile stamped onto her lips, but she seemed sweeter now. Her cheeks rosy from the heat and the effort of dancing, she was truly curious about the story of his nickname. Who knows what her cousin had told her about him. At the very least, the story of the maestro, Costantino thought, and he didn't have time to think about anything else because the Romana had invited him to dance, confusing him even more, and soon after she had placed her arms around his neck, turning his world upside down. Awkward, and with a heart bursting with emotions, Costantino initially placed his gaze on unthinkable points in the room, accidentally catching the watery eyes of the other dancers.

Then she broke the silence: "So . . . when were you supposed to have seen this bicephalous eagle?"

It was the first time Costantino heard that word: bicephalous, the proper term, not double-headed, like he had been saying. The Romana wasn't hostile anymore, nor was she arrogant. She was all ears and eyes. Brown eyes. Lovely and sincere eyes.

"I saw it on the day of the fair, in the sky of Marina. I must've been eight or nine years old . . ." the boy replied. And he told the story of that day, of which he preserved mental snapshots, vivid and blue, but they were disjointed from one another: the heavy mugginess of a summer day, which enveloped grandpa, Baialardo, the goats, and himself, the boy, Costantino; the sweat that poured into a sea of blue-white waves; a tender kiss on the shore of the sea; the old rhapsode with the face and the lahuta of the serenade; an eagle with two immobile heads and four vivid and proud eyes.

For the Romana—who at one point had told him "My name is Isabella"—for Isabella, then, it was hard to link the various snapshots, but she seemed fascinated by the magical halo that enveloped them. She stared at Costantino, enchanted, in between his eyelashes, and on his lips, from which she seemed to hang, and she no longer heard the music, the words of the songs, the invitations from other boys when the record ended. She had only interrupted him once, to tell him he was the only one who didn't suffocate her while they danced, and in saying that she grazed his ear with her lips, accidentally, and all of a sudden her rosy cheeks became first purple, and then blood red. Finally, now she seemed really *kupilia e bukur si gjaku e gjiza*, the girl as beautiful as blood and ricotta from the fable, his favorite princess as a boy. It was a shame that the last snapshot, the clearest one, the one in which the majestic flight of the double-headed, or rather, bicephalous eagle appeared in the blue sky, spotted with puffs of clouds, had already passed.

Isabella smiled, and for a moment pushed her perky breasts against Costantino's chest, smiled again, and then laughed: a dry and unexpected laugh. Finally, just before leaving with her cousin, she became serious and said: "Visionary bullshit!"

Baialardo died of old age in his sleep, without bothering anyone. The next day, nani Lissandro gathered up all his strength and tossed him into the Varchijuso ravine: he watched him bounce off the rocks four or five times, and then sink into the bramble for good. No one in the family shed a tear for him, they had other things to think about. Only nani Lissandro felt a little emotional in his own way: "*Jeta ësht si fjeta*" Life is like a leaf, he said; he removed his hat and placed it over his heart.

From that day on he became even more taciturn than usual. He even stopped repeating that old age was a pain, because, in the face of his trembling hands that had forced him to give up his hobby of carving, his superstitious complaints were worth nothing. The disappearance of the double-headed eagles from his doorstep reminded everyone, as if there were a need for it, that old Lissandro already had one foot in the grave and that a gust of freezing or muggy wind would be enough to sweep him away forever, like a leaf.

Costantino was the only one who didn't notice the daily changes that nani went through: the dark splotches that spread over his skeletal face, the fading pupils that became lost in the dirty whites of his irises, the mouth that, now that his lips had disappeared, was caving in toward the cranium, so that the chin poked out sharp and prickly. To Costantino, nani was the same as ever: the man who calmed him when his father left and who one day had brought him to the fair in Marina. He hadn't even noticed the tremor in nani's hands, which had manifested itself the day after the wounding of the maestro, taken as he was in the grips of anguish and disappointment, a feeling that wouldn't even relent once he was in his bed at the castle. He retraced the lines of the walls, now more twisted than before, with the hope of forgetting what had happened. But the lines were cruel: there it was, a *gurgullea* like Signor Maestro; so, he would switch eyes and perspective: among the lines, Isabella's upturned breasts appeared, and her sardonic phrase echoed: Visionary bullshit.

It would be nice, Costantino thought, if the events that had happened had been visions like those that appeared on the cracked walls of the castle: you switch eyes, and you erase them forever; you erase the bloodied maestro, and the lines close in a perfectly round circle, just like the vallja: in the center, the vision of Isabella.

Thirteen

The Mericano hadn't returned to Germany again because he worried that, without his scrupulous protection, a storm of gossip and slander could be brought down on his family, veiled or not. At first, he had asked the factory to grant him more of his earned vacation days; then he made up illnesses he didn't have; in the end, he received a polite pink slip. He didn't bat an eye. He threw himself head-first into his work and stayed at Castello del Piccolo all day, helped by his wife. He went all day without saying *kështu* or *ashtu*.

Lucrezia saw to all the domestic chores, listening to the radio from morning until late at night, when her parents came home for dinner. The whole time, she sang along with the songs being broadcasted in her whistle like a desperate nightingale. The whistling was probably a way to avoid thinking and suffering, because it required her, as she had always said so, a great deal of concentration. As a matter of fact, while nani's hands trembled, and Costantino melted into endless anxiety, and his parents had exiled themselves to Castello del

Piccolo, she blossomed before everyone's eyes like a striped carnation. She had bleached her hair to hide the white lock of her disappointment, and a few months later a blue mane had blossomed on her, streaked with straw yellow. Her eyes, after those endless tears of the early days, had become deeper, green most of the time, but the dark green of cypress trees, without even a hint of light. When she walked to church, alone, wearing fashionable high heels, a fire-red sweater, and tight jeans that clung to her thighs and made her seem slender and firm, she turned the head of every man in Hora.

She was really a beautiful girl, Lucrezia, a special girl, even that arrogant Isabella had said to Costantino, on the second time that they had seen each other by chance at the Kriqi. She, with her inseparable cousin, out for a stroll on that cold, humid night, and he, with Mario and Vittorio, leaning on Skanderbeg's bust and talking about soccer. Isabella was the first to greet him, as one does with an old friend, and immediately flooded the group with the discussion about his sister, as though it had been stuck in her throat for some time. "I've never seen eyes and hair so . . . so unique before. She doesn't look a thing like you; you're so different!" she had finally said to Costantino, and then she invited him for a stroll.

The other three followed them like puppies, stopping now and again so as not to pass them. Isabella walked lazily, throwing one leg here and the other leg there nonchalantly. She was in no hurry. She was very interested, she said, in the story of his sister's fiancé, stabbed, they said, for love. It seemed impossible to her that things like this still happened. Was it true, or had her cousin told her a fable from other times?

This time it was Costantino who was in no rush to talk. Isabella scrunched her neck into her shoulders like a turtle, and only a lock of black hair poked out from the collar of her white coat. "It is a little cold, isn't it?" Costantino said, to derail the conversation.

"A little cold?" Isabella had taken the bait. "It feels like we're in Siberia! Luckily this is the last night I'll be in this frozen hellhole; I've already packed my bags. Tomorrow we finally leave!"

"What, don't you like it here with us?" Costantino asked to bring the subject as far as possible from the embarrassing discussion about his sister and Signor Maestro.

"Of course. I like it a lot. A lot, a whole lot. Especially during this season," Isabella answered, ironically. "I think if I had to stay here another week, I'd lose my mind," she then added, seriously. "This exasperating slowness; these eyes like boiled fisheyes always glued to me; this spiteful gossiping about people behind their backs. If you knew what was said about you . . . These absurd rules: women prohibited from bars . . ."

"Excuse me, what should I know?" interrupted Costantino, who was now in a rush to listen. Isabella's head had poked out from her collar: "Come on, you already know!"

"What? Are you going to speak: yes or no?"

Costantino waited impatiently. He had opened his eyes wide, as though he had to hear the answer through his dilated pupils. They were the eyes of a hardened dreamer, Isabella noted, too big in that moment, too innocent and lost.

"They say you're the one that stabbed that maestro," Isabella let out with an exhale, and a moment later added: "But I don't believe it." Maybe she had been crude to talk to him about that matter; if she had been able to predict his feverish gaze, "if I had known it would hurt you to talk about it . . ." But now it was done, and she could do nothing more now than take his hand and squeeze it a bit in between hers as a sign of apology and solidarity.

Isabella's cold little hands had the effect of a miraculous balm on Costantino's wound. That gesture was priceless, those little hands had penetrated his heart, and they no longer felt cold to him but smooth as velvet. The velvet caresses lasted until the end of the walk—muted caresses, since they both were mute—and they warmed Costantino's heart for the rest of that miserable winter.

In March, the Mericano agreed to go work with his cousin Demetrio on construction sites in Ludwigshafen. "The work is rough, but the pay is excellent if you do overtime; here you bust your ass for nothing," he repeated to his relatives in Demetrio's effective words. Then he promised to bring them to spend the summer in Ludwigshafen, just as soon as he secured a decent home; and he forced himself to appear calm at that departure like never before, and to smile, squeezing the corners of his eyes so intensely as to reveal wrinkles upon wrinkles, grimaces upon grimaces, like a sulky child on the verge of tears. He left the town behind him with the relief of no longer having to fear people's inquisitive looks and left also behind him all the worries that had accompanied him day and night in those long months. And so, the message hidden in those wrinkles was clearly understood only by his son, who, as soon as he saw the bus disappear with his father, under a heavy spring shower, had felt himself invested in his new duty as protector of the family.

In the long evenings of April, he would silently join the gathering of old men in the piazza and the small groups of young people that livened up the bar, while the juke-box blared the raspy cry of "What do you know about a field of wheat . . . and of the whole world contained in one street, what do you know?" echoing off the walls of the bar stuffed with bottles of liquor, and crashing against the noisy sky, already speckled with the black of the swallows. He stayed for a few minutes with each group, just enough time to catch the drift of the conversation, and then he would scurry away.

If his sister or mother were still up, he would have to endure the artificial, unnerving whistle of the former and the old-fashioned fatalism of the latter. Hunched over from the weight of her shame, his mother was the only one in the family to externalize her pain—to the satisfaction of the townsfolk, as her daughter said. Not knowing whom to be upset with, the maestro having already been punished enough, she took it up with their bad luck: "Things always go wrong for us, they put the maestro under a spell, he changed from this to that, someone's evil eye is behind all this; I know them, some jealous people, who would burst like Trabekku if it were true that any justice existed in this world."

Aside from this Trabekku, mentioned by zonja Elena without ever explaining who he actually was and why he had burst, Costantino was bothered by his mother's lack of reason, with her fatalistic complaints, and by his sister's whistled indifference. In a paternal guise, he would alter his tone, playing the moralist, "Come on then, knock it off, aren't you ashamed? What will the neighbors think? With all this breath you're wasting, your goiters will grow just like the old women of Palacco." And he would enter his small bedroom, sometimes without having touched any food, slamming the door behind him.

From the next room over, nani Lissandro, already in bed for some time, would mutter something, some random curse, complaining that they didn't let him sleep. Just to say that he existed, too.

Fourteen

Lucrezia's hair burned under everyone's eyes, and Costantino tried unsuccessfully to put it out because the fire had grown as big as the Christmas bonfire, and Lucrezia laughed in the middle of the crowd, alive and healthy, with her midnight-blue hair in its rightful place; but Costantino kept trying to put out that bonfire, assisted by his sister Orlandina who had suddenly emerged with a bucket of water, and ate plump snails that were cooked by crackling away in the coals.

He woke up when Orlandina, who had arrived with the nine o'clock bus, kissed him on his sweaty cheeks and said, beaming, to her three-year-old son whom she held in her arms: "Paolino, this is uncle Costantino, give him a little kiss."

The child moved away from Costantino, furrowing his brows in disappointment, but a minute later changed his mind: he smiled, and Costantino tickled his bare feet.

Paolino was suffocated by the affection of his neighbors and relatives. Lucrezia would have liked to have eaten him raw, she said, and zonja Elena would have covered him in kisses from morning until night. Even nani Lissandro, who had never liked small children, was won over by the little nasal voice of his great-grandson, who when in front of those massive plates of pastina in dove broth, repeated stubbornly, "*Jo jo, non dua io, non dua*," no no, I don't want it, I don't want it, mixing his Arbëresh and Italian, and then happily grasping the nursery rhyme recited in the bilingual version: "*Ki do bukë*, this one wants bread/*ki ngë kemi*, this one says we have none /*ki vemi e vjedhmi*, this one says we'll steal it."

Orlandina was truly pleased with her little son who understood Arbëresh because at first for her up there by herself, she said, not having anyone to speak with *si neve*, like we do, was the worst thing, second only to missing her loved ones. Early on, her husband would scold her if he heard her speaking to the boy in, he said, that Moroccan language. The boy was already two and couldn't yet say mama or papa because, according to the husband, he was confused by the two languages he was hearing. Then the parish priest from his town had explained to him that two languages meant two cultures, dear Narciso, and two cultures enrich one; it makes people sharper once they grow up. Thus, her husband no longer grumbled and, in fact, after hearing Paolino chirping in Trentino dialect and *si neve*, he had the grace to admit he had been wrong and to apologize for the incident.

Orlandina was the only one who noticed the pounding swirling of her brother's heart when the mailman handed him an azure postcard, which he nonchalantly placed in a corner of the cupboard, after glancing at Isabella's signature. He had forced himself not to scream in joy, but he hadn't managed to contain an abrupt batting of his eyelashes, which scared two little spring flies that had landed on his forehead.

"Did your sweetheart write you?" Orlandina dared to ask, in Italian. Costantino was taken by surprise and tried to bluff, camouflaging his embarrassment with an arrogant response: *"Nanì fièt puru litisht!* Now you also speak Italian! A sweetheart! *Vre këtu!* Look here! A sweetheart!" And he headed for the piazza, leaving the postcard unattended and at the mercy of the two curious sisters, who gave an indifferent glance at the aerial shot of Imperial Rome and then read the message aloud so that their mother and grandfather could hear: "'My dear Aquila, last night I saw you fly in a lovely dream . . . with love. Isabella. P.S. Happy Easter and see you soon.' Who in the world could this Isabella be?" they asked themselves, and read it again out loud, laughing.

They had lots of fun on Easter Monday in the countryside, eating cold *pasta al forno* and *kucupe*, the Easter sweets. Nani Lissandro had made a swing out of the old reins from his mule, making use of a branch from a giant oak. And now he pushed Costantino, who had Paolino on his lap, with all his strength.

The women chatted, lying on the grass, and Lucrezia lazily grazed on the fresh grass like a little goat. What could they say other than that they were really enjoying that moment? Truly enjoying it. That this must be what paradise is like. The air was not too hot, not too cold. With a sun that you could stare right into the eyes of. With the loved ones united shoulder to shoulder, mind to mind. And all three of them thought of the Mericano, who was surely paving a road near Ludwigshafen at that very moment. The thought lasted just a moment because it was interrupted by the laughter of nani and of his grandsons, tussling together in the grass.

They headed back home at dusk, with their cheeks reddened by the sun and the excitement. The first day spent in happiness after many months.

The next day, early in the morning, nani Lissandro filled the house with the *tac tac* sounds of years past, from his doorstep.

He wanted to make a present for Paolino, he said. A nice double-headed eagle to bring to Trentino.

He hacked away until the eve of the guest's departure, under the critical gaze of the boy, and it was the only time he painted his eagle, red talons, brown wings, and four celestial-blue eyes. Holding it in his hands, Paolino said, "T'anks," echoing his mother: "*Thuaj gracie nanit!*" Say thanks to nani! He turned it over and over, and he smiled and made nani smile in satisfaction. Finally, he convinced himself that it was a wooden hen. In fact, he said: "*B'utta pula*" Ugly hen, and he tossed it down the stairs like he did with all the things he disliked.

Orlandina picked up the dented eagle, with one of the heads broken at the base of the neck and one wing completely snapped. "I'll glue it properly," she said with her face flushed, to her grandfather. "This son is a devil," she yelled angrily at Paolino. But the grandfather and the son started laughing, amused.

Fifteen

Costantino didn't pass Italian and Latin class, and while he was waiting to take the makeup exams, he spent the afternoons playing cards in front of the bar, in the warm shadow of a green and white-striped awning. Isabella saw him there a few days after she arrived in Hora, his sulky face turned toward the cards and his eyes opened too wide from the effort of concentration, shaded by lashes so long and curved they seemed fake. She greeted them with a simple "Hi guys" and shot Costantino a smile and a look just a tiny bit longer but enough to make him lose his concentration on the game, sending him soaring.

Isabella was standing behind him, with her inseparable cousin, tapping her fingertips on the blue plastic strings of the chair, as though following the rhythm of a song she was singing in her head. Costantino stared at the Neapolitan cards without seeing them, and he tossed them haphazardly onto the coffee table, making his friend despair because at that point he knew how it was going to end. Sure enough, they lost the game and now, according to the winners Mario and Vittorio, at the very least they had to be gentlemen, and aside from the lost drink, they had to buy a nice ice cream for the two girls.

"What gentlemen! These two are idiots," Isabella said, with her usual frankness. "We'll play you for our ice cream, if you're up for it."

Costantino felt her hand on his shoulder and her voice in his ear: "Could you move over, please?" He moved, and like everyone else, he could barely believe his eyes: that was the first time two girls had played cards in a bar in Hora, and they knew how to play *tresette* and *briscola*, demonstrating a mastery of moves so perfect, made of little signs with the eyes and lips that were so swift that the surprise was doubled, and then tripled when they started to win, in between the double entendre made by the young spectators—"Are you also this good playing *scopa*?" Screwing?—and the criticism a little ways away by a group of old men; and eventually the surprise quadrupled when a voice came booming powerfully enough to open a passage in the wall of upright bodies: "*Vajzarè me tij pra bëmi kundet!*" Girl, we'll settle this later! It was Aldo, Isabella's cousin's father, up to his head with rage at his daughter and at his niece, to whom he accorded merely a passing glance, but it was full of anger, as if to say: it's all your fault. Then he headed straight for the Kriqi, with his hands in his pockets and his chin in the air, as if passing by chance and not, as everyone thought, sent there by some soul from hell.

Aldo's daughter had turned the color of clay, on her arms, her face, and even the pupils of her eyes, and she sat there dumbfounded under the perplexed gaze of that little crowd, waiting for a sign from Isabella on what to do. The gesture didn't take long to come, and it was one of anger, while the cards were flying in the air: one finger, the one in the middle, piercing the sky, her gaze pointed at *lal*, uncle, Aldo who was barely visible, one stinky word in pure Arbëresh, spat in the direction of the Kriqi: "*Mut!*" Shit!

In the late afternoon, Isabella was walking around on her own in the piazza immersed in the sunlight, with the look of a bored tourist. Costantino approached her with a smile like the best of Sundays. "So, you can even speak *si neve*," he said to her just to strike up a conversation.

"Just the swear words, when I'm angry; but I understand everything," she replied, politely this time; it was obvious she was looking for company. Sure enough, she added, "Shall we walk?"

"Sure, let's walk. With you I would even go to the end of the world," Costantino said, unaware that he had used one of the banal phrases most hated by Isabella, without any hint of ironic tone, as were his intentions.

Isabella walked, with her arms protecting her upturned breasts, losing her balance a bit; she would have really let herself be guided to the end of the world because, she said, she wanted to vent to someone. She couldn't stand being treated like a little girl from a reformatory anymore, and you can't do this in Hora—in Hora we do it like this and like that—she would have strangled *lal* Aldo, on more than one occasion, and even her father was hateful in Hora. He changed completely from this to that. In Rome she had every possible liberty; in Hora she was under every possible control; at the seaside, it depended. If there were people from Hora, then: wear a more modest bathing suit, don't get chummy with this guy and that guy, because then in Hora they will judge you poorly. But, she said, at the beach, she didn't care for whining because as soon as some ballbuster opened his mouth, she would just dive into the water and come back to the shore an hour later, with her hands pruned and her lips purple. It was in Hora that she had nowhere to dive into.

Now, Isabella seemed like a common mortal to him, with everyday problems, on the small lane lined by dusty thistles. She was also sweating, like him, on her forehead: minute droplets the color of the sky and of light. A good sign, Costantino thought, because people that never sweat put him in awe. She kept talking: "You're not listening to me, though. Am I boring you? Tell me Costantì." It was the first time she called him by name, and this too was a good sign, Costantino thought, and rushed to deny it: "No, no, what are you talking about! Keep going!" And she continued.

"Where can one dive in Hora, where? In the little alleyways, like cats? You can drown in boredom in the . . ." She interrupted herself abruptly, and it was like suddenly raising the volume of the countryside: choruses of cicadas, with sudden highs and lows, solos from sparrows hidden in the olive trees, swallows with aluminum-foil wings, the slithering of lizards and snakes, bells of sheep in the distance, gusts of wind blowing through the holm oak leaves and . . . "is that a castle?"

At last, the little white castle was before them, so shiny that to look in its direction you had to shield your eyes with your hand.

"Welcome to my palace," Costantino said, smiling. He opened the rusty gate and, walking along the cobbled pathway, he responded impeccably to the slew of questions Isabella posed: Whose is it? Whose was it? Why is it so white? Why is it so little? Then he led her into the courtyard covered with river gravel and explained to her his father's project: rebuilding the stairway to the top of the tower and building the brick terrace. Isabella's eyes lit up. "Beautiful, wonderful, dazzling," she repeated the entire time, and meanwhile she leaned tiredly on him, with her arms crossed over his right shoulder, her perky breasts against his arm. "So, you'd be a good catch, as they say in Hora. Well, if one day you come to live here, I'll marry you," she concluded, amused.

Costantino really liked that what-if game the girl had come up with, but he didn't know whether to laugh, or to look her in the eyes, or to remain motionless, following the undulating heat of her breasts on his arm. In the end, he decided to play: "Consider yourself my bride already, because I've lived here for some time. And now that we're here . . ." He lifted her in his arms and headed toward the little front door, with superhuman effort, wobbling, just four more steps. Isabella was heavy—who would have thought?—she was heavy and was laughing and predicted: "Now we're going to fall!"

They fell, luckily, on the new flooring. Costantino did it. They fell one on top of the other, roaring with laughter, with no desire to let go of each other, instead twisting their legs together, their hands in each other's hair: "How crazy, how crazy," Isabella was repeating, laughing by herself now, because he was looking at her in silence, very seriously; he liked her little kitten teeth, she was excited, this Isabella, her cheeks and lips were red, her chin and forehead white, *e bukur si gjaku e gjiza*, as beautiful as blood and ricotta. "Don't look at me like that," the lovely blood and ricotta said to him, while her gaze landed on Costantino's lips.

It was a kiss with open eyes, a brief contact of the lips. It was a kiss with eyes incredulous of what had occurred.

Isabella was the first to stand up. She brushed off her clothes and her hair with energetic hands and then looked around her. She did not like the restored buildings at all; they were tasteless, they lacked style, lacked even a minimum of respect for traditional form, she said, not to mention that atmosphere of decay that ruled everything, even before the restoration work was complete: broken tiles, missing bits of broken baseboard, deep cracks in the plaster, patches of mold on the ceiling, shutterless windows. Not even a word about the kiss from before. Nor a word about it at the castle, nor on the way back, nor during their following dates.

Sixteen

The Mericano kept his promise and by July 7th he awaited his wife and daughter in Ludwigshafen because, by some turn of events, he wrote, I found a little apartment that will be available exactly on July 6th, and I can't wait to hug you both again. What a shame, what a real shame that you don't want to come, father Lissandro, but knowing you it's useless to waste more of my breath: if you've said no, no it is. You will keep him company, my dear son Costantino; this way you can better prepare yourself for your exams in September. And I hope this is the last time you bring such a disgrace upon me. If it happens again, you can sell your books and buy yourself a hoe.

For the first time, Costantino reacted to his father's scolding and punishment with a cry of joy. He hugged his grandfather and said to him under his breath, "It will be an exceptional summer!"

Busy packing their bags and reapplying makeup to their souls, zonja Elena and Lucrezia didn't notice that Costantino was spending all morning in the bathroom powdering himself, spraying cologne, fixing the comma-shaped curl of his hair with hair spray, combing his eyebrows, his sideburns, and his thin mustache. Later, at lunch, he ate his spaghetti Bolognese slowly, from the first steaming forkful to the last with three hardened strands of spaghetti, staring at the wall clock waiting for it to strike two, the time set for his date with Isabella.

Aside from his friends, the only person who almost instantly understood that Costantino had lost his mind over that girl from Rome with the tan and always naked thighs was nani Lissandro. On occasion, he had seen him spin like a top, making weird theatrical gestures and laughing happily with his mouth closed; or with her, observing the little pepper and tomato plants that grew right before their eyes, talking tirelessly in the castle courtyard, she would barrage him with questions, and he would recount to her the life and times of all his family members, hiding nothing from her, not even that his father suffered from hemorrhoids. Both of their gazes looked like those of crazy people, but not their gestures; they didn't lay even a finger on each other, because maybe, thought nani, the times have changed; back in my day, with a girl like that around not a soul would have held himself back. But that was exactly what Costantino wanted to avoid, being an old-fashioned man, a deprived country boy who had never seen a beautiful girl, even though he knew full well that if his friends saw him wasting time talking instead of acting, they would have labeled him as fruity for the rest of his life.

Costantino had lost track of that game of what-if, and Isabella wasn't helping him find it again, maybe because she hadn't perceived that he was head over heels for her or maybe because she didn't care about him and his open-eyed kisses. Maybe she just wanted to spend time with someone now that *lal* Aldo had forbidden his daughter from hanging out with her. One thing was certain: with Isabella one had to be patient, to wait for another magical opportunity to casually draw close to her lips and her breasts, or to reveal to her the consistent presence of her little hands in his heart, ever since Christmas. Yes, an endless patience, seeing that the traditional methods didn't work with her. He had told her that on some night he would serenade her, and what did she do? After the first of three records chosen with care for an entire morning, all love songs from that summer, she opened the balcony door of her house, scaring the wind out of him, Vittorio, and Mario, convinced that her father was about to come outside, or worse, her uncle, the shiver of fear, while the needle of the record player skipped brusquely forward: "how many kisses that night . . . blackberries, and to the river, I brought you . . . that night, how many of them," and then back again, "it was the blackberry season . . . cornflowers and poppies . . . up . . . and up . . . ," and if that weren't enough, she yelled, breaking the thick darkness and silence of the alleyway: "Costantinoooooo, where are you running off to? It's me, Isabellaaaa." So, from that night, everyone knew that Costantino Avati, the so-called Eagle, was flirting with Isabella Barbato, the so-called Roman.

And then even nani Lissandro butted in, albeit unwillingly, erasing any chance of a magical opportunity. In fact, he stayed at the Castello del Piccolo from morning until night, tending to the little pepper and tomato plants, and fertilizing them with care. Isabella wanted to meet him, intrigued by Costantino's stories, and now they spent their free time with him, who worked with exasperating slowness but talked fluidly and quickly, like a radio sports commentator: about the past, the distant past and the past-perfect of Hora and of the surrounding area. If they happened to be left alone, Isabella continued to ask Costantino for clarifications about nani's stories, as she also called him by now, and she seemed to have lost any interest with regard to the boy. "I've grown fond of nani Lissandro," she admitted, "because he reminds me of grandpa Renzo from Rome: the same rosy face of a skinny newborn, the same little lively eyes." She would even kiss nani to show her fondness when she arrived and when she left. So, it didn't take long to win him over, to the point that he felt the duty to tell his grandson to take care of her, as if there had been any need: "I recommend you tend to her well; Isabella is a *vaizë me kripë*, which is good for you: good and smart, with a delicate face, like that of the beautiful blood-and-ricotta girl from the fairytale."

It was extraordinary that nani Lissandro had also noticed that resemblance. It was so extraordinary that he wanted to tell Isabella, the very day his mother and sister were leaving for Germany and his grandfather was home absorbing his daughter's final instructions, as though he were indeed the newborn Isabella was talking about. Finally, the two were alone, one in front of the other. Isabella hung happily from Costantino's lips, kneeling like him on a sack of corn husks in the largest room of the castle.

"Now I want to tell you the fable of the girl that looks like you," he told her, even though it was already late and the bus to Crotone was due to leave within the half hour. "So. Once upon a time there was a king's son who ate ricotta. While he was cutting bread, he also cut his finger, and so the ricotta was stained with blood. As soon as he saw the blood on the ricotta, he was fascinated by the scene, and he said: I absolutely must find a girl as beautiful as blood and ricotta. And then . . ."

Perhaps because she already knew the fable, at that moment Isabella placed the palm of her left hand over his mouth and closed his eyes. He brushed his mouth on her open hand and then reached his mouth to hers, sucking lips, saliva, teeth, tongue like one sucks a pomegranate, and he delicately held her head in his hands, afraid of piercing that face of blood and ricotta with his fingers. Isabella slid off her red under-shirt, and since that moment, Costantino couldn't decide whether to keep kissing her or to admire for his entire life those black nipples that arched up superbly toward the ceiling. There was an instant in which she, intimidated by those wide eyes, covered her breasts with her arms, but then they rolled onto the sack, crushing the dry husks and barraging the sky framed in the window with hot breaths, so much so that the cicadas in the olive trees out front briefly fell silent. Right when he also began to unbutton his own shirt, the voice of Vittorio broke the spell: "Costantì, hurry because it's late, the bus is leaving in five minutes; your mother and sister are turn-ing the town upside down to find you. Did you forget you're supposed to accompany them to the station?" He had spoken while huffing and puffing from the great run, but it was when he glanced at Isabella's breasts out in the open that he com-pletely lost his breath.

Costantino didn't even check his watch so as to not lose more time. "*E nanì, e nanì?*," he repeated.

"Well, now if you run you'll make it," Isabella said, get-ting dressed.

He scurried outside in a flash, and in a flash was back in again; he had forgotten to tell her something important: "*Të dua mir*," I love you.

"Me too," Isabella responded, but he was already a cloud of dust on the road, huffing, with the weight of that trip in his stomach, which he could've done without just then, look-ing for any excuse for his lateness, with which he would attempt to appease those furies of women who could already be heard yelling in the piazza, while the bus, with its motor running, grumbled impatiently under the July sun.

Seventeen

The house stunk of old air and garlic, and it made sense because nani felt the cold even during the heatwave, and not having anyone to account to, he kept the windows closed even when he was cooking dishes based on the deadly garlic from Castello del Piccolo.

Costantino studied in the small, stifled kitchen and ate that salad of tomatoes and garlic, and bread with onions and lard without complaining. Never had he felt as free as he did in those days of self-imposed seclusion. He made his presence known the day of the feast of Saint Veneranda, next to Isabella, and after the makeup exams, which he passed with the highest marks. He was thinner and pale, but his eyes expressed great serenity.

The old Lissandro seemed reborn in those months of life with his grandson: his small face turned rounder, and his back had straightened and stretched a palm higher since he could sleep the way he wanted: on a mattress on the ground. So, as soon as the two found out that zonja Elena, a week before her scheduled return to Hora on the first of October, had fallen ill and therefore was forced to stay in Hamburg with her daughter, they hugged each other with joy. And they turned deaf ears to the voices that hinted at what they already knew: the illness was an excuse, a way to save face, since zonja Elena had had the barbarous courage to leave an old man and a boy alone.

To see them walking, they seemed just out of a naive painting: the old Lissandro, with a black wide-brimmed hat and an unbuttoned waistcoat, and Costantino with an oleander cane in hand. Then they would immerse themselves in the autumn forest, bathed in rain and in light, behind the castle, and they would step back into that painting with no frame. Nani would pick the quince apples, and after having smelled them, Costantino carefully cleaned them of their fuzzy coat of miniature hairs; they made bunches of yellow-red rowanberries, and before they filled up the basket, they picked at the acidic pulp of the jujube and the sweet of the azaroles, imitating the larks; then came the dog rose and myrtle berries, and finally some red fruits of the strawberry trees, with the taste of strawberries and the sea.

Costantino liked helping nani with his little projects: he closed his schoolbooks without giving it another thought when it came to making jams, or reorganizing the storehouse, or harvesting olives from Castello del Piccolo. And now, more than ever before, he liked talking to him because he treated him like a man by then.

He talked about Isabella without shame, about his love for her, the only one in the world he missed at that moment: with her, he said, right here, right now, it would be paradise. He even read him the scented letters, in which they cursed their distance, kissed each other all over, and couldn't wait to hug each other again.

Nani Lissandro understood him, *po po po*, how he understood him, because he had married for love, an exception for his time. He and Sidonia had risked stabbings just to meet up, at night, in some stable. To move the date of the wedding up by a month, the young Lissandro had gone to Cariati on foot to have the bishop sign his papers, seven hours of walking for love, and on his way back he almost ended up dead. In fact, around ten at night, when he was just a few kilometers from Hora, in a place called Dera, he heard the sound of a pack following him. He listened carefully and realized that they were wolves about thirty meters away. All he could do was pray: blessed feet of mine, help me flee, he hurried off the mule path and climbed an olive tree. The wolves, twenty of them or close to it, found his hiding spot immediately with their acute sense of smell and howled below the tree. The young Lissandro held his breath, but he was so afraid that he nearly soiled his new pants. With trembling hands, he pulled the revolver that he always carried on him from his pocket and started shooting six shots at the pack of wolves. The wolves, intelligent animals, slowly backed away.

The risk was worth it. They married, they enjoyed a month more of happiness. Sidonia was a *grua me kripë*, capable of keeping her word, hard-working, beautiful, healthy, always ready with a funny punchline and a laugh from the heart. Maternity didn't wear her down; quite the contrary. She was prettier and fuller than before, and Elenuzza looks just like her. Who knows how she would have turned out if her mother had raised her. But *jeta ësht si fjeta*, life is like a leaf.

This is the phrase that Costantino still remembers today and that nani cried to himself in moments of discomfort, having nothing else to cry about: "Life is like a leaf," it seemed to be the essence of his existential philosophy. Because for him, any kind of disappointment or pain like the death of a friend, like the loss of Baialardo or the fire in the wood were like stones thrown into the swamp of his memories, and the trembling concentric circles lasted much longer, as the stone thrown was bigger. *Jeta ësht si fjeta.* And it hadn't been a stone but a boulder that sunk into the deep blue of his heart when Sidonia had died, at the age of twenty-seven, of bronchial pneumonia.

The best doctors of the Crotonese had come to see her and had prescribed her rest, syrups, and pills, paid for with her life savings. He would have sold his soul to save her. But Sidonia had passed, with the hope of recovery imprinted in her tired eyes.

His mother-in-law had even called the sorceress of Puhërìu, so as to not leave any option unattempted, and she, after having observed her for a moment by herself, had gone back to the kitchen and said with an arrogant assurance: "She cut the throne of the fairy queen. It happened in the Krisma woods. It was a big, exposed root of a heather; after the first strike, the ax fell out of her hands and she heard a cry. But she didn't suspect a thing: she insisted, she cut down the throne and heard a woman's wail. It's all clear, then: vendetta. That same night her fever rose. There is no escape for her. The fairies know how to be evil with the same intensity they have to be good."

Nani Lissandro didn't know what to say to that bird of ill omen with bold eyes, who was accusing him and his whole family: they should have called her earlier, she was saying, maybe then she could have appeased the fairies with pasta and cookies, just as she had done many times before. At this point, it was too late.

The only truth in the tale of the sorceress, according to nani Lissandro, was the circumstance that one day he and

Sidonia had gone to collect wood in the woods and that evening she had felt ill: she was sweating and raving, her fever was extremely high. Well, yes. She had also cut the heather root; she grew stubborn, not wanting to let him do it: Sidonia was hard-headed about these things; they amused her, and she could have let loose her great laugh all of a sudden, like she did that morning, and if the fairies really existed, they would have rejoiced too. The rest, nani Lissandro says to the sorceress, the big root that cried out, the cut throne, the fairies that must be appeased, it is all nonsense. And he asked the woman to leave the house immediately, and he grew angry with his poor mother-in-law for having summoned her.

He has no doubts: if his wife passed at such a young age, it was because *jeta ësht si fjeta*. For her before us. But for us too. *Fjeta*. The sharp turns of the living, happy, green warbles. And then the damp earth.

And what are you doing now, Sidonia? What are you doing, Isabella?

Eighteen

They barely recognize her, she's tall in high heels and wears a fur coat that reaches above her knees. Under the fur coat, she wears black velvet pants and a celestial-blue silk shirt. Her breasts are round, and even though they are bound by a bra, they oscillate with her every slight movement. Viatrice Sciales is there, in the Mericano's apartment, excusing herself a thousand times for the unexpected surprise, but the reason for the visit is quite important. She speaks in Italian, at first, "Kind Signor Avati, dear zonja Elena, dearest Signorina Lucrezia," and she smokes; but then, when she realizes that even the women, especially Lucrezia, dabbled a bit in German, she continues in this manner to allow her companion to understand her: "*Ich bin mit meinem Mann gekommen, um euch mein Haus zu verkaufen.*" Essentially her companion was her husband, and they had come to sell the old house in Palacco. The man had smiled throughout the entire visit, widening the arc of his big black mustache. He was the Turk the paesani had been talking about, owner of two restaurants and an *Imbiss*, a cafeteria, in Mannheim. He is polite and well-mannered; he smokes as well and lights his wife's cigarettes with a golden lighter; he tastes the wine from the Castello and says *super*, zonja Elena's strong coffee and says *sehr gut*, very good, even the pork sausage preserved in fat and says *lecker*, yummy. A truly good Turk, beyond criticism, a gentleman—who, apart from the compliments, kept out of the discussion.

Why was Viatrice selling the house? Because she didn't want to return to her hometown, not even dead. Why specifically sell to them, out of all the paesani in Ludwigshafen? Because to her, people dear to her come before everyone else. She will never forget the good deed Signor Avati did for her. How much did she want? asked the Mericano impatiently. The cost of the official stamped paper to notarize the deed of sale, Viatrice Sciales answered immediately.

They are all dumbfounded, him, his wife, his daughter. But Signora Viatrice does not even want to be thanked. She makes an appointment for the next day at the notary's office in the consulate and leaves with her arm linked with the smiling Turk, leaving a small cloud of jasmine perfume in the living room.

The Mericano's eyes shined green like in the old days, now that he was in the piazza telling of Signora Viatrice Sciales's visit. His plan was to demolish the old house, made of a single room and a doorstep at the front door, and to make a garage out of it. "Great idea," his friends said to him, "a nice garage, that you could even rent out, if you wanted."

The Mericano was full of plans again, enthusiastic, active. He talked and shook hands with everyone, he laughed, he said his wife and daughter were doing well in Germany, nobody could complain, thank you. Lucrezia was working in a laundromat, and zonja Elena spent her time raiding the supermarkets in Ludwigshafen with his money: she had bought a present for each relative and every neighbor, a chest full of things she would bring in the summer, with his nearly new Mercedes, comfortable as an airplane. He was in Hora in the off-season for work because people like him, wallowing in self-pity and fishing for compliments, were born to slave away. Yes, it's true: life ends but work never ends.

He didn't even notice the stench of garlic and stuffiness that filled the house, nor the old father-in-law's good health, nor the dark whiskers his son had grown. He had arrived like an earthquake, without warning, at the beginning of April, and like an earthquake, he would have disappeared ten days later, leaving piles of rubble behind him.

Instead of completing all his restoration projects at the castle like he had said he would various times in the past, he was convinced by the surveyor of Marina, whom he had turned to for the project, to demolish it entirely. The motive? It is less expensive to build a new house than to restore an ugly ruin like that one. How many millions had he already spent on restoring it? Many. What was the result? The Mericano didn't respond out of shame. But he was still in time, the surveyor said, if he wanted to properly invest his money. A nice three-story house, one floor for each child, with a lovely square shape, so that he would gain more space from the same number of cubic meters. And, with a skillfully drafted sketch, the surveyor demonstrated the veracity of the concept to him. He himself would oversee the work. Signor Avati could rest assured while abroad; by summertime, he would find the garages ready, as well as the frames of the three apartments: pillars and suspended slabs.

The excavator only took one day to demolish the castle, tossing the rubble into the ravine.

That day, Costantino was at school and nani Lissandro was in the countryside. When that night the dusty Mericano told them euphorically that, where the castle once stood, now there was an open piazza as big as the *rahj*, the two didn't know where to point their eyes full of rage.

The next morning, the Mericano emptied Signora Viatrice's house: from the old loom he made firewood, the walnut table he brought to his house, and the worm-eaten chairs and blankets he gave to the neighbors; the rest was worthless, in his opinion, and could be buried in the rubble without worry.

In the early afternoon, a smaller excavator than the one that demolished the castle made Viatrice's house disappear forever, after an old woman with a black coha came to gather all the snapdragons from the wall.

The Mericano left again for Germany that same evening, leaving his son and father-in-law with mouths full of dust.

"This is the fate of the Mericano: return, leave, demolish, build, return, demolish, leave," said nani Lissandro, "not even he knows what he wants."

"*Kj ësht fati i Merikanit: vjen, vete, çan, ngren, vjen, çan, vete, ngë din nemenu ai atà çë do.*" The tape recorder on high volume reproduced the voice of the old man, who jumped at the marvel. Costantino smoothed his whiskers with satisfaction. At least the Mericano had the brilliant idea to give him—other than the dust—an easy-to-use Grundig CR 485 stereo tape recorder, with a built-in microphone.

In the first few days, Costantino spent his free time recording songs from the radio, and he listened to them a thousand times on the bus to school. Then, one afternoon, he had the idea to record nani Lissandro's voice recounting the stories he had told him the day of the fair so many years ago. It was nani who pointed him to the old zonje in their and other gjitonì, who were better and had better memories than himself, for he had exhausted his repertoire of fragments of rhapsodies in prose and verse with only half a cassette.

The old zonje didn't mind reciting or singing the ancient rhapsodies into the microphone on his tape recorder, but they wanted to know what he needed them for and why he was collecting them. His friends insisted as well: "*Pse? Pse bier mot me keto shërbise?*" Why? Why do you waste your time with these things? "Was it really a waste of time?" Costantino asked himself. He liked the rhapsodies, wasn't that enough? Maybe he was looking for whatever it is a boy looks for in a story: adventure, heroes, similarities to his own life. "*Pse? Pse?*" Costantino answered with a smile, and if that wasn't enough, he would sigh: "Kështu," just like that.

Collecting rhapsodies became his favorite pastime. He did it with the same passion some boys have for collecting shells, stamps, postcards, and figurines of soccer players.

That spring was full of work for Costantino. In the morning, he went to school; he did his homework on the bus; and at three on the dot, he was home, ready to devour the onion frittatas nani Lissandro made for him. Then he would wander around town until late at night, searching for rhapsodies.

When Isabella came back in mid-June, two weeks early, she found him with his tape recorder under his arm and with the absent-minded air of a visionary. That day, Costantino had collected, from the childlike voice of old zonja Mena, the rhapsody about Skanderbeg's death "Vdekja e Skanderbekut," and he was enthusiastic about it. He wanted to translate it, he said, because it deserved it. And he had the girl listen to it.

Isabella admitted she didn't understand a thing: "It is just a mournful lament that gives you the chills," she said. "I don't like it." Costantino grew gloomy. Half an hour later they had their first big fight.

At first, Isabella was speechless. They arrived at Castello del Piccolo, and the castle wasn't there. In its place was an erected three-story construction of pillars and suspended slabs, the base of which was walled off with cement blocks. "Horrible," Isabella said, disappointed. "Who was the idiot who had this mess done? He deserves to be arrested."

Costantino blushed and lowered his gaze. But Isabella didn't show signs of letting up: "They must have the brain of a chicken . . . What a fool . . . is it even possible! To sweep away a little castle . . . moron. . . ." Costantino wanted to make her stop: "Look, you're talking about my father." But instead, this made her even more angry: "Ah, it's your father; then he is doubly moronic." The first slap landed full on her face; the second on the back of her head. "Bitch, you will not talk about my father like that!"

Isabella became furious: she threw kicks, punches, she scratched; she cursed, "asshole, not even my father has the audacity to slap me!"

They tumbled in the dust, without stopping the insults, and if nani Lissandro had not arrived, they would have torn each other apart. "Ah, so this is how you demonstrate affection these days," the old man said while separating them, and he didn't even want to know the reason for that violent fight.

They didn't speak for four days. When they ran into each other by chance in the piazza, they lowered their heads and walked on.

On the fifth day, Costantino kicked his pride aside and apologized to Isabella, with the voice of a beaten dog.

They started going back to Castello del Piccolo, which in those days had been reduced to a dusty construction site, and they said no more about the Mericano, or the monstrous construction of reinforced concrete. They kissed each other, they kept nani Lissandro company in the dusty vegetable plot, they kissed each other, they watered the little tomato plants, they kissed each other, and they laughed. They had beaten each other up; Isabella hadn't given an inch; Costantino had trampled his own pride; and it was as though nothing had happened. It would always be like this between them: "If we get married one day," he said, playing the "what if?" game, "we'll live in Hora;" and she offered a hundred counter-reasons: "I would even live on the moon, but in this town of lunatics, not even dead!" He would act offended, she would kiss him, and they would laugh.

One night the games came to an end: walking back to town, they, too, captured the news that had for hours paralyzed the strolling of the elderly in the piazza, the game of cards in front of the bar, and the housewives with grocery bags in hand in the licks of shadows in the alleyways: from Somalia, the maestro, Signor Maestro Carmelo Bevilacqua, had returned.

Nineteen

A wave of hot garlicky stagnant air stopped Isabella at the threshold of the Avatis' house. She saw nani over the lit hearth, lost in the sluggish stirring of the yellowish gruel in a stewpot and in his thoughts. "And Costantino?" she managed to ask him, suffocated by the oppressive heat. "*Ësht atje mbrënda,*" he's there inside, the old man replied, pointing to the large bedroom with his ladle.

Costantino was rolled up on the bed reading comic books. The room was kept nice and tidy by nani, so the comic books strewn across the floor bothered her: she gathered them and stuck them in a cabinet in order not to see them; then she kissed Costantino on one ear and messed with his curls. The boy let himself be cuddled; it was clear he needed it, but he couldn't go on like that, snuggled up on the bed like a cat, "you can't, there's no reason for it," she told him. "You haven't been outside in three days, let's take a walk, come on, otherwise you'll get scoliosis."

He lied, looked her in the eyes and lied: he wasn't doing so well, he said. He had a continuous headache and didn't want to go out. So that's when Isabella ran out of patience: "Ah, you have a headache? I'll make it go right away; it's because it smells like a hospital kitchen in here. Air, air is what you need." And she opened the French doors that led onto the balcony, she climbed on a chair to unlatch a small window that had been closed for a year, and she finally made way into grandpa's inferno. "Air," she said, "you need air, you're suffocating here" and threw the kitchen door open.

Costantino had followed her barefoot and was awaiting nani's reaction. But the old man didn't lose his composure: he was still bent over the embers of the fire, with his usual rosy face, not at all flushed or sweaty, and he spoke to Isabella from that uncomfortable position: "In a bit, we'll eat *bath e buk*, fava beans and bread; it's a specialty: fava beans give you blood, more blood than meat; you'll eat with us."

Isabella happily accepted the invitation, as she was famished. Every now and then Costantino's gaze would land on her, forcing himself to seem annoyed, but she would smile at him and boss him around: "Go get the wine, there's no bread, the tablecloth needs to be changed . . ."

The fava beans had become a steaming cream, and now they were to dip pieces of bread into the plates, as nani had recommended, when someone called up from the doorstep of the house: "May I come in?"

The fava cream froze in the mouths of nani and his grandson, because both of them understood that it was the voice of the Maestro Carmelo Bevilacqua; sure enough, the elegant blond who stood before them a moment later was precisely he, hard to recognize for how much he had changed, but it was him, by his mannerisms, affable and polite, it was him. He began with an enigmatic; "If Mohamed doesn't go to the mountain . . ." left in suspense and smiling and giving a warm handshake to each of them, he dispensed compliments ("I find you well, Signor Alessandro; what a handsome young man you've become, Costantino; and who is this lovely girl?") and more smiles, as though they had parted as good friends two years before, with a rose pinned onto his heart.

Costantino kept his eyes on his steaming plate: he was worried that nani might do something rash, that he might rudely throw him out of the house, giving the neighbors an excuse to gossip. He had forgotten that hospitality is sacred. Sure enough, the old man, betraying no signs of nervousness, like his grandson's forced or restless smiles, or like the abrupt movements of Isabella's hands from the table to her hair, invited Carmelo to sit down and eat with them.

"You are as kind as ever, Signor Alessandro," said the maestro, "and I accept the invitation because I know that otherwise you would be offended." Yeah, what a real offense, Costantino thought, what a son of a bitch, what a smug face on him.

Isabella brought another plate of creamy fava beans to the table and said politely, "Grandpa cooked these, they are a specialty."

For a few minutes, the only thing that was heard was the sound of the spoons drowning in the cream of favas. The Signor Maestro's face appeared serene and bright, not at all bothered by the thoughtful silence of the old man and the boy, nor by Isabella's flurry of glances. What she saw before her was a handsome man in his thirties with fashionable glasses, no extra rolls of fat but rather a lean and athletic body, a face the color of coffee, an elegant outfit of celestial-blue linen worn with a figure of confidence, with blue shoes and a blue shirt; in other words, he looked nothing like the oily, bald piglet Costantino had described to her. Even his sparse hair was nice and luminous as a field of ripe wheat under the sun. Isabella smiled at him politely. But after some time, she couldn't stand that silence wrapped in the volcanic fumes of the creamy favas, which made the wrinkles around the maestro's eyes tremble. "Did you find yourself well in Somalia?" she asked, breaking the steamy silence.

It seemed like the maestro hadn't been waiting for any other question for the entire duration of the dinner. Did he? He was having a wonderful time in Mogadishu, he earned a boatload of money, like five times an Italian salary, and he could afford to rent a villa by the sea. But he wasn't there for the money, he eagerly pointed out. He was there to help the Somalis, offering them his culture, clearly demonstrating his friendship toward people who lived in misery; even though to them, he was and always would be a *gal*, a stranger. They are suspicious, ooh, those Somalis are so suspicious, but they are polite and welcoming.

For the first time, nani Lissandro raised his rosy face toward the maestro and spoke: "We say: *Dirq e litì, mos i këllit mbë shpi, se te çajnë poçë e kusì*, Pigs and Italians, don't let either in your house, because they will break your clay pots and cauldrons. Being welcoming isn't always rewarding; quite the contrary."

The maestro didn't have time to ask about the meaning of the proverb because Costantino had erupted in a belated defense of the Somalis, as though it had been on the tip of his tongue for some time: "They are right to be suspicious. Up until now, foreigners have gone there with just one thought: to colonize them, to suck the blood out of those poor people, to erase their culture. Everyone. The Italians, the British, the Americans, and now the Russians, after the socialist coup a few years ago."

Well, Costantino knew his facts, but the maestro was struck less by his competence and more by the aggressive tone of his ex-student, struck to the point of muttering something incomprehensible, stumbling over his multiple attempts to pronounce "that is," "let's see," and "even though." Then he cleared his throat and spoke more clearly: "You're right, even though only partially: the gals have, and are, exploiting Somalia. But not us Italians; in other words, we've only given to Somalia, without earning a cent from that hole . . ."

"Please don't make me laugh: it's only because there hasn't been a time or a way to suck anything out!" Costantino interrupted him, with a tone of arrogance and challenge.

Luckily, a new question from Isabella (perhaps about the attractions in Somalia) cut short the "what the fu . . ." a furious reaction of the maestro who was losing his self-control.

The maestro quickly found his smile again and displayed it with impressions, sensations, and information about Somalia, like an actor who has rehearsed his part a thousand times.

At the end of dinner, he thanked them, and with a bow he wished them good night.

Later on, Isabella had Costantino accompany her home; that way, finally, he would get some fresh air, she told him, and he could stretch his legs.

"Yes, I could use that," he admitted; then he didn't say anything else. Swarms of the maestro's words were playing in his head, and he didn't even notice the lovestruck eyes of Isabella, who for the first time in her life, she said, was leaving for the beach reluctantly.

The maestro had talked so much!

But he hadn't said he was back in Hora with the intention of marrying Lucrezia.

Twenty

The maestro hung out in the piazza at night; you could see him walking arm in arm with the mayor or in the middle of the committee for the feast of Saint Veneranda, impeccable in his outfits of crinkled linen, the only one in a jacket and tie and therefore easy to spot from far away, so much that Costantino could avoid running into him well in advance. He hadn't dared set foot in the Avatis' house after the coldness reserved for him the night of the dinner. He was waiting impatiently for "those who matter," he was telling everyone, meaning Lucrezia and her parents, because old Lissandro was an old-fashioned man, with a thick shell, incapable of forgiving and being forgiven, and Costantino was a boy who was easily influenced by his grandfather. In the meantime, he was helping out with organizing the celebration, and was happy to do it, because he was an altruist, he said, and he had a big surprise for Hora that only the mayor knew about, a precious gift, enclosed in a giant aluminum foil egg, that would be opened just on the evening of the celebration on the stage.

The more curious ones began courting him to find out more about it: they would wink an eye in hopes of getting the secret out of him: "Come on, I won't tell anyone, I'll be as quiet as a mouse, like a tomb I'll be, come on," but the maestro let nothing slip, and the mayor, like the shrewd man he was, would pretend not to hear the question or would immediately change the topic. Odd as he was, the maestro could've stuck anything in the aluminum foil egg, but one had to be as brainless as Partù to come to the conclusion that the egg was full of a bunch of dollars. The reason? To replace the off-key church bells that the now wealthy maestro had said more than once were unworthy of a town like Hora.

The maestro laughed with pleasure the first time he heard Partù's comical idea, but he kept repeating, with a certain maliciousness: "The most I can do is to show the shape of the egg."

The house had been tidied up for his return, Signor Maestro had explained to the more curious visitors, who were mainly his former students; they had offered it to him for twenty-five million lire and he might have purchased it out of affection, even though he would only use it for vacation. His former students were listening to him distractedly, so the maestro understood: he took the big egg in his hands, dazzling them with the aluminum foil, and placed it with care in a large box. They would see the rest shine, he said, on the stage under spotlights, along with the famous band I Ricchi e Poveri. He had made the yellow flier advertising the party himself, booking the ten o'clock spot in bold letters: Wonderful final surprise thought up by Professor C. Bevilacqua.

Two days before the start of the feast, stalls filled every corner of the piazza and the Kriqi; they hid Skanderbeg's bust under a green tarp and left a round space vacant where the stage would be built.

Just like every year, Isabella arrived with her family on the eve of the feast, her tan legs placed in plain sight with a white miniskirt. Costantino saw her again the next day, during the procession, and glued himself in front, behind, to the left, and to the right of her, trampling on her shadow for the good part of the day. At nine that night, he was still next to Isabella, in the middle of his group, all standing before the stage.

Nani Lissandro had gone to work at Castello del Piccolo even on that day, firstly because the plants and the chickens were calling him loudly, he said, then also because the procession is for young people, the games in the piazza are for children, and the musical soirée was to rob people of their money: with all the millions collected each year, passing in front of the houses with the Saint, you could buy a combine harvester or an ambulance or something else the town actually needs. But with the exception of nani and the families in mourning, all of Hora and many people from nearby towns had crowded the piazza and were now applauding because the band's concert had ended and the Signor Mayor and Signor Maestro Carmelo Bevilacqua, with the aluminum foil egg in hand, had taken the stage.

The mayor, on behalf of the town administration, thanked the organizing committee of the celebration and then greeted the sons of Hora, the emigrants who after a year in the cold north, had come back to the fold. A first burst of applause interrupted him. The mayor smiled, flattered, then pulled a sheet of paper from his coat pocket and continued: "Your kind applause also goes out to the sons of Hora scattered around the world, who, although they are far away, wanted to be here close to us, contributing to the success of our celebration with generous monetary donations." A second burst of applause.

And he began to read in alphabetical order names, places, and sums of money. Barrages of applause. Then he asked for absolute silence. "We also welcome Professor Carmelo Bevilacqua present here, who has returned to us, bringing us a precious gift. I give the floor to him."

Signor Maestro shone under the spotlights, not at all intimidated by the hundreds of gazes he felt upon him. In fact, he spoke with a clear voice, slowly: "I would like this gift to be like the first stone Saint Peter placed in the spot where the famous basilica would be built that carries his name. In other words, I would like a nice beautiful ethnographic museum to be built in Hora, where it would be possible, in other words, to preserve the cohe, the quilts, the loom, the artisanal tools, and all the beautiful things that are disappearing. I worked on this for a long time to surprise you, I hope you like it . . . let's see . . . voilà." With a little knife, he cut the red ribbon that wrapped the aluminum foil egg, and the shell split open in two equal parts. "The majestic symbol of Arbëria!" Signor Maestro announced.

The precious gift was a brown taxidermied eagle, double-headed with shining beaks, two long, pathetic necks, and little yellow eyes made of glass, which seemed to be ready to burst into tears.

An embarrassed silence fell over the piazza. Costantino didn't know what to think or where to point his gaze, and if he should laugh or whistle. Ah, so was this the surprise? And what kind of surprise was this? From the perplexed eye-rolling of his friends and people around him, he understood that in that moment many were feeling the same uncomfortable sensations as he. All of a sudden, he felt a strong itching in his fingers and he began to rub them with anger to the point of wearing away the skin, as he would do from then on in moments of severe nervousness. It was obvious: he didn't know whether to believe his eyes or what to do.

Dazed by the lights and the bicephalous eagle, Isabella noticed his skinned fingers only later, when she squeezed his hand.

"I understand your amazement," Signor Maestro felt the need to add. "This eagle is a little miracle of craftsmanship. That is, I purchased two little brown eagles in Sudan, and I sewed the neck of one onto the neck of the other. Now I will hand it to Hora's head citizen, but it is as though I am giving it to all of you. May this bicephalous eagle of yours, or rather, ours, find his nest as soon as possible, in the long sought-after museum."

Between the maestro's auspicious words and his donation of the eagle to the mayor, a deafening burst of exclamations erupted, which made the heads of the maestro, the mayor, and the eagle bow. Behind them appeared two young couples, with their arms raised to greet the crowd: one blond and one brunette, dressed like rich people, and one blonde and one brunette, dressed like poor people: "Ladies and gentlemen, I Ricchi e Poveri!"

The youth went wild: they clapped, whistled, yelled bravi, hooray bravi, singing along: Town of mine that sits on the hill/ laid out like an old man sleeping/boredom, abandonment, nothingness/are your disease/town of mine, I'm leaving you, I'm going away.

It was obvious that the Germanesi and the other emigrants felt goosebumps on their skin. They were words played by the speakers at full volume that stuck in their guts like a stab: Nearly all of my friends have gone away/and the rest will leave after me/too bad because I felt well in their company/but everything passes and everything goes away.

It was obvious that Vittorio had a lump in his throat. He had to leave at the end of August: destination Frankfurt, where his older brother had emigrated a few years ago; in that time, he would roam the construction sites and countryside asking for work the way one begs for money: he had to pay his own train ticket as well as the promissory notes on a Vespa 50 . . . What will come of my life, who knows/ . . . but it will be, it will be what it will be.

Costantino put an arm on his shoulder, and it was just what he needed at that moment, the arm of a friend on his shoulder. Now he also had a lump in his throat. In November, he would leave town to go study at a university in Rome; Mario would go to work in Hamburg; half the people filling the piazza would be spread around the world within two, three weeks. Maybe this was the cause of the lump in his throat: the suffocating feeling of being surrounded by future ghosts, by fake bicephalous eagles, by promises sung over and over: I only know that I'll be back/ . . . I only know that I'll be back.

Twenty-one

The Mericano parked his celestial-blue Mercedes in the only sliver of shade on the town road, around two in the afternoon. The first to get out was Lucrezia, who took in her world with a sweeping glance, to then detach herself from it, exposing her face to the warm sky with an attitude that was both haughty and endearing. The sun was a yellow light with blurred edges, dotted with swarms of crazed swallows. Zonja Elena touched the humid air with her hand in the direction of the little church of Saint Anthony, which could be seen in the distance, and kissed her crossed index and ring fingers, thanking *i bekuar*, the blessed saint, for getting them home safe and sound. She wiped the sweat from her face with a handkerchief and tried in vain to tidy up the hair that had gotten stuck on her neck and face.

"A shame, such a beautiful perm, which cost forty marks, ruined by the trip," her husband teased as he unloaded suitcases, boxes, plastic bags, bags of food, bags of gifts from the car, all in all twenty-two things, twenty-three with his daughter's little brown leather purse. The Mericano continued to sweat. His white undershirt had turned straw-yellow, due to old and new sweat, and left exposed along his shoulders and chest two crescents of gray hair, curled around little drops of sweat.

All of a sudden, the Mercedes was surrounded by a pack of tail-wagging dogs, sleeveless and smiling neighborhood women, and children of all ages. "You look so rejuvenated, *ndrikulla* Elena, *kupile je bënë*," you look like a young girl, said Mena with the echo of the other women, "*kupile, kupile*. Just like your daughter."

"*Jam e lodhur, jam e dekur*," I'm tired, I'm dead, zonja Elena kept repeating, to justify how ugly she knew she looked at the moment. Lucrezia, who couldn't stand her mother's complaints, nor the compliments that she felt showered on her in hot bucketfuls by the neighborhood women ("*Po po po, ç'je bënë e bukur, si djelli, si hënëza, si . . .* ," Wow, how beautiful you've become, like the sun, like the moon, like . . .), grabbed one of the suitcases and started down the narrow alleyway, followed by children, the neighborhood women, and her parents, each with a piece of luggage in hand.

In the house, despite Costantino's foresight to open all the windows from early that morning, the stink of garlic and stale air still ruled, stinging the nose and eyes of the small crowd and the little clouds of flies that buzzed through the air, never resting. "*E zeza u, mizat!*" Dear me, these flies! She had forgotten the flies, zonja Elena said at first, and then kissed her elderly father and Costantino.

The people left politely, "You must be tired, you have to eat a bite." Rather than eating, they drank: fresh water, wine from Castello del Piccolo with ice, and orange soda; they drank and talked about the trip, about the work at the castle, about Costantino passing his graduation exams, about

Ludwigshafen. Of the Maestro Carmelo Bevilacqua, nani Lissandro said: "He arrived three weeks ago; he had the nerve to come visit us."

"We know everything," the Mericano replied. And that was it. Then they gave each other compliments, everyone looked younger; Costantino, obviously, had become *i madh*, *një burri*, a man, all grown up.

The Mericano's eyes were closing on their own, *i shkreti*, poor guy, he had driven for over twenty hours; so he threw himself fully dressed on the bed and a moment later could be heard snoring heavily.

When the relatives' visits began, Lucrezia also retired to her room, because she was seeing everything foggy, she said, because of her exhaustion. So, the burden of welcoming the relatives fell on zonja Elena's curved and sweaty shoulders until late in the night, when she was finally able to unpack the bags, because otherwise, she repeated, she would never be able to rest with her soul at peace.

She awoke early the next morning with a strange sense of anguish in her chest, exacerbated by the small cup of strong coffee, since it had the same aroma of the coffee she had drunk a year before, exactly on the day of the trip to Germany. In other words, it was as if she had lived through the year spent in Germany in a dream that night. Strange indeed. In other words, it was as if the year had passed in reverse, backward. Strange.

Lucrezia began to laugh: "Oh ma, are you going senile too?" and she shut herself in the bathroom to wash and do her makeup.

Costantino listened to the voices of his mother and sister from his bed. Then he closed his eyes and in that half-asleep state he heard his mother's heavy steps, the sound of the broom scraping on the floor, and his sister's nightingale whistle.

Maybe his mother was right: the year had lasted only the length of a long night's dream.

He awoke in good spirits two hours later: he had dreamt of Isabella. He waited for his underwear to deflate, then pulled on his shorts and headed to the bathroom. It was still occupied by Lucrezia: "Duchess, madam duchess, are you planning to spend the holidays there?" But Lucrezia didn't respond. So, Costantino began to dip slices of bread in the chocolate milk his mother had prepared for him. His father and nani had left early that morning for Castello del Piccolo to complain about the slow pace of the construction on the new house and most of all about the irreparable damage caused by the hot desert wind.

"*Po po po*, such damage, all that effort gone with the wind, what great damage," the Mericano noted on the way back. "It all looks like it was burnt with a low flame. Without seeing it with your own eyes, you wouldn't believe it. But we might be able to save something," he concluded hopefully.

"Little. Very little," replied the old father-in-law, discouraged.

At that moment, Lucrezia came out of the bathroom: she was wearing a jean skirt that left her bony knees uncovered and a red sleeveless blouse. She walked gingerly on her bare tiptoes and bowed in front of her brother, displaying her usual midnight-blue hair: "The bathroom is all yours, Duke Costantino of the Avatis." The tiredness and wrinkles from her expression that the trip and life had marked on her face had been erased with a light foundation, almost rosy, and by a shadow of pearly rose on her eyelids; her lips were just brushed with a touch of lipstick, which allowed their perfect shape, like a fleshy heart, to show through. "You look like a lightbulb," her brother told her, who had looked her over carefully. And she smiled proudly.

Later on, the relatives and neighbors who stopped by the house to greet them would see her the same way Costantino had. "*E bukur si drita*," zonja Elena bragged about her daughter when she noticed that everyone was devouring her with their eyes. "Yes, she is a little crazy, this daughter of mine, but she is as beautiful as sunlight."

That night they were still there, sitting in a circle, with new companions that changed every hour, repeating that in Germany things were good and things were bad, or rather things were bad and things were good; bad because of the distance, you know, good because where there is work, you know; and that Lucrezia was reborn there, she earned fairly good money at the laundromat, she had German and Italian friends with whom she went dancing on Saturdays, and even though she was a little crazy, like all today's youth, she was *e bukur si drita*.

Illuminated by the vertical light from the lightbulb and from the horizontal light of Lucrezia, Giorgio Taruscio began to rehearse his part when only the empty chairs and the Avati family remained in the room.

Giorgio Taruscio was a small man in his sixties, with reddish hair and a shrewd gaze, deft of tongue and hand. He spoke with impressive fluency, drawing his concepts and words with quick movements of his hands. He was considered the most skilled olive tree pruner in town. He bragged that he could have been a lawyer if he had had the chance to study. But he felt satisfied with himself all the same, he said, because he always brought good news to good people's homes.

Everyone understood what news he was talking about because to the town Giorgio Taruscio was known as the infallible wedding matchmaker.

"For Signor Maestro, I had chosen a young teacher from Kona, but he is all caught up with Signorina Lucrezia: he came back from Africa just for you, Lucrezia." Giorgio Taruscio always spoke his mind, he said, and he listed the maestro's good qualities, stressing each of them with a light snap of the fingers: "He has money, education, and youth. He is a gentleman, and here in Hora he is well-liked. You all know him better than I do. I've thought it over long and hard: Signor Maestro and Lucrezia were, and always will be, a perfect couple, both born for one another. Actually, I'm sure that a hundred years from now, when they die of happiness, they will be reborn as lovers from the ancient songs: he will be a cypress, she the white grapevine, wrapped around him forever." Giorgio Taruscio smiled like a saint, inhaled deeply, and concluded: "What happened, happened. I came here tonight to hear a 'yes' from Lucrezia and the marriage will take place."

Lucrezia jumped up. She drew everyone's anxious glances with an undecipherable smile, then she slowly half opened her heart-shaped lips. Her grandfather and brother hoped to hear a nice, sharp jo; her mother and father feared hearing an ugly, equally sharp jo. And in fact Lucrezia said: "Jo. No, he has to come here himself to ask me officially."

So it was a yes.

Shkoi një ditë mjegullore

A day of fog went by,
of fog and sadness,
as though the sky wanted to cry.
And then, it became a day of rain
and from the piazza a shout was heard,
which entered and spread mourning
in the hearts and in the buildings.
It was Lek Ducagin.
He was beating his forehead with one hand
and pulling his hair out with the other.
"Tremble, Arbërìa!
Come, ladies and gentlemen,
come, poor women and soldiers,
come and weep in sorrow.
Today you are made orphans,
without the father who guided you,
guided you and helped you.
And the honor of the maidens
and the joy of the neighborhoods:
he who protected them, you have no longer.

The father and Commander of Arbërìa,
he died this morning:
Skanderbeg is no more!"
The houses heard and shook,
the mountains heard and split;
the church bells
rang the mourning song on their own.
But in the open skies entered
Skanderbeg the unfortunate.

The Final Vallja

The long days of summer became sticky due to the desert wind that ran through the town far and wide, leaving a veil of Sahara sand on the soft asphalt and a myriad of little butterflies that went crashing into the hot walls of the houses. Those were seaside days, Costantino thought, tired of swallowing boiling air when he opened his mouth and of writing addresses on the wedding invitations in the stifling little kitchen. He would have happily gone to Tredici beach with Isabella, with his feet in the water all day long, because the water even refreshes the soul, and he needed it. Every now and then he would stare at his family with an enigmatic gaze, which could have been one of irritation or of commiseration, but no one noticed. They had a thousand things to do, and in their little moments of spare time, they tried to convince themselves and others that it was as though "the bad events of the past" had never happened.

Only nani Lissandro didn't play the part: he kept silent and to himself, his little clear eyes following the moths drawn by the lit bulb. He wouldn't even answer when addressed directly, nor was he moved, like everyone else was, when the maestro said he forgave whoever had injured him, he hadn't seen that person's face since he had been hit in the dark, but he forgave him, and he too wanted to be forgiven and was humbly apologizing, apologizing to Lucrezia and the entire family.

Lucrezia looked at her future husband with her big, done-up eyes, without a trace of darkness and bitterness; but a minute later, without even asking for his opinion, she set the wedding date for the last Sunday of August, when the town was still full of Germanesi who would bring her in their cars to the restaurant by the sea.

On the day of Ferragosto, in the all-encompassing heat of the kitchen, a joyous nursery rhyme pierced through: *Neja neja nga Picuta/u martua lalë Karmelluci/e mori cinë Llukrè/pu pu çuramè*, Fog, fog from Picuta/uncle Karmelluci got married /he took aunt Llukrè/*pu pu çuramè*. It was Paolino's nasally voice, trapped on the doorstep of the house in between boxes, packages, suitcases, and his sweaty parents.

Orlandina, now eight months pregnant, wobbled around the house wishing to help, but then was forced to park herself in an armchair, sweaty and panting. Caringly, her husband would cool her with a Japanese fan, and she, instead of thanking him, would scold him: "You're always hovering around! Get out, go to the bar, go with papa, go with whoever you like, just get out of here!" So this would end in a fight, because at that point he wouldn't hide the fact that he had been dragged to Hora; he didn't want to be there, with her in that condition: "Who forced me to do this? You've brought me to Africa." And she would retort that he was a mountain man, that he wasn't worried about her health but about the health of the apple trees. They would only stop fighting when they saw the Mericano's shadow appear at the front door. Yet he didn't do anything special, the Mericano. He would politely greet them, dry off his sweat, and then recall that he still had to hoe twenty or so olive trees, that he had to hurry, he had to, or there was the risk that even his entire olive grove would go up in smoke, in those hellish days: there were too many fires to keep count of them all.

Paolino, on the other hand, wasn't afraid of the Mericano's shadow or his gruff voice. He had become a little five-year-old devil, who, when provoked, would unleash every possible curse word in Arbëresh, and never sat still. An hour after his arrival, he had already broken around ten ceramic wedding souvenirs, gondolas with little couples in love, all sitting peacefully in a big box. Hence, after two days of this mess, to get him out of the way, his mother entrusted him to his great-grandfather Lissandro.

Paolino seemed bewitched by that old man with the baby face and would let himself be led everywhere by him, to Castello del Piccolo, the piazza, the Kriqi, never objecting. Then, with his mouth wide open, he would listen to his stories of women, men, and children who came from the sea following the flight of a big double-headed eagle, about a man named Skanderbeg, so strong that, with a hit of the sword, he would split an oak as tall as Don Morello's building in half, so strong that his enemies would tremble just at hearing his name: Skanderbeg, ooh so scary. And he would show him the bronze bust in the courtyard in front of city hall.

"*E pra?* And then what? *E pra?*" Paolino would start to chant, the moment nani allowed himself a pause.

And then one morning Skanderbeg fought his last battle, the battle against his dark destiny. This here is the shadow of wind, and it has no heart in its chest and it is called Death.

Your life is over, Death tells him. But Skanderbeg doesn't cry, because a man never cries, but he becomes sad because he thinks about the times to come, about his son who is still too young and already without a father, about Arbërìa in mourning. And then . . .

When the guest list had been double-checked, Costantino noticed that the name of the rhapsode of Corone was missing. The wedding was just a few days away, so it was necessary to go to his house to invite him, make the appropriate apologies, said Signor Maestro, and he had the consent of the entire Avati family, with the exception of nani Lissandro. The old man kept shaking his head: "It is all useless," he said, "Luca Rodotà—may our own health endure—is dead."

"Dead?" they replied, almost as if in chorus.

So nani told them about how he had seen the eagle in a dream, yes, the double-headed eagle from the legends, flying over a crowd dressed in black that was still dancing, feasting, laughing. Even the sounds of the lahuta can be heard, but the rhapsode isn't there. The eagle flies and flies and flies, never tiring, and it has the same eyes as his friend Luca Rodotà, celestial-blue and shining like the sky after the rain; and therefore, Luca is dead.

Costantino felt the little dormant bubbles of his anguish sting him in the stomach. The Mericano, on the other hand, erupted in an artificial and arrogant laugh. "And you, pa, in your old age, believe in dreams? Any chance you've turned into a wizard?" he asked his father-in-law, still laughing.

"No," the old man answered without losing composure, "I am still the same old Lissandro."

"Anyway, we have to go invite him. Dreams are not infallible," said Signor Maestro decisively.

The next day, just after noon, the Mericano, Costantino, and the maestro were in Corone, and having parked the Mercedes in the main piazza, they started off on foot down a muggy, dark alleyway. The rhapsode's house was shuttered. They knocked a few times until finally a woman in her sixties, dressed in black, opened the small front door.

"We're looking for Signor Luca Rodotà," the maestro said. The woman led them to the living room, and between silent sobs, she began to speak: "My father has flown away."

The three men looked at one another perplexed, as though they had completely erased old Lissandro's dream from memory; then they shook her hand as a sign of condolence.

"E si ka qënë? E kur?" And how did it happen? And when? the Mericano asked with a heartfelt voice.

"Eh! It happened three weeks ago. It happened because of that," the woman replied, pointing to the lahuta hanging on the wall. She had immediately rushed down from Stuttgart, but her father hadn't even recognized her. He had fallen off his mule while he was going to Spixana to sing. Actually: some youngsters from Corone had made him fall. They wanted to take his lahuta from the *duako*, how do you say that in Italian? from his knapsack. Four or five of them surrounded him, and they took turns poking the crazed mule, who was spinning in circles like a top. Now they say they had no intention of making him fall, that they loved *zoti* Luca, that they only wanted to try and play the lahuta. But they laughed and made fun of him. "Let us play it, come on!" Come on, come on, come on; her father had lost his balance in the effort to protect the lahuta and had fallen with his back on the rocks. He remained motionless, with his eyes wide open. At ninety-two years old, he still had a strong will to live. In fact, his soul did not want to leave his body. He was in agony for eleven days, saying neither *vdes*, I die, nor *rronj*,

I live. His eyes were absent, becoming more and more sunken and celestial-blue, that shining celestial-blue of the sky after the rain.

The woman was now sobbing loudly. But this didn't stop her from offering her guests some cold beers. They drank in silence and slowly. At last, they went out into the humidity, and the beer returned in the form of droplets of sweat.

When they popped out into the piazza, Costantino felt his head suddenly being emptied out and his legs turning as soft as ricotta. Perched on the hood of the Mercedes was a double-headed eagle who moved its talons back and forth, as though it were dancing, to keep from slipping.

"*Mbe, ngë vjèn?*" Well, aren't you coming? asked his father, who had arrived at the car.

"But aren't you all seeing anything?" Costantino said, with his voice quivering.

"What is there to see?" Signor Maestro answered, looking around. And, having confirmed that there wasn't even a stray dog around, in that piazza with the steaming asphalt at two in the afternoon, he opened the door of the Mercedes. A moment later, a violent gust of wind inflated the shirts of the three men and smacked them in the face, messing up their hair.

The double-headed eagle had disappeared behind the tufts of whiteish clouds that dotted the sky.

The Mericano noticed some fresh scratches on the hood of his Mercedes and immediately blamed the children of Corone for it. Sure enough, before he got in the car, he said: "Now look at what a bunch of sons of bitches live in this town."

A surreal calm swooped down in the Avatis' house from the early morning. Everything was ready; the happy ending was just about twenty hours away. The house was clean and tidy, the ring of chairs set for the guests in the big empty room, the table with a variety of liquor and shot glasses, a big wicker basket with the wedding souvenirs and a smaller, empty one to gather the envelopes of money, new clothes hanging nicely in the armoire, the white bridal gown laid out gently on the twin size bed with a plastic cover protecting it from the fly poop. Even Paolino seemed calm and patient: he was playing cards with nani Lissandro, without sneering. For lunch and dinner, they ate panini to avoid dirtying the clean and fragrant kitchen. Lucrezia and Signor Maestro were cooing, leaning against the railing on the house's doorstep: after the party, they would leave for Rome, where they would spend a few days of their honeymoon, and then fly to Mogadishu.

In the empty calm of the large room, a thick heat was dominating, which was cut to pieces by Costantino's sharp glances. If she doesn't come to the wedding, I swear I'll leave her, he thought, and he was obviously referring to Isabella, who was undecided about giving up a day at the beach to go to a wedding that promised to be intense. Anyway, she would have talked about it with her parents; that she had promised him. In those days they had seen each other just once, at the beach, and Isabella had shown herself to be insensitive to the excuses of Costantino, who was complaining about not being able to visit her like he had promised because his help was needed at home. He thought of her every moment, every moment, but . . . "Where there is a will, there is always a way," Isabella had interrupted, annoyed, and she had refused to pay attention to him anymore: she had lain out on a floating air mattress, and she happily let herself be teased by Costantino's heavy glances, her upturned breasts poking imperiously above the surface of the water.

The next day, during the exchange of wedding rings, Costantino sighed; he sighed so heavily that his parents and

Orlandina turned to look at him: their cheeks were wet, either with sweat or tears. Lucrezia, on the other hand, was still fresh, not at all moved. She had a circumstantial smile marked on her lips, and her eyes, of a superb green, were dry. When he kissed her in congratulation, her brother felt a sense of relief, as though his spirit had been freed of a heavy weight.

After him, it was Isabella's turn. She had arrived at the end of the ceremony with her parents, and so she excused herself for her tardiness, and with a wink she said to the bride: "Congratulations, sister-in-law." Then she kissed Costantino too, mischievously grazing the edge of his mouth. And so as not to lose him in the stifling throng of guests, she took him by the hand and took him up to her parents' Alfa Romeo Alfetta.

The Mericano's shiny Mercedes started on the road to Marina, followed by a long line of cars that drowned out the screeches of the cicadas with the honking of their horns. In front of the restaurant, a collective stampede took place that scandalized Isabella's father. "Bunch of savages!" he exclaimed. "They'll never learn good manners!" That was how Isabella's family, being the last to enter and finding no open seats, ended up being invited to sit at the table of the betrothed. "*Eni, eni këtu*, come, come here, sit with us," said zonja Elena, aglow with happiness.

There was a double menu, one meat-based and one fish-based, because the Mericano didn't want anyone to be unhappy and one could order, stomach permitting, from both of them, "*Hani e pini*," eat and drink, he kept saying, roaming around the hundred set tables, with his green eyes, "*Pini e hani të nuses e të profesorit!*" Drink and eat to the health of the bride and of the professor!

But right after the third helping of pasta, Paolino ran outside, toward the sea, followed by nani Lissandro. He seemed enchanted by the colors of the water: an intense blue, splotched with white foam and of little celestial-blue waves. It was the first time he had seen the sea so close, and who knows what emotions he was feeling in that moment. Surely, he didn't fear the water, because he ran right into it without taking off his shoes and the fancy suit from the ceremony. Then he pushed on slowly toward the horizon.

Nani Lissandro, who was trudging behind him, dragging his feet in the sand, called him, short of breath: "Paolì, *eja këtu, nanì nanì!*" But Paolino didn't listen and continued walking in the water.

Now the old man was running and yelling in desperation. He could see a fog in front of his eyes, and in the fog was Paolino: he was completely soaked, shoes, pants, shirt, jacket, up to his heart. "You really gave me a scare!" said nani, his voice cracking, pressing his hands against his chest.

Without speaking, they walked on the wet sand of the shore, looking around. The stretch of beach in front of the restaurant was deserted, but some fifty meters to the right and to the left, a dozen or so brightly colored umbrellas swam through the haze, as well as women, men, and children, half-naked and noisy. After a time, nani began to press his sides with his hands to support his thin, trembling legs as they kneeled down. He wanted to kiss the shore, as he had done so many times before, for the first time at the age of six, imitating his father. But old age is a bitch, he kept repeating in that contorted position of a centuries-old olive tree. So he gave up on the idea of kneeling and asked his great-grandson, who was watching him amusedly, to gather a fistful of sand.

Paolino didn't have to be asked twice: he dug his hands into the sand and offered his great-grandfather an overflowing fistful of grainy sand and small colorful stones. The old man stuck his sharp bony face in the boy's hands and closed his eyes in ecstasy, as though the sand tasted good. Paolino stared at him with two large, enchanted eyes, almost breathless. To him, that kiss was probably a strange game. One wasn't supposed to talk while it was happening. But as soon as nani raised his face dotted with wet grains of sand, Paolino improvised in his own way: all at once, he hurled the sand at the old man, dirtying his new shirt. "*Të kam zënë*, I got you," he started shouting, running a few steps from nani. So the game was clear: Paolino was waiting to be chased.

"Ah, *bir putërje*, if I get you . . ." nani said, and he threw himself into an unlikely chase, moving his dry old branches in slow motion.

Paolino couldn't stop laughing. Nani, at that speed, would have never ever caught him. So he decided to wait for him in front of a brightly colored boat. When nani reached him— even though he was out of breath and his eyes were wet with tears from laughing so much—he managed to lift Paolino off the ground and spin him around. Who knew what corner of his body he stored all that hidden strength in! Finally, exhausted, he leaned his back against the boat and let himself slide down to the sand. Paolino sat next to him, propped his elbows on nani's legs, and stopped laughing.

All of a sudden, a burst of clicks made them both turn their fixed heads in the same direction. It was the photographer wildly capturing pictures of the newlyweds and their relatives, of Costantino, of Isabella and her parents, and even of Vittorio and Mario who were nearby with their girlfriends. Hundreds of poses, with the sea and the small harbor as the background in that deadly afternoon haze.

"Ok, that's enough," the groom said. "Let's go back inside, they are going to serve the cake."

"Just one more moment please," the Mericano intervened. "Let's take one last picture all together, in a circle, as though we were dancing a vallja, like this . . ." Maybe the Mericano was drunk, or more simply, he was just happy. He felt light, and he moved lightly. He was the one to start singing *Lojmë lojmë, vasha, vallen/Kostantini i vogëlith/vet tre ditë dhëndër-rith*, Let's dance, let's dance, girls, the vallja/of Costantino il Piccolo,/married for only three days, to the amazement of his wife and kids, who knew how much he detested those old chants. Everyone else followed with a simple la-la-la, sometimes singing the few verses they remembered: *Tè ku vete zoti pjak?/Vete të gramisi jetën*, Where are you going, old father?/I am going to throw my life away.

From where nani Lissandro and Paolino were positioned, the circle must have looked perfect, but the song was a jumble of off-tempo voices.

The first one to start laughing again was the old man; he laughed so hard he could be heard from the vallja, and while laughing he said: "They sound like bleating sheep. They look like donkeys braying as they crush the fava plants in the barnyard . . ."

Paolino's laugh was as sharp as the blaring of a trumpet. "And then what?" he began to ask in Italian. *"E pra?"* he repeated in Arbëresh, since nani kept laughing without answering.

"They sound like broken bells . . ."

Nani was clutching his belly with his hand from laughing too much; but now the laughter came silently from his mouth. He hadn't laughed this hard in years.

"And then what? *E pra?*" Paolino insisted.

"They are like ghos . . ."

The old man couldn't finish the word and probably didn't hear the end of the song: *Hani e pini më se vini/se m'erdh*

Kostantini, Eat and drink the more you come,/because Costantino has returned, nor did he see the vallja break up. His eyes were like two little glass beads the color of the sea. His mouth, with neither lips nor teeth, was a perfectly round little cavity, a third dark eye, as motionless as the other two.

"And then what?" Paolino shook him impatiently. "*E pra?*"

Author's Note

From the very first pages, the narrative rhythm of *The Round Dance* follows the echo of the rhapsodies recited or sung by the old ladies of my childhood. Like Costantino, the protagonist of this novel, I am fascinated by them: they are juicy stories, fast and light, and full of simple but effective metaphors.

The first rhapsody, the one of Costantino il Piccolo opening the book, I had heard recited as a boy by grandma Veneranda, the sweetest Moma-pó, and I had even attempted a transcription of it, dubious since I was illiterate in my native Arbëresh. The Italian translation of *Vú spërvjeret Skandërbeku* is instead taken from the very beautiful book by Girolamo De Rada, *Rapsodie d'un poema albanese* (Rhapsodies of an Albanian Long Poem), Florence, 1866. Over time, I obtained the collection of rhapsodies of Antonio Scura and *papàs* Giuseppe Ferrari that, together with those of De Rada, allowed me to integrate, with single lines or entire stanzas missing, the increasingly incomplete versions collected in my town and utilized here and there in this book.

I would finally like to mention—for allowing me to enter more deeply into the intricate world of Arbëria—the experimental research of Carmelo Candreva and Carmine Stamile, the precious books of Giuseppe Gangale, the studies of

Francesco Altimari and Ernesto Koliqi on the myth of Skanderbeg, as well as the ethnographic material published by papàs Antonio Bellusci and the cyclostyled ones by Delfina Rossano. To Francesco Altimari, I also owe a debt of gratitude for having helped me correct my shaky Arbëresh orthography.

My affectionate gratitude goes out to my parents for all the beautiful stories they told me and made me live out.

A special thanks and a kiss to Meike, who read the numerous drafts of this novel, including the German version, always giving useful suggestions.

And lastly, a warm thanks to my readers. To all, *arrivederci*, until the next dance.

—Carmine Abate

Notes on Contributors

CARMINE ABATE was born in Carfizzi, a town of the Arbëresh (Italo-Albanian) community in the southern region of Calabria, Italy. As a child, he spoke only Arbërisht, a variant of the Albanian language. After obtaining his degree in Italian literature from the University of Bari, Italy, he moved to Hamburg, Germany, where his father was working. In Germany, he taught at a school for immigrants and began publishing his first stories. In 1984, his first collection of short stories appeared under the title *Den Koffer und weg!* It was a socio-anthropological study conducted jointly with his wife Meike Behrmann that speaks about the Calabrese community in Germany. It was subsequently published in Italy with the title *I Germanesi*. After more than a decade in Germany, Abate returned to Italy and settled in Besenello, Trentino, in northern Italy, where he taught middle school. Abate has published several acclaimed novels and short story collections, including *Il ballo tondo* (1991). Three of his award-winning books have been translated into English: *Tra due mari* (*Between Two Seas*), 2002; *La festa del ritorno* (*The Homecoming Party*), 2004; and *Il banchetto di nozze e altri sapori* (*The Wedding Banquet and Other Flavors*), 2016. His work has also been translated into several European languages and into Arabic. His book *La collina del vento* (The Hill of the

Wind) was awarded the 2012 Campiello Prize (in Venice). Among his other novels are: *Il bacio del pane*, 2013; *La felicità dell'attesa*, 2016; *Le rughe del sorriso*, 2018; *L'albero della fortuna*, 2019; *Il cercatore di luce*, 2021; and *Un paese felice*, 2023.

MICHELANGELO LA LUNA (Harvard University and University of Calabria Phds) is a professor of Italian Language and Literature at the University of Rhode Island, and director of the Italian International Engineering Program and the URI Summer Program in Italy. He is the author of articles and books on Italian and Italian-Albanian writers and poets, such as Carmine Abate, Dante Alighieri, Luigi Capuana, Girolamo De Rada, Dacia Maraini, and Pier Paolo Pasolini.

As director of the series SOPHIA, Michelangelo La Luna is the editor of Dacia Maraini's *Taccuino americano (1964–2016)*, 2016, and of the collection *Writing like Breathing: An Homage to Dacia Maraini*, which is divided into five volumes: *Beloved Writing. Fifty Years of Engagement*, vol. I, 2016; *Mafia and Other Plays*, vol. II, 2017; *USA 1964–2017: An Italian Reportage*, vol. III, 2018; *Dacia Maraini and Her Literary Journey* (co-edited with Angela Pitassi), vol. IV, 2020; and *A Life Devoted to Writing: Festschrift in Honor of Dacia Maraini*, vol. V, 2021. Moreover, he edited and wrote the Introduction to Dacia Maraini, *Writing Like Breathing. Racconti Romanzo Poesia. Sessant'anni di letteratura* (Writing Like Breathing. Short Stories Novel Poetry. Sixty Years of Literature), 2021; Dacia Maraini, *Sguardo a Oriente* (Gaze to the East), 2022 (the sixth edition of the book was published in April 2023); and Dacia Maraini, *Sguardo al nuovo mondo* (Gaze to the New World), 2023.

In addition, Professor La Luna's research activity focuses on Girolamo De Rada (1814–1903), the major Italian-Albanian poet of the Romantic period, about whom he wrote and edited the following volumes: *Invito alla lettura di Girolamo De Rada* (Invitation to the Reading of Girolamo De Rada's Opus), 2004; *La corrispondenza inedita tra Girolamo De Rada e Niccolò Tommaseo* (The Unpublished Correspondence Between Girolamo De Rada and Niccolò Tommaseo), 2006; *Autobiografia* (Autobiography), 2008; *Opere letterarie in italiano* (Literary Works in Italian), 2009; and *La corrispondenza tra Girolamo De Rada e Angelo De Gubernatis (1870–1900) et alii* (The Correspondence Between Girolamo De Rada and Angelo De Gubernatis et Alii [1870–1900]), 2016. In addition, Michelangelo La Luna is the co-editor of *Atti del Convegno Internazionale "Codex Purpureus Rossanensis: problematiche scientifiche e prospettive di valorizzazione." Palazzo della Cultura San Bernardino, Rossano, Italy, May 25–26, 2017* (International Conference proceedings on "Codex Purpureus Rossanensis: Scientific Issues and Valorization Perspectives." Palazzo della Cultura San Bernardino, Rossano, Italy, May 25–26, 2017), 2018; and he published the critical edition of Luigi Capuana's *La Reginotta* (The Little Queen), 2020. He is one of the editors and translators, together with Susan Amatangelo and Tullio Pagano, of Giovanni Verga, *Per le vie*, 2023; and an editor, together with Dagmar Reichardt, Domenica Elisa, Laura Fournier, Colbert Akieudji, and Carmen Van den Bergh, of *Benvenuti al Nuovo Sud*, Proceedings of the International AIPI (Associazione Internazionale Professori d'Italiano) Conference, Palermo, October 26–29, 2022 (forthcoming 2024). Currently he is also preparing a critical edition of an unpublished manuscript of Dante's *Divine Comedy* (forthcoming 2024).

FRANCESCO ALTIMARI is a professor of Albanian language and literature at the University of Calabria. He is the editor of the *Opera Omnia* of Girolamo De Rada (1814–1903) and author of several books and articles on topics concerning

Albanian philology, linguistics, and literature. He is an honorary member of the Academy of Sciences of Albania and the Academy of Sciences and Arts, as well as the president of the Academic Foundation Francesco Solano, which promotes Albanian language and culture in Italy, fosters cultural exchanges between historic Albanian communities in Italy and in the Balkan area, and supports didactic and scientific activities of the University of Calabria in the Balkans.